KATHRYN TROY

A VISION IN CRIMSON

FROSTBITE BOOK ONE

A VISION IN CRIMSON
Frostbite, Book 1

CITY OWL PRESS
www.cityowlpress.com

Cover Design by Fantasy Book Cover Design by Keylin Rivers. All stock photos licensed appropriately.

Edited by Tee Tate.

For information on subsidiary rights, please contact the publisher at info@cityowlpress.com.

Print Edition ISBN: 978-1-64898-431-0

Digital Edition ISBN: 978-1-64898-432-7

Printed in the United States of America

BOOKS BY KATHRYN TROY

Curse of the Amber

The Shadow of Theron

A Vision in Crimson

PRAISE FOR KATHRYN TROY

"Exciting and engaging from the first page to the last, *The Shadow of Theron* is a high fantasy filled with romance, magic, and twists and turns that will keep the reader enthralled from beginning to end." — *Elayna R. Gallea, author of Tethered*

"Major Zorro vibes... excellent writing with gorgeous vocabulary." — *R.M. Krogman, author of The Keepers of Midgate*

"A vibrant, vivid world with a rich culture and complex religious system that draws the reader in... *The Shadow of Theron* is an exciting and riveting fantasy novel with an intriguing plot and well-developed characters that will keep the reader engaged until the end." — *Briar Boleyn, USA Today Bestselling author of Queen of Roses*

"Brimming with pulse-pounding adventure and sweet romance, this retelling of Zorro was such a joy to read." — *Olivia Wildenstein, author of House of Beating Wings*

"A wonderful book, fantastic action, a detailed and rich living world, and full of a passion you don't see too often in the genre. A can't miss!" — *Joshua C. Cook, author of Blood of a Fallen God*

"The heart of *Curse of the Amber* has the ability to steal the reader's breath and not return it until the very end. With the amount of details, as far as not only the story but also the glance into archeological procedures, the audience often feels they are living a different life rather than merely reading... There is a solid hook from the very start that no one is able to resist- pulling one in and giving them the ride of their lives." – *InD'tale Magazine*

To Annabelle & Adrian: That you may never stop dreaming.

1

THE UNFORGIVING SUN BORE DOWN ON THE DESOLATE VALLEY BELOW, focusing its energy on the only thing moving as it slowly sank into the horizon. A tall, slim figure, clad all in black, cast a long shadow in the grass as he approached the remnants of a crumbling castle. His shadow was faint. He pulled his wide-brimmed hat low on his head, protecting his pale face from the last vestiges of the sun's rays.

Just a few more minutes. He awaited the setting of the sun with the anticipation of the condemned beneath the executioner's axe, eager for a single, forceful swing so that you could at last be done with it. Being half-human, he could bear the daylight, but on especially hot days like this one, it made his skin feel as if it were being peeled away from his flesh. The night brought sweet release from constant torture. But the day's torments didn't register on his face. Emotions rarely did. Half-vampire and cursed with eternal life, he had experienced it all. Most of it pain.

The sunset brought its own complications. Killing vampires at night, at the height of their power, was a fool's errand for even the strongest hunters. With his horse being shod at the town that had hired him, he'd had little choice than to reach the ruins on foot, and it had taken longer than he expected. Abandoned for thousands of years, only a few heavy stones half-sunken in the dirt belied the layout of what was once a grand complex. But the solitary man had tracked down enough vampires to know that the one he now sought was nearby. Ruins proved too strong a temptation for the ancient beings. Their natural affinity for the old over the new attracted them without fail to the myriad shells of castles that dotted the countryside rather than more industrial, durable structures.

The hunter's keen eyes spied an entrance to a subterranean passage, obscured by dense undergrowth. Whoever was there was bound to already be awake. In the end, it mattered little. He took one uncaring step forward, then paused.

Why am I doing this again?

The little village he had passed through was one of the few places to hire a dhampir hunter, even begrudgingly. The majority of the town had wanted to wait for another hunter to come along, but one young man was desperate to get back his bride of only a few days, pleading with the village mean to hire the dhampir.

They had balked at the price the hunter had quoted them. It was steep, given this particular vampire's formidable reputation and the fact that there were several hostages. But the newlywed had assured him that the town would be able to pay him the minute he returned, that they just needed some time to collect the money.

The personal circumstances of his employers didn't matter to the hunter. But he had envied the look in the young man's eyes, full of worry for his beloved. In all his years, he had never been fortunate enough to have loved someone, or to be loved. There was no reason for both of them to be miserable, the dhampir reasoned, if he could help it.

Plus, he still hadn't found the one vampire he really wanted to kill. With every job he took, he hoped finally to encounter the monster who had caused his wretched existence and destroy him. He was always disappointed. Still, there was nothing else for him to do but keep trying. The hunter took a deep breath, reached for the long, thin blade at his back, and crossed the threshold into the hidden crypt.

The hunter descended a narrow, winding staircase that led to underground catacombs. When he reached the bottom of the stone stairway, he entered a long hallway lined with dead bodies set into the wall. His eyes shone in the darkness as he sought out the vampire's lair. His determined footsteps were silent, creating no echo that would give away his presence. In a few minutes' time, his ears picked up the sound of women crying. Their wails emanated from an offshoot corridor to his right. He noted its location and continued forward into a broad, open space with a low curved ceiling.

The unpaved ground was littered with wooden boxes. He ripped the top off each and inspected their contents. He left a sole grave undisturbed; a rotted slat on the side of the box revealed a decaying arm in tattered clothing encased in dirt.

The overall impression of a grave that had been quitted for the night meant nothing. If his prey *had* left, the hunter would have seen him. Like it or not, dhampirs excelled as hunters. Especially this one, for he was so very thorough. He had outwitted even the most cunning vampires because he didn't trust his eyes alone. He emptied every coffin, finding nothing but human remains. Even the box he'd left unmolested earlier seemed ordinary.

As he stared at the human husk within, contemplating his next move, he noticed that the box was unusually tall. Twice as tall, in fact, as the other coffins. He bisected the box lengthwise with his sword and kicked at the top half with his foot. The box and its contents toppled over, revealing a second coffin underneath, lined with a pristine fabric dyed a luxurious shade of red. It was empty.

"Very clever," a deep voice echoed from behind him. The hunter turned to face his opponent. Across the dark expanse, the dhampir noted the vampire's subtle similarity to his own facial features. They had the same nose, the same chin. His overall build was bigger but did little to mask the truth. The hunter had lost count over the years of how many of his victims had reflected a family resemblance.

The vampire saw it as well.

"So, you're one of *his* mongrels, are you?" the vampire drawled, unfazed by the hunter's swift discovery of his hideout. "I guess even the best of us get bored *some* of the time."

To full-blooded vampires, dhampirs were nothing but the products of vampires' attempts to entertain themselves in their eternal existence. They raped human women for the psychological thrill of it. It delighted them to instill fear, and it allowed them to exert lifelong control over their hapless victims, for endless hours of amusement.

The insult was meant to sting. That was the creature's second mistake.

The hunter lunged at his opponent. Unarmed the vampire dodged the dhampir's blade with incredible speed. He clawed at the attacker's throat, but that was equally unsuccessful. The hunter was just as fast, and just as strong. And in the case of *this* hunter, his mixed nature gave him the advantage over human and vampire alike. The full-blood's arrogance, underestimating the dhampir as even less than human, was the mistake that was fatal.

The vampire's movements were slow, relatively speaking, his muscles relaxed and his attention lax at best.

"Although my mother was no mere worm, I, too, am related to —Augh!"

In less than a second, the skilled hunter had pierced him through the shoulder, pinning him to the wall. The vampire grabbed hold of the blade, and growled when he could not yank it free. The sword was lodged firmly in the wall, held in place by a physical and supernatural power far superior to the vampire's.

"Where is he?" the dhampir demanded.

The vampire flashed the hunter a cruel grin in response. "If you haven't figured that out yet, then you never will."

The young man sighed as he pulled a wooden stake from inside his coat. The full-blood's voice could not hide his fear in the face of his distant cousin's determination.

"Now wait a minute. I said wait. Please! *Don't!*"

The vampire's pleas fell on deaf ears. The hunter retained his blank expression as he impaled the vampire through the heart. In the same moment, the full-blood drew a hidden blade and stabbed the dhampir in the chest. He saw it in enough time to twist his torso and avoid being pierced in the heart, but just barely.

"Why?" the vampire sputtered. His flesh dried up and fell away without an answer, until all that was left was a dusty skeleton, hoisted to the wall by the wooden stake lodged between its ribs.

I don't know.

The slim figure retrieved his sword from the bone and returned it to its sheath. He'd lost a lot of blood already. His wound refused to heal as he expected it to. It continued to agitate him as he retraced his steps, coming upon the hallway where the late vampire's victims were being kept.

He found all eight women, trapped in an alcove that had been outfitted with heavy metal bars. They were huddled around a small fire they had made with some of the straw and grass strewn over the floor of their tiny prison. The group screamed as they saw the dhampir approach. In the dark and covered in blood, and with the flames lending his skin an eerie glow, he could almost understand.

"Don't be afraid," he said. "My name is Luca. Your husbands sent me."

"Bullshit!" an elderly woman cried. "Why would they send one monster to rescue us from another?"

"I'm not a vampire," Luca answered as he bent the bars of their cage open with minimal effort.

"Half a vampire is *still* a vampire!" the crone snapped back as she walked through the opening.

Luca held out his hand to help the others through the bars, only to have each one of them ignore him in turn. He returned his arm to his side.

When they were all gathered in the hallway, he asked, "Is everyone here?"

"Yes," a young woman answered. She was being supported by two other women, her breath labored. Though none of the women had been bitten, this one had suffered a serious injury to her leg. Luca approached and asked the two women assisting her to help her to a sitting position.

Her head shot up and her eyes bulged. "Why?" she asked. "What are you going to do?"

"I'm going to heal your leg, if you'll just sit down."

"Oh no you're not!" she shouted, her voice echoing through the passage. She seemed to want to climb deeper into the embrace of the women holding her upright.

"It's bad enough we've been manhandled by a vampire. I'm not *about* to let a dhampir put his paws on me too!"

He just stared, contemplating the depths of her stubbornness.

I'm not contagious.

"It'll only take a minute," he offered again in a quiet voice.

She said nothing.

"You'll be permanently crippled otherwise."

She shrugged. She didn't care. Hobbling around for life was preferable to being touched by a dhampir.

Luca sighed. "Suit yourself. The exit is that way." He pointed down the hallway, allowing the group to walk ahead of him. Some sneered at him as they passed by, while the younger ones shrank away, scurrying quickly by him as if at any moment he might snap at them.

"You're welcome," he muttered under his breath as he turned to follow them out. He shook his head and put his hand to his still bleeding side.

They had better pay up.

2

IN THE HEAT OF THE LATE AFTERNOON, LUCA SHUFFLED THE DEAD GRASS between his feet, and kept the hat on his head pulled down low. His raven black hair hung limply past his shoulders and down his back, flat and sweltering in the absence of a breeze. His face, almost always devoid of expression, just now looked haggard.

He had been walking for hours. He had returned to the village, with all eight abducted women safely in tow, only to discover that the townsfolk had, predictably, decided to stiff him after all. The young newlywed who had pleaded with him earlier had said nothing, kept his eyes on the ground as Luca had argued with the other villagers, who denied ever having agreed to pay him. While he stalked off to collect his payment from the mayor, some of the men had gone to the town stables and slaughtered the horse he'd left there to be shod, leaving him to wander in the intense heat. They hadn't even let him stay the night in the village inn to recuperate, citing a local rule that forbade dhampirs from traveling unaccompanied. The faint shadow he cast at his feet was stained with his blood. His shirt and coat were soaked through, sticky and rancid under the sun's glare.

Luca stumbled. He paused to catch his breath, but he felt the sun's oppression all the more. He needed to hide, or he'd be boiled alive. He blinked away the sweat in his eyes and saw a blurry valley ahead. It gave rise to a line of thickly forested hills. He could take refuge there if he didn't collapse first. Luca put his hand to his side, letting fresh blood seep between his fingers. With trembling muscles he brought his fingers to his mouth and sucked them greedily dry. The rush made him sway in place, dizzy with hunger. It was the only thing he could do to stop from dropping dead in the field.

There was no pleasure in it because the blood was his own. Sheer force of will and his unbreakable self-loathing prevented him from ever drinking, except in an emergency. And even then, he had only ever drunk his own blood, as now. Luca had never taken a single human victim. Not out of hunger, and *not* out of lust. Though he had been sorely tempted.

Using the last of his strength, Luca climbed into the hills, found the darkest spot possible, and started chipping away at the soil with his sword. The stubborn wound, not to mention the sunstroke, was enough to best him. The sun had won. Again. The only way he would survive was to rest in the earth.

His vampire nature was dominant, though he hated to admit it. He was nocturnal but being a vampire hunter meant he had to conduct business with humans during the day *and* hope to kill vampires while they slept. He was usually not that lucky and was often engaged in bloody warfare all night. He rarely got a good day's sleep.

It wasn't deep enough. But it would do. He practically fell in, with just enough sense left to cover himself with the dirt he had disturbed, leaving only his head and neck exposed. He closed his eyes and had to wait only a matter of minutes to feel his heart rate slow and his skin begin to cool. He shuddered as he took in a long, deep breath, and reflected on the situation in which he found himself.

His existence had been bleak for longer than he could remember. His condition today—overworked, abused, feared, and hated—was but the repetition of ages wandering from place to place in search of work. Wherever he went, he was inevitably met by countless leering faces, a combination of horror and disgust, and sometimes outright mockery. His age had numbed him to this constant rejection, and he had long ago resigned himself to his status as a permanent outcast. But his apathy went even deeper than that. For someone living as long as he had, seeing the same scenes playing out over and over again, Luca did not express emotion because nothing moved him. His eyes only ever dimly reflected his eternal sadness. He could not remember if he had ever laughed. Or cried. Or cared.

Except once. A young, naïve girl had hired him to rescue her from a vampire who had bitten her. She'd had no money and had offered to pay him with her body. She was too young to know him for what he was on first sight. When he had told her he was a dhampir, to ensure she knew exactly what kind of bargain she was striking, the color had drained from her face. But she had grown attached to him over time, and he to her. He remembered their brief, chaste kiss fondly. He had left without collecting his fee, or even a proper goodbye.

That must have hurt her terribly, he contemplated. The night before he left, she had begged him to stay, and he nearly had. He craved physical intimacy as much as any man, moreso because of his millennia-long abstinence. But his sexuality and his bloodlust ran parallel to each other, which kept him from acting on either. Beyond his physical desires, he yearned for an emotional bond. He had never felt respect, appreciation, friendship, or love. He wanted them all, but they were irrevocably out of reach. What the girl had offered him couldn't begin to satisfy him. And he couldn't bring himself to simply take what she had been offering. She had already been defiled once, bitten by a vampire. Sleeping with a man like himself, he thought, just for the sake of it, would have completely ruined her, and his already abysmal self-esteem would have ceased to exist. He didn't want that. As painful as his sudden departure must have been, in his mind, his intentions justified his actions.

How much could she have really cared for me, anyway? He rationalized. They had only known each other for about a week. And though she had thrown herself at him on that final night, he had never forgotten the look of sheer horror that had crossed her face when he told her what he was. A dhampir. Untouchable. Unlovable. What had seemed like genuine affection at the time, he knew, was probably nothing more than a teenage infatuation with the forbidden. It had been over a century since then. Deep down, he did not regret his decision to leave, but knowing that she was probably the closest he would ever come to feeling loved turned his thoughts melancholy.

Just what was driving him? His hunt to kill his father, who had condemned him to this horrible life? Even if he could finally locate and kill him, what then? It wouldn't change his fate. The best he could hope for was to be killed himself in the process. In the absence of hope, he longed for oblivion.

It was in this sorrowful mood that Luca finally drifted off to sleep. After a while, he began to dream. Disjointed images flooded his brain.

He dreamt of a majestic castle by the sea, and felt elegant finery brush past his skin.

He was sitting at a table with what felt like a close circle of friends, though in reality he had none. He was laughing with them but couldn't decipher why. A beautiful red-haired woman, cloaked in black and gold, smiled beside him, leaning in close and resting her hand on his upper thigh. He felt happy.

His vision swam in a blend of white, gray, and red.

He smelled the ocean. The fragrance slowly turned into the stench of garlic being smoked.

A blast of icy wind stole his breath away.

He felt himself pushing up against a tree in the middle of a thick forest, something warm beneath him. He looked down to see the gorgeous, now naked red-headed siren moaning in the throes of passion and calling his name. His real name. He felt his bare abdomen rubbing against hers, her full, soft breasts pushed tightly against him. The sensation made every strand of hair stand on end. He had never been so close to a woman. From her ivory throat spilled two pools of blood. He craned his neck and tongued the wound, then clamped down with the full force of his fangs, pinning the girl to the tree and drinking her in. It was so real he could taste her. Blood rushed to his head, and he felt feverish and dizzy. He was drowning in a sea of red. He shifted in his grave and let out a low moan. He licked his lips.

His dream was broken by the feel of something soft against his mouth. He opened his eyes and blinked, thinking for a moment that he was still asleep. Flooding his vision was the red-haired siren of his dream, crouched above him.

Her dark brown eyes were staring straight into his. He held her glance for a long while, then took a minute to glimpse at the rest of her. Her features were well defined and graceful. Her long luxurious hair, braided in a few places, spilled over her firm, ample curves onto the ground in front of her. Looking at it now in reality, he saw a unique, vibrant shade of red, darker, and almost auburn in the shade of the trees, with strands of pure copper and gold highlighted by the sun through the forest canopy. Her large eyes sparkled. They were alight with intrigue and kind concern, but Luca saw a touch of the tired sadness that he was accustomed to seeing in his own dim reflection. Too much for someone her age.

Luca puzzled over her age for more than a few seconds. Her beauty and slender frame suggested a girl nearing her thirties, yet her countenance told him she had been through more than her share of life's troubles, even for a woman of the rough and unprotected countryside.

She stared at his clear crystal blue eyes, framed by thick dark brows. A straight nose, tightly pursed lips and strong chin completed his face. Despite his pale complexion, he was dark and beautiful. She didn't let it show on her face, but the woman had become immediately enamored of him.

Her fingers rested lightly on his mouth. After a silence that lasted a bit too long, she was the first to speak.

"I'll have you out of there in just a minute," she whispered. "I won't hurt you, but we have to be quiet."

She turned her head to the side to get a glimpse of the valley below.

"I'm looking out for a friend, and just spotted you here a minute ago. Once I'm sure he's okay, I'll start digging."

Luca said nothing. When she was sure that he wouldn't make a sound, she removed her hand from his lips and moved closer to the hill's edge, looking for her companion. Luca got a better look at what she was wearing.

A plaid scarf in sapphire blue with hints of gold thread was wrapped around her neck and waist, covering a tunic dress of the same shade. Her legs were covered by high, soft leather brown boots and blue leggings, but Luca spied shapely thighs at the edge of her skirt. She wore a utility belt across her chest which hinted at her generous cleavage despite her modest neckline. Above, his gaze traced the silhouette of her long, pale, comely neck with excitement, but he quashed the flutter in his heart before it developed and redirected his gaze.

At her hips she wore two short swords, and the hilt of a dagger peeked out from the top of her boot. She was certainly well-armed and didn't appear the least bit threatened by Luca. She didn't react to seeing him for the first time in the manner customary to women, and even scores of young men. They usually succumbed quickly to his outward charms—his dark aura and hypnotic stare, two of his many vampiric qualities. But she didn't gasp in fear or swoon in ecstasy. It puzzled him.

A small part of him was disappointed that she hadn't exhibited an immediate response. He chalked it up to her finding him covered in dirt from the neck down. But he knew that shouldn't have stopped her from surrendering to his trance-inducing stare, even for a moment. More puzzling was that she had just happened to appear as his dream self was making love to her.

Her garb made her even more of a mystery. He only noticed such inconsequential things, because the fabrics, colors, and design of her wardrobe were infinitely superior, and foreign, to anything he had ever seen, including some of the priciest fashions available in the biggest cities. He much preferred the naked version of her, which had dissipated with her actual presence. But even in all her gear, chosen for its rugged functionality, she looked regal. She gestured to her friend, then she turned to face him once more.

"Okay, it looks like whoever did this to you is gone. I'll have you walking around again soon. Who *did* do this to you, anyway?" she asked, as she began to claw at the earth with her hands.

"I did."

His voice was as toneless and nonchalant as ever. Her hands paused for a moment, still holding clumps of dirt. She looked at him quizzically.

"You buried yourself? Why on earth would you do a thing like that?"

Here came the part he always dreaded.

"I'm a dhampir."

"A what?"

He waited for what he had said to sink in, but it didn't. She was still honestly waiting for an answer. He repeated himself.

"I'm a dhampir."

"What's a dhampir?"

He just stared at her, his eyes going wide.

"I'm not from around here," she explained, "so you're going to have to fill me in."

Now it was Luca's turn to pause. Never in his entire life had he been asked to explain this term. In a world whose entire existence revolved around the struggle between vampires and humans, to find someone who was not familiar with this word was truly unheard of. He experienced an emotion he had almost never had occasion to experience. He was, in a word, stunned.

"I'm part human, part vampire."

"Oh. Ohhhh."

She finally got it. He waited now for the standard response. Instead, a look of embarrassment swept over her face as she began hurriedly replacing the soil she had disturbed.

"I am so sorry, I didn't realize. I didn't mean to intrude on your resting. You looked like you were having a hell of a dream."

If you only knew. But, was she actually apologizing for bothering his rest? Luca's revelation hadn't fazed her in the slightest. His amazement at her response only piqued his interest in her more.

"I was just getting up."

"In that case, would you like me to help you?" she asked.

"Do what you like."

She resumed her exhumation. "My name is Kate, by the way."

Luca stretched his muscles and sat upright, the remaining earth above him falling away. He took her outstretched palm with his freed right hand, and they both stood up.

"Call me Luca."

"You're hurt! That looks really bad."

Her fingers touched the cut on Luca's clothing where the vampire's sword had pierced him. Luca inhaled sharply at the touch of her fingertips to his side.

"I'm fine."

"Are you sure you're alright? You look so… sad."

Luca remained silent.

"It's written all over your face," she continued.

He averted his gaze from her scrutiny, so intense that she had noticed the echo of emotion in his eyes where everyone else saw nothing.

"I'm sure."

"Can I give you a ride home at least?"

"I don't have a permanent residence."

He blinked. He'd answered her without thinking, and now couldn't take it back.

"Then I'd like to treat you to a warm bed and a bath, to help you clean off."

"It's not necessary." Again, he regretted his words. Being wary didn't feel right, given her demeanor. But neither did being careless.

"Come on," she replied. "I know what it's like to be weary of traveling, tired and hurting. It will make me happy."

Luca paused at that last bit. Her eyes implored him.

"All right."

She beamed.

"Thank you," he added. When exactly had he lost his footing?

"You're very welcome," she said. "Good, that's settled. Come on, Dracula."

Luca started. "What did you call me?"

"Huh?"

"Where did you hear that name?"

She knew his name. The one she had called out in his dream. The name his mother had called him, not caring enough to give him one of his own. He had only ever told anyone that his name was Luca.

Suspicion washed over him. He grabbed her by the shoulders and asked his question again, this time more insistent.

"Where did you hear that name?"

"It's the name of a famous vampire. *Dracula* was a popular novel when I was young. It was a joke! How do *you* know that name?"

Luca looked deep into her eyes for any hint of deception. He could find none. But he knew it was no coincidence. He wanted to know more, wanted a chance to pick her brain for any information that might be useful to him. He promptly released his grip.

"I didn't mean to hurt you."

"You didn't."

He hadn't answered her question, and it was clear he wasn't going to.

"Let's go, they must be waiting for me," she said.

"I'm sorry if I startled you."

"Just forget it, okay? I shouldn't have said it. It was in bad taste. Let's get moving, it'll be dark soon."

As they emerged from the tree cover, Luca noticed it was late afternoon, around the same time when he had first dozed off. He'd been unconscious an entire day.

3

Luca tried to banish the dirt from his clothes, but it refused to budge from the worn creases at his elbows and his knees. The tear from the vampire's blade had already begun to shred, and the edges were caked in blood. The shirt couldn't be saved.

He pulled the lapels of his jacket closed to hide it. But his dream girl, as it were, wasn't looking at him. She was poised at the edge of the hill, staring into the distance. She seemed cowed by the sight of the wasteland below.

"Is something wrong?"

Why do you care?

He didn't know what was wrong with him, but he was having the hardest time keeping his mouth shut.

"Can I ask you something?" she said, still not turning to look at him. "It might seem like an odd question, but…what year is it?"

He narrowed his eyes. "Don't you know?"

She'd claimed not to be from the area, but what did that have to do with the year?

"I wouldn't have asked if I did."

He couldn't think of a reason not to answer.

"12,205."

She let out a breath he hadn't noticed she'd been holding.

"And how long has it been like this?" she said.

"Like what?"

"Completely destroyed."

Luca had questions of his own, but she stopped him before he could say anything more.

"No, don't. I've changed my mind, I don't want to know," she said. Her gaze met his for a moment as she turned to face the opposite side of the hill, as if to distract herself from the vision of desolation. "Come on, let's go," she said. "I've wasted enough time already."

"Where are you from?" Luca asked as they walked downhill.

He wanted to know a lot more than that, but that would come after. He needed to get *her* guard down.

"I was born here in the year 1884," she answered. "But for the past three hundred years, I've had the good fortune to live..." she caught herself, and cut her sentence short. "somewhere else."

Three hundred years old and still gorgeous? So she's not human.

A succubus was his first thought. The dream, the desire, it all made sense. That theory lasted about a minute.

She *would be attracted to me, not the other way around.* The admission caught him off-guard, even if it happened only in his own head. Maybe she had her talons in even deeper than he realized. But then, why not strike when he was in the ground and defenseless?

"What's your business here?" he asked.

"We're just passing through."

Another clipped response. Just like his. Luca's experience with casual conversation was nonexistent, but this was getting him nowhere.

She groaned as they approached the bottom of the hill, and the slope became steeper. "Actually, we could *all* use a meal and a warm bed. I promised them they'd be home by now." She shook her head. "I hate breaking promises, but I have no choice."

We?

Luca spied a solitary man waiting for them at the foot of the hill.

Not a succubus, then. Definitely not attracted to me. Somehow, this was worse than his suspicion that she meant to destroy him.

"Your husband?" he asked, gesturing toward her companion.

Kate smiled. "No, just a friend. I am unattached. But thank you for asking."

Luca responded with characteristic stoicism. But her answer was tinged with hope, possibility, and something else he couldn't put his finger on. It was worrying and exciting, in equal parts. She had caught his interest, this woman he still knew nothing about. But he couldn't help it. She was so pretty, and so far, she hadn't run away or tried to kill him. That alone made her special.

They were met at the bottom of the hill by a man who towered over Luca. The breadth of his shoulders would put any giant to shame. Sandy brown hair fell just below his broad shoulders, which were covered by a mangy-looking vest fashioned out of a golden animal skin and trimmed with dark brown fur. Extra folds of the hide gathered around the man's neck, culminating in a hood made from a lion's head. The lion skin, like its owner, had seen better days. The lips on the lion head curled back in a menacing fashion, revealing gums blackened with time and exaggerating the length of the single canine that remained stubbornly attached to the mouth.

The start of wrinkles on his face and hands suggested he was past his prime, but it did nothing to diminish the sense that this man was a force unto himself.

He stood arms akimbo, not a single sharp edge on him. It was as if Kate were carrying weapons enough for them both.

"Luca," Kate began, "this is Hercules, one of my closest friends. Hercules, this is Luca. He'll be joining us tonight."

"Uh, okay. It's nice to meet you, Luca."

Like Kate, the man had no visible reaction to Luca's presence. No shock of horror that a woman had brought a monster into their midst. Her companion's expression was clear and open, not an ounce of suspicion. He offered his sword hand in greeting without so much as a thought.

Luca had never actually shaken a man's hand before. It was…surprising.

"I thought after me, you were going to stop picking up strays," Hercules said.

"I know. I lied," Kate said.

"Hmm, I wonder whatever could have changed your mind…"

His gaze darted between them, as if the reason were staring them in the face. Hercules was trying, and failing, to suppress a smile.

Kate pursed her lips. "You finished?"

The shift in her expression made the man she was with, a man twice her size if not more, stand up straight.

"Yup."

"Good."

Luca, for his part, had observed the slightest flush rise to Kate's cheeks.

She turned to look at him, and caught him staring. She met his gaze full on. She didn't blink or turn away like most people, if they dared to look in his direction at all. For a moment, they drank in the sight of each other.

This open, silent interlude brought a stronger rush of color to her face. She must have realized it, for she broke the connection and rubbed her cheek. Her blush faded, and her breathing came easy again.

Under the shadow of his hat, the corners of Luca's lips upturned in a rare and miraculous fashion that no one saw.

"So what's the story?" Kate asked, directing her attention back to her companion.

"There's definitely a system here," Hercules responded.

"Can you tell how much quartz is there?"

"It's hard to say."

"All right." Kate looked up at the sky. "It's a bit late to be setting up our equipment now. I say we get some food, and some sleep, and start early in the morning. We'll keep a low profile, and hopefully we'll be out of here before anybody notices us."

Hercules looked at her, then looked at Luca.

"Okay, before anyone *else* notices us."

"And then we're going *home*."

Kate didn't answer. Hercules pushed the issue.

"*Right?*"

Tension rippled in the air between them.

"That depends," she answered at last.

"Come *on*, Kate," Hercules protested. "How much longer are you gonna drag this out? We're exhausted and have almost nothing to show for it. We need to go home. Regroup. Can't your brother figure out an alternative?"

"I'm *not* going home empty-handed," she said. "I can't."

Hercules growled, but it was obvious even to Luca that the more they argued, the more she would dig in her heels. Hercules shrugged and threw his hands up in the air.

"Yes, your h—"

"*Don't,*" she cut in, quashing the word in Hercules's mouth before he could form it. "*Don't.*" Her gaze darted in Luca's direction. His expression was unchanged. But he *had* heard something.

The whinny of a horse echoed above their heads. The three of them looked up.

"There's Philip now," Kate said. Hercules let the conversation drop, and Kate let out a sigh as he turned his back to her.

Asking his questions now would vex her further. If he was going to get her talking, she needed to relax. He leaned over and spoke into her ear so only she could hear.

"Are you okay?"

Kate turned to face him. She was so close now the warmth of her breath on his face as she answered sent a shiver across his skin.

"Yes. Thanks." Her whole countenance brightened with a smile.

Gods you're beautiful.

A flying horse of the purest white descended nearby. The wind generated by its broad feathered wings buffeted against the trio's faces as he touched down. He tucked in his wings and trotted over to join them. The horse was not carrying a rider. Then it spoke.

"There's a small village with a sizable inn a few miles to the east, but other than that, there's not anyone close enough to bother us," Philip said.

"Good," Kate replied.

"Your horse flies *and* talks?" Luca asked. This girl was full of surprises.

"Oh boy," Kate mumbled, turning her eyes skyward.

"I am *not* a horse! I am a pegasus. I am *the* pegasus. The last of my kind, I'll have you know." Philip turned to Kate and stomped the ground with his hoof. "How many times do I have to explain this?"

"Take it easy, Philip. He didn't know."

Philip snorted.

"Philip, this is Luca. Luca, Philip. He's my constant traveling partner. And usually he's in a much better mood." Kate tilted her head in Philip's direction. He snorted again.

"I'm just so tired of having to explain myself. You have no idea what it's like."

"Actually, I do," Luca responded.

"Oh?" Philip inquired.

"I'm a dhampir...part vampire," he added when the same confusion Kate had expressed earlier settled on Philip's countenance.

"Oh!" Philip cried. "Really? I always thought vampires were a myth."

"That makes two of us," Kate responded.

"So you know what a vampire is, but not a dhampir?" Luca asked Kate.

"I know *now*," Kate said.

"Well *I* don't understand the word 'dhampir' *or* 'vampire,'" Hercules said, arms crossed.

Kate thought for a second, then said, "*Vrykolakas.*"

Hercules raised an eyebrow. "Oh. Hmm."

Luca could see the wheels turning in his head. "What?" Luca asked. It appeared that Hercules's friendly demeanor was about to disappear. But the man dismissed it with a shake of his head.

"Nothing," he said. "You just don't look like a monster to me. And I've seen more than my share."

"Of vampires?" Kate asked.

"A few."

"You never told me that," Kate said.

"You never asked," Hercules sneered. "It was before I met you."

"So you're not afraid of me?" Luca asked. The second the words had left his mouth, he second-guessed them. His question was too earnest. But he just couldn't make sense of Kate and her cronies. Their openness was something he'd never encountered before. He wanted to know why.

Philip whinnied. "It should be the other way around, don't you think?"

Kate's gaze slid in his direction, a warning glance. The grin on Hercules's face had noticeably widened. It put Luca's hackles up.

Kate broke the tension that had bubbled up from nothing.

"What Philip is trying to say, although not too nicely, is we can hold our own and then some. You could have easily attacked me on the hill, but you didn't. Second, I've only ever read about vampires, and I'm not about to judge you based on *that*. I really meant no offense before, honest."

"None taken."

"Plus," she added, "it wouldn't be the first time I'd encountered a living myth." Hercules chuckled, and Philip let out a soft whinny.

"I remember thinking humans were a myth, before I met you," Philip said. Kate simply shrugged.

She is *human*, Luca thought. *How does a human get to be three hundred?*

"Are we just about finished with the introductions?" Philip asked.

"They better have everything set up already, I'm starving," said Hercules.

There's more *of them?*

"Let's go then," Kate said, and the four of them re-entered the forest, heading back the way Hercules had come.

No matter how hard he tried, Luca just couldn't figure them out. They didn't seem to care a whit about his being a dhampir. They didn't shrink away. Kate had introduced him, and the others had welcomed them, like they might any other person. In all his long life, this was a first. He'd seen and heard enough to want to know more. What sealed the deal though, in Luca's decision to accompany them, was Kate's silent confession of their mutual attraction. The way the blood in her face had risen to the surface at the sight of him—he would follow that rush of excitement, of wanting, of *her*. He would follow her anywhere.

4

BEFORE ENTERING THE FOREST CLEARING, KATE SLOWED HER GAIT, allowing herself and Luca to fall behind. Hercules and Philip turned around for a quick glance before continuing forward, giving her a minute alone with the hunter. She put her hand on his forearm and stopped them from walking altogether.

"What you're about to see," she said, "you can't unsee. And I can't afford to be wrong about you. Can I trust you?" Her gaze bore into him, searching the depths of his crystalline eyes for an answer that would ease her anxiety. She seemed to look right through him; it wrenched his gut that he couldn't give her what she wanted. His response offered little comfort.

"We can part ways here if you want." Letting her know that he wouldn't follow her if he wasn't welcome was all he could do.

"It's not about what *I* want," she said.

Luca saw the strain of sadness in her eyes that he had first detected upon meeting her grow, ever so slightly. He became a bit melancholy himself at the prospect of having to walk away now. In less than an hour, he'd taken a great interest in this woman, and his heart ached to spend more time with someone who so far seemed willing to accept him, even if just as a friend. The pair remained silent for a moment, as Kate decided. She hung her head and took a deep breath.

That's it then.

He wasn't surprised. But this time, it hurt, in a way that it hadn't done so in a very long time.

She lifted the mood hanging over them like a storm cloud with a soft smile and took his hand in hers.

"Come on," she said.

Luca's eyes shined. At least for now, he was welcome. She had welcomed him. Something unfamiliar bubbled up in his throat. He swallowed hard.

"Thank you," he said.

She nodded in acknowledgement, and they stepped into the clearing.

Hercules and Philip were standing in the open. But other than that, the clearing appeared empty. What struck Luca, though, was that the space seemed more alive than any other part of the wood. The forest floor was a vibrant shade of green, shimmering with dew that adorned the underbrush and the rich bark of the trees. Even a boulder looked animated as a light wind blew through the shaggy brown moss that covered it.

"There's no one here." Luca turned his attention back to Kate, his suspicion rising again. His senses came alive, and he sensed motion on all sides of him. He began to think better of his last statement.

"Isn't there?" Kate's mouth curved in mischief.

Tempting as her mouth was, Luca kept his eyes trained on the forest. His vision darted back and forth, trying to detect an anomaly in the environment. Just then, a cluster of small leaves fell from the canopy. They drifted to the ground in a peculiar pattern, swirling around themselves and forming what looked to Luca like the shape of a woman. The silhouette grew more and more defined until, finally, the woman made of leaves spoke, her voice the sound of rustling foliage.

"Welcome back, Kate."

What the—

Luca tilted his head, trying to understand how he could possibly be seeing what he was seeing, but the tree to his right caught his attention.

Dew drops glistening on the bark ran together into a single puddle that clung to the tree before it and the trunk peeled away. Underneath was a second tree, the *real* tree, and what floated before him a more vibrant copy. The dew and bark split apart in midair, forming two female shapes, one made of water, the other tree bark. The dew on the ground collected itself in the same way, forming a second woman made of water. The pieces of the forest slowly took on more tangible, humanoid shapes, their skin shining in the greens, browns, and blues of their surroundings. The water women looked slick, and the tree-like skin of the third retained a rough, cracked texture.

Several mossy rocks that were clumped together shifted, and Luca realized that they weren't rocks at all. The largest boulder uncurled itself and stood up. A bipedal, hooved creature with the head of a bull covered in shaggy brown fur was what Luca had mistaken for moss. A man with the horns and legs of a goat, and a giant of a man, whose trunk terminated in the body and legs of a workhorse, followed suit. Luca had killed countless monsters in his time as a hunter, the grotesque horrors that served as mindless minions of the lords of the dark. But the creatures he looked upon now were of an entirely different class.

"You sure keep interesting company," Luca said. Hiding his amazement no longer seemed necessary, or even possible.

"That I do," Kate replied. "But someone is missing. Someone who's in an awful lot of trouble." Louder, she called out: "Corbin! Report!"

From the tree cover above, an oversized rat dropped onto Kate's shoulder. A large scar ran down the length of his left shoulder, and his left ear was half chewed off. Despite that, its dark coat was remarkably well-groomed.

"Hi, Kate. How's it going? Who's your friend?" Luca was going to introduce himself, but Kate cut him off.

"Never mind that," Kate said. "Did you forget something?"

"Forget something?" Corbin asked, his pupils shining. "Oh, of course, you mean our equipment! Not to worry, it's all safely tucked away."

Kate bit down on the inside of her cheek. "The camp, Corbin. Where's the camp?"

"The camp. Right. Well…" Corbin scratched the spot on his head behind his ear.

A narrowing of Kate's eyes got him talking.

"After you left, Cato said he was really tired of sleeping on the ground and suggested that maybe we could find a place to stay *here*. There was no motivating them after that." Corbin turned then to Luca. "Hello. I'm Corbin, Kate's second in command. And you are?"

A giant, talking rat is second in command. Of course.

"Luca. It's nice to meet you," he managed to say.

Kate shifted on her feet. "I said we would find a place to stay at our *next* stop," Kate told the rodent.

"I told them that. They'd rather not wait."

"Did you explain to them that this world is not going to welcome them with open arms?" she protested.

He chittered at her with his long front teeth. "Of course I did. But they won't listen. They were hoping you could arrange something, seeing as it's your home planet and all."

Home planet? Are they aliens? This he couldn't let slide.

"What do you mean 'this world'?" he asked Kate.

"This one. This one world," she answered, and pointed at the ground.

"You're saying there's more than one?"

"More than you can imagine. What I was saying before, on the hill," Kate explained, "was that a long time ago, I was fortunate enough to stumble into a world that suited me better than this one. Theirs." She gestured to the array of creatures that now populated the clearing plain as day.

It was so much to take in. Luca was overwhelmed by the new, and his mind flooded with questions. After age upon age of the same, this band of wanderers sparked his curiosity. Kate especially. As a human who had chosen to live among such creatures, it wasn't a stretch to think that, maybe, it was possible to be more than just her friend. He clung to the chemistry he felt whenever their eyes or hands met, alert for an opportunity to engage her in some sort of contact.

"Back to the issue at hand," Kate said, returning to her conversation with Corbin. "How am I supposed to do that? *Where* am I supposed to do that?"

"Philip mentioned something about an inn…" Corbin murmured.

Kate narrowed her eyes at him.

He bunched his shoulders behind his head. "I'm just the messenger."

She clucked her tongue. "Fine. I'll try. But the lot of them will have to sneak in the back door. Understood?"

"Aye-aye, captain."

Kate walked toward the center of the clearing with Luca in tow. "Everyone," she shouted, "this is Luca." She patted his upper arm. "Holy smoke! What are you made of, steel?"

"What?" He asked, confused by Kate's question.

"Your arm, it's as hard as a rock."

She moved her hand to test the top of his shoulder and found it just as implacable.

"My god, you've got the weight of ten worlds on your shoulders," she exclaimed.

"If you're really tense," Hercules suggested to Luca with a mischievous grin, "you could ask Kate here to give you a massage. It wouldn't take much convincing on your part, I'm sure." Hercules flashed her a toothy smile as Kate stared at him, wide-eyed. "Isn't that true, Kate?" Hercules asked.

She just rolled her eyes at him, then caught Luca's gaze again. Hercules's suggestion suddenly seemed more serious.

"I suppose I could, if you like."

Luca considered Kate's offer. He'd just met her. And wasn't accustomed to people touching him. But he didn't want to outright refuse. The memory of her touch still lingered on his skin. In his dream, her touch had felt incredible. And here she was, offering to turn that sensation into reality.

"Thank you."

"Not a problem. You won't regret it, I promise."

What did I just agree to?

Luca's brain was spinning so fast, his thoughts were in a jumble.

Kate grabbed a blanket with a geometric design in bold primary colors from a pile of their belongings and called Philip over to her.

"Can you take Luca and me over to that inn you saw? If by some miracle I'm able to secure sleeping accommodations, you can come back here and get everyone else."

Philip whinnied in the affirmative. Kate then looked to Luca. "Okay?"

"I don't know how much help I'll be." His presence would be the opposite of helpful. But Kate wouldn't hear it. He was in no mood to argue.

"Nonsense. It'll be good to have a local with me."

He shrugged. "Okay."

Kate mounted Philip then turned to extend Luca a helping hand.

At this, Luca hesitated. Riding together would mean he'd have to squeeze in close behind her, pressed against her backside. Kate was either oblivious to the situation into which she had just invited him, or she didn't care.

"Hop on," Philip said, pawing at the ground. "Let's get going."

"Philip rarely lets people other than me ride him, so you'd better take him up on his offer before he changes his mind."

If you insist. Self-control was something he possessed in spades. But this was an altogether different kind of test.

He grabbed Kate's hand and swung his leg over Philip's back to settle in snugly behind Kate. He sat up as straight as possible to keep a comfortable distance between them. He wrapped his right arm around Kate's slender waist, but held her with as light a touch as he could.

Kate glanced back at him. She cupped her right hand over his, pulling his arm tight around her.

"I wouldn't want you to fall off." Her eyes gave off a devious light.

He left his arm where she had placed it. When she tried to uncurl her fingers from his to take hold of Philip's mane, Luca held on, testing the waters. He held her stare as long as he could. Mischief spread across his features as he watched her throat bob, and color once again raced to her cheeks, lending her a tantalizing flush.

She was open to his eyes on her, his touch. It was so much more than he'd ever expected. He reveled in it. She cleared her throat as he released his grip on her fingers and took firmer hold of her waist.

"Ready."

Philip raced along the ground lightning quick. Though his wings were tucked in all the way, the wind still rushed through them, making it feel as if his hooves galloped on the stream of air just above the ground. Kate's hair filled his view as it flowed behind her. He was surrounded by the scent of her, sweet and heady and *female*. Any questions he had thought to ask slipped away into the silence. He tightened his grip and leaned in, closing his eyes and letting the intoxicating scent of her tresses overtake him as they gently brushed against his face.

5

THE INN SAT AT THE EDGE OF A TOWN. IT WAS A SIMPLE, TWO-STORIED brick structure with a bar and kitchen serving dinner on the main floor. Only two of the dozen or so windows on the second floor appeared to have lights on inside them. The inn was modest in size. Kate's crew would have to squeeze in.

Luca dismounted first, giving himself the chance to grab Kate by the waist again to help her down. She needed no assistance, but she accepted his offer anyway. Their eyes locked as he lowered her to the ground. It was a simple thing, but being able to look into the eyes of a beautiful woman, one who was willing and eager to look back, filled him with content. Kate stretched the blanket along Philip's back to hide his wings. The pegasus took to grazing as Kate and Luca made their way toward the front door.

"What do you put in your hair?" Luca asked. It was rather forward of him to ask, but he *had* to know.

"Hmm?"

"Your hair. It has a wonderful fragrance."

"Oh." She was blushing again. "I don't know, a mix of things. Orchids, honey, a touch of cinnamon."

"Mmm."

"Sorry, I didn't realize my hair would be blowing in your face like that. I'm not used to having another rider with me."

"I didn't mind."

Kate and Luca entered the inn and stepped up to a wooden bar where a young man stood reader to greet newcomers. As the pair approached, the man's gaze shifted from one of them to the other.

"Evenin.'"

"Hi," Kate said.

"The name's Rick. How can I be of service, little lady?"

The way he leaned forward and smiled at Kate made it clear that he was attracted to her. Luca took an immediate dislike to him. He was satisfied to know that Rick's lousy attempt at flirting with her had fallen on deaf ears.

"Do you have any rooms available, *Rick?*" Kate asked, all business.

"One hundred denarii a night. Will *he* be staying with you?"

Rick jutted his chin in Luca's direction, but pointedly avoided looking straight at him, just like always.

I knew this was a bad idea.

Kate didn't bother to acknowledge the question. "How many rooms do you have?"

Rick laughed at that.

"So you *are* looking for two rooms. Good, saves me the trouble of trying to talk a sweet thing like you out of spending the night with the likes of him."

Luca ignored the impulse to turn Rick's shit-eating grin into sheer terror.

Kate turned to look at Luca. He read the incredulity in her eyes, and saw it steadily replaced by a simmering anger.

Fury rippled off her skin, but she persisted much as she had before.

"Just answer the question. How many free rooms do you have?"

"A dozen altogether."

"I'll take them all."

Kate opened a drawstring purse that was tucked at her waist.

Rick scoffed. "Is *he* getting his own room?"

"What different does it make?" she shot back.

"It makes a *big* difference to me," Rick said. "Folks like him ain't allowed to rent rooms on their own. They gotta have an employer or somethin' to vouch for their good behavior."

"Folks like what? He's a big boy, he can be responsible for himself."

It was obvious to everyone but Kate what the innkeeper was referring to. He had tried his luck at enough places to know how this was going to play out. What interested him was how heated Kate was allowing herself to become.

"I told you I wouldn't be much help," Luca said.

Kate turned her intense stare at him. "Are you serious? Folks like *what?*" she demanded of Rick.

"Dhampirs. Can't trust 'em. They're as likely to suck you dry in your sleep as look at ya."

"Did I miss something? Is the word 'dhampir' tattooed on his forehead?"

"I know a half-breed mongrel when I see one," Rick sneered. "Now, if you plan on his stayin' here it's gonna cost you a thousand denarii extra. For insurance. And it's non-refundable."

"That's ludicrous!"

"If you can't afford it, sweet thing, then why don't you ditch this guy, and I'll see about finding you a room, free of charge." Rick leaned his elbows across the table, and raised one eyebrow at Kate, eyeing her cleavage.

She stepped back to block his view. Rick licked his lips and continued.

"If it's male companionship you're lookin' for, why not let a real man show you how it's done? I'll make it worth your while. I'll double whatever he's paying ya. I just *know* a monster like him's gotta be paying a pretty steep price to get a girl like you to jump in a coffin. Hell, if you're any good, I might even give ya a tip."

That's it.

It was one thing to insult Luca, to insult his masculinity. It was downright un-original to deride the sexual ability of dhampirs as only "half men." But what he had suggested to Kate—that he wouldn't stand for.

But before he made his move, Kate brushed past his arm, drawing Luca's attention. Her skin had gone cold. Luca put one hand on her wrist to stop her as she advanced. Her temperature had dropped so low his fingertips burned with it.

`She quickly jerked her wrist free. Without a word, she made herself clear. If one of them was going to set this guy straight, it was going to be her.

"You know, Rick, I've got a tip for *you*." She inched closer.

"Oh, yeah, what's that?" He awaited some dirty suggestion, oblivious to what was about to happen to him. Kate hid her intentions behind a flirty smile.

Luca tried one last time to stop her. Something was wrong. He had lost his taste for a fight.

"It's not worth it," he said.

"Oh yes it is," she said, her eyes gleaming. Her face was inches away from Rick's now.

"Lay it on me, baby," Rick said.

"Desks are hard." Without even giving Rick time to think, she grabbed him by the scruff of his neck and shoved his face down onto the wooden counter. It resonated with a horrible crunch and did not give way at all to make room for Rick's face. A second later, he rose to reveal the unyielding surface, slippery with blood.

"Fuck! You broke my nose, you bitch!"

Kate leapt over the counter, still holding Rick by the neck. She lifted him off the floor with one hand. Her other hand held one of her short swords tight against his balls. For all Luca's super speed and heightened senses, he hadn't seen her draw the weapon.

"You want a monster, you got it! If you so much as blink, you'll be squatting to piss for the rest of your days!" Her voice had devolved into a low growl.

Luca did not like this at all.

"Now," Kate roared, "you're going to apologize to me, and apologize to my friend."

`Go to hell!"

Kate tutted, disappointed, and tightened her grip on his neck, breaking the skin. Her blade began exacting its own toll from his between his legs.

"Augh! Stop! *Stop!*"

Piss and blood ran together as Kate brought her head closer to Rick's. Her pupils were dilated, drinking in the sight.

"I'm sorry, what was that?" she tittered. "I couldn't make that out, you'll have to speak up."

Rick choked on the blood streaming from his face. The more he sputtered, the tighter she squeezed. Rick's cheeks took on a distinctive shade of purple.

She's enjoying this.

"I'm sorry, okay? Oh, God, I'm sorry! I'm sorry! Please, *stop!*"

"Enough." Luca's voice was quiet, but firm. It was flattering, how she'd defended him, but he preferred her kindness, and wanted to banish the strange expression on her face.

He held her gaze until, finally, she relented. Kate returned her blade to its sheath and dropped Rick on the floor like a broken doll.

Luca placed his hand on the small of her back and led Kate out. Once the fresh air hit her face, Kate's anger began to leave her. Luca tried to lighten the mood.

"That didn't go so well."

Kate turned to face Luca. "I am so sorry," she said, panting. Her eyes were wide, and she sounded dead serious.

"It's alright. You shouldn't get worked up like that. I told you, I'm used to it."

"No," she said. The warm demeanor that had caught him off-guard the moment his eyes first met hers returned with all its vigor. "I can't even imagine the pain you've had to bear. No one should *ever* have to get used to that."

Luca had no idea what to say to that. She really meant it.

"Thanks." It seemed so inadequate for how her passion moved him.

"Don't mention it."

The tips of his fingers buzzed with the realization that his hand was still on her back. He drew her closer to him. She didn't resist.

Philip stopped nibbling on the weeds nearby and rejoined them.

When he came closer, Luca relinquished his hand, and took a step back. Kate was still trying to catch her breath.

"Is everything alright?" Philip asked.

"Everything except Rick..." Luca responded.

His offhand comment made Kate crack a laugh. She bent down and grabbed her knees to compose herself.

"I'm sorry I wasn't more helpful," Luca said.

"Oh, you helped. You stopped me from turning that kid into a eunuch. I didn't mean to... I lost control. Thanks for pulling me back." She smiled at him.

Luca smiled back. He didn't like seeing her so upset. Still, it *was* nice to see her stick up for him like that. She cared. He could trust her.

"Yes," Kate finally said to Philip. "Everything is fine, but we're going to have to set up our own camp tonight."

"What a shame," Philip sighed. "This place looked promising, and it's late to start setting up camp now."

"I know," she said. "I'll take care of it."

"Are you sure?"

"I'm sure."

"You're really not supposed to do that that often."

Luca's eyes narrowed. He was missing something.

"I'll be fine. Don't worry so much," Kate said.

"It's my job to worry about you," Philip insisted.

"And it's *my* job to worry about them. They're out a good night's sleep, a warm meal, and I owe Luca here a bath and a massage."

"You don't owe me anything," Luca said.

He didn't know what they were talking about, but Luca decided he didn't like anything that was going to come at the expense of Kate's well-being. Which is what Philip seemed to be suggesting.

"Sure I do. And I keep my promises. Everything will be alright. Anyway," she said, "this will give me the perfect opportunity."

"Opportunity for what?"

Kate's eyes gleamed in the twilight.

"To give you a taste of Icarya."

6

Hercules was the first to greet them. Kate noticed that Cato, the minotaur, was not in the camp.

"Everyone's ready to go. And ready to eat. Cato went off to look for food, but hasn't come back yet," he said.

"Hold that thought," Kate said.

It was the oddest thing. She'd brutalized the innkeeper without blinking, but now she was wringing her hands?

"Why, what's wrong? Did everything go okay?" Hercules asked.

"Perfect. I broke some guy's face."

"Okay, good, so—wait, you *what?* Oh, Kate…"

"Sorry, Herc. It couldn't be helped."

Hercules sighed.

"What was it *this* time?"

"He called Luca a monster. And me a whore."

"Oh! Well, Then by all means, *break* the guy's face," Hercules said, throwing his hands up in the air. "The gods know we've never been called *names* before."

"All right, Herc, you've made your point."

"Have I?"

"Yes, Dad," Kate retorted. "Shall I go to my room now?"

"What room? We've got *no* rooms, and we're stuck setting up camp in the middle of the night. Again."

"Hey, the guy was a real jerk," Luca interrupted. "Take it easy, okay?"

"Look, I put us in this position," Kate said as she laid a gentle hand on Luca's arm, "and I'll fix it. Just make a fire."

Hercules stared at her, then hung his head.

"You don't have to do that. We'll be fine. I wasn't suggesting that you—"

"I know you weren't. But they're cold, and tired, and they've been away from home too long already. Cheer up, it'll be good for morale," she replied.

"And what about you?"

"If they're happy, I'm happy."

Hercules just kept shaking his head.

"Relax, will you?" she said. "It's not that serious."

"Kate?" Luca asked.

"Yeah?"

"Why is everyone so concerned about you making camp all by yourself? You've got plenty of people here to help. And I don't mind pitching in."

"No, you don't understand. This I've got to do on my own. I just need some space. Why don't you go mingle, okay?" Kate pressed on his forearm again, then released him. "I'll be back in a bit." With a final glance at Luca, Kate walked off into the woods.

Luca turned to Hercules. "Are *you* going to tell me what's going on?"

"Kate is going to cast a spell, give us a better camp than one we could make ourselves."

Of course. She was beyond beautiful, older than a century, and talked to animals. He felt stupid not to have realized it before.

She was a witch.

"Is it dangerous?" Luca asked.

"It's magic, so there's always danger. But the mirage is all in Kate's head, down to the very last detail. It takes an enormous amount of mental energy, and—"

"And?"

"A blood sacrifice."

That's a problem. He was having a hard enough time as it was keeping his fangs to himself. Smelling Kate's blood might put him over the edge if he wasn't careful. And he had to be, because he liked her so much. The last thing he wanted to do was hurt her if he lost control. Or scare her away. Anything but that.

"Are you going to be okay?" Hercules asked.

The abrupt turn in the conversation left Luca vulnerable. He tried to play it off.

"What do you mean?"

"You know what I mean. Will you be able to control yourself?"

And just like that, the open welcome he'd received earlier had evaporated.

"Yes," Luca answered.

"Don't lie to me. If you can't guarantee that she'll be safe, just walk away."

Hercules was more perceptive than Luca gave him credit for. Luca knew he was taking a risk by staying. The more time he spent with Kate, the more he wanted her. Wanted her body. Wanted her blood. But most of all, he wanted to bask in her open acceptance. For that, he was willing to sacrifice the rest.

"I would never do anything to hurt her."

"No, I don't believe you would." Hercules's tone softened, and he smiled. "Had to ask, though. Standard big brother type stuff. Plus…"

There's more?

"Kate can get very emotional."

"I noticed."

Hercules nodded. "And when she gets emotional, her magic can be…volatile."

"Then why do you let her do it?"

"Let her do it?" Hercules laughed. "Let me tell you something about Kate. No one *lets* her do anything. She just does it. Look, if she says she'll be fine, she'll be fine."

Luca still didn't like it. It was risky for her, so her friends believed. It was undoubtedly risky for him. But he had already seen firsthand how headstrong Kate could be. If her closest friends couldn't stop her from endangering herself, he knew he wouldn't be able to either. And he was *not* about to admit that if he caught the scent of her, of the liquid velvet rushing through her veins, he might, in fact, lose his mind.

"I've got to start collecting firewood," Hercules said. "Why don't I introduce you to some people?"

"Okay."

Luca stood in the middle of a crowd of creatures, while Hercules went off to find proper kindling. The dhampir did his best to make small talk. Everyone was kind and welcoming, and no one seemed to mind that Kate had brought him into their camp without asking anyone.

That's what everyone he talked to seemed to have in common. They adored Kate, and trusted her without hesitation.

A short while later, Hercules returned and began making a fire in the center of the clearing.

A fire that small isn't going to warm anybody.

He was about to say so, and offer his help, when Kate returned. Unlike before, when her compatriots had rushed upon her, they all kept their distance. The forest fell quiet, and no one looked directly at her.

She walked right past Luca without seeing him and headed toward the fire. She didn't speak to anyone. She knelt by the fire and studied the flames before grabbing a long, thin branch that poked out of the center. The end of it was still lit. Without lifting the branch off the ground, Kate dragged the smoldering end in the dirt, creating a large spiral that bordered the entire clearing.

Luca saw those far to the edge step closer, making sure to stand inside the inner curve of the spiral.

When the outer edges of the spiral met in a closed circle, Kate dug deeper into the dirt and left the burning stick upright in the ground. She returned to the fire, walking back the way she had come, rather than crossing the lines and going straight for the center. Luca could hear the slip of a whisper, and her lips were moving, but couldn't understand her words.

When she arrived at the center, she knelt again before the fire. From a pocket on her belt she pulled out a small blue orb and held it out in front of her with her left hand. Eyes closed, she used her right hand to draw the dagger from her boot.

Luca's breath came faster. His heart raced.

I don't know if I can do this.

He wanted it. He wanted it so bad his whole frame buzzed with anticipation of the moment her skin would lie open to the sky.

He was a monster. She was on the brink of hurting herself for the sake of others, and all he could think was how badly he wanted it to happen.

Damn him. He should have left. Just turned around and disappeared into the forest. It would have been easier before, when Kate had walked off. He wouldn't have had to face her.

He could hide himself in a hole somewhere and sink the teeth that were pressing against the inside of his gums into his forearm. It had always been enough, before.

There was no moving him now. He was rooted in place, watching with pulsating pupils as her fingers rotated the orb, placing the blade in her left palm between the orb and her hand. Her chanting continued, and the fire glowed stronger and brighter.

Luca heard Kate take a sharp breath, and in the next moment she ran the dagger across her palm. She squeezed the orb. Hard. When her blood dripped into the fire, it reacted like gasoline. The blaze traveled the path of Kate's spiral in the dirt.

In the haze created by the flames, a caravan began to take shape. A series of red and gold tents slowly materialized along the perimeter of the spiral, their doors flapping in the breeze to reveal the rich décor inside. The tents were populated with lush pillows and fabrics, cups and bowls made of silver, and incredibly soft-looking beds.

Kate's blade was still biting into her hand, which had begun to quiver. When the orb dissolved into the ashes and the tents took on a physical form, Kate dropped her dagger into the dirt and balled her cut-open hand into a loose fist. With her good hand, she retrieved the plaid scarf out from around her neck and wrapped it tightly around her wound. She picked up her dagger, wiped the blade on her lap, and returned it to its place alongside her leg.

But Luca saw none of this. From the minute Kate had opened her flesh, his nostrils had been filled with the scent of her blood. He didn't see the caravan appear out of nowhere, didn't hear the fire crackling past him as it spread around the clearing. His consciousness was filled with her blood, and nothing else. For once, it was his turn to be hypnotized. He had closed his eyes to hide the blood that had rushed there in his excitement, causing his pupils to shine bright red. His nose detected the tawny and sweet notes spilling into the fire. He had tried to steel himself for this moment, but her blood possessed a luxurious quality that made its owner absolutely irresistible. He stood immobilized, enrapt. And incredibly thirsty.

When his breathing returned to normal, and he was sure his eyes had cleared, he opened them to find what her blood had purchased.

"Pretty amazing, huh?" the faun standing beside him said.

"Yes, she is," he replied in a dreamy tone. The forest seemed to be spinning. Luca felt unsteady on his feet.

The faun turned to him.

"I meant the camp."

The dizziness subsided, and Luca finally felt in control enough to approach Kate. Though the others had begun to move about and settle into the tents, she hadn't moved from the center. She sat with her legs folded, staring at the ground in front of her.

"Hey," he managed, clearing the feeling of being parched from his throat.

Kate looked up at him, then looked down again at her hand, nursing her wound. "Hi."

"Are you alright?"

"Peachy. Help me up."

He assisted Kate to her feet. When he reached for her left hand, she shrunk back with a grimace. With the lightest of touches, he turned her hand in his, and placed his left hand on top of the wrapping.

"May I?"

"Go ahead."

Luca uncovered her wound and placed his hand over hers. Luca held his breath to stop the hypnotic smell from permeating his brain. There was uncertainty in her eyes. But no fear. After a moment, he released her hand. The wound was gone. Only a light smear of crimson remained as evidence that she had even cut herself at all.

"How did you do that?" she asked.

"I accelerated the healing process in your hand."

"I thought regeneration was something vampires could only do to themselves."

"For most vampires and dhampirs that's true. It's just an ability I have," Luca explained.

"Thank you," said Kate.

"You're welcome."

She wiped her hand on her clothes.

What a waste, a sinister inner voice reflected. Luca shut out the thought.

"Huh. I feel a lot better. Not just in my hand, I mean. I feel energized," Kate said.

Luca nodded.

"I'm still hungry though," she added.

Me too.

The faun approached them. "Sorry to interrupt, but Cato *still* hasn't come back yet."

"Still not here?" Kate asked. "I wonder what he's been doing all this time."

"Catching this!" The minotaur Cato strutted into the circle and dropped the enormous beast he had slung over his shoulders by the fire. Cheers erupted from the entire camp.

"Oh ho ho! It's shaping up to be a good night after all!" Kate smiled, rubbing her hands together. "I want those ribs. Torrence, do you have that nice spice rub you make on you, by any chance?"

"I never leave home without it! You never know when you might need an Icaryan barbecue," the faun answered.

"Excellent. Hop to it then! And tell Lena and Varya that there should be some fruits, vegetables, and wine in the tents. See if they can't whip something up."

"With pleasure." Torrence left the couple alone again.

"It's going to be a while before dinner is ready," Kate said. "That should give us enough time."

"For what?"

"Your massage. Or did you forget?"

He had not.

She cocked her head at him. "Still want it?"

More than I can stand.

"Mmhmm."

"Right this way." She took hold of his hand and turned to lead him to a tent at the edge of the circle, keeping their clasped hands on the small of her back.

7

THE TENT WAS FURNISHED WITH A BED, A FEW CANDLES, A WOODEN DESK littered with papers and scrolls, and haphazardly thrown jewelry. The minute she let the flap drop behind her, Kate unloaded her satchel and sent her weapons clattering to the floor.

"God, that feels so much better," she said with a long stretch. Without the scarf and the satchel, which had obscured her figure, Luca found toned, graceful arms that retained their soft femininity.

"After dinner," Kate said, "I'll clear out of here and you can sleep in my bed."

"You can dream up a whole camp but can't add one more tent?" he asked.

"This is only a replica of a camp," Kate explained. "I can see it all in my mind's eye, but I didn't build it, and I can't change it. Except for one thing."

Kate held the back flap of the tent open. What should have opened onto a rear view of the forest instead led to an inner chamber of stone.

"After you," Kate gestured.

The candlelit room smelled of fresh flowers, and deeper, headier scents Luca couldn't name. In the center was a large shallow pool.

Kate came to face him. Luca could feel his heart tapping out a rapid beat as her palms grazed his shoulders and slid his arms out of his coat sleeves. It was more human contact than he had ever had. He kept his gaze on her, and felt his pupils pulsed when she held his stare. After a beat, her attention lifted upward, and she removed his hat.

"You can put the rest of your clothes here on this stool, and I'll have them washed."

"Don't bother."

Her brows furrowed. "Are you sure?"

"They're not worth it."

She inspected their condition and hummed in agreement.

"I'll come back in when you're ready," she said, and disappeared back into the tent.

He stood there, alone again for the first time since he'd woken up, and took a moment.

Am I really doing this?

He pulled the buttons open on his shirt. It peeled off him like a second skin. His belt didn't even make it, but snapped in half at the slightest tug. Luca tested the waters with his fingertips first. Warm, but not scalding, and still. Still was good. If there had been a fountain, they would have had a problem.

When seated, the water rose to cover his chest, leaving his shoulders dry. Between the dark color of the stone and the dim lighting, his submerged half was sufficiently obscured. He stretched his arms out, resting them on the outer rim of the bath. Scented steam surrounded him. He inhaled deep, and breathed it in.

Kate's voice echoed from the tent beyond. "Are you ready for me?"

Not nearly.

"Yes."

His fingers tensed. He braced his fingernails against the stone, waiting for Kate to catch a glimpse of him undressed.

Kate headed first for the pile of clothes Luca had discarded.

Good gods woman, will you look at me already?

Why had he agreed to this? This was absolute torture.

Two small, dark red pills fell out of Luca's pocket as she picked up his pants.

Luca almost leapt out of the bath, but remembered that she was holding his pants.

"Uhhh..."

Kate's eyebrows rose. "Do you need these?"

"No. *Yes.* They're...uhhh..."

A flush spread over his skin like a fever. She was looking at him, waiting for an answer. He wracked his brain for something to say.

"They're...food."

She looked down at the capsules in her hand. Luca wanted to disappear.

She didn't say a word. She just handed Luca's clothes, and the pills, to one of the water women standing on the other side of the door. Then she came toward him.

"I'm sorry," he said.

"Sorry for what?"

Her voice was quiet, and soothing. He leaned back in the bath again and let the issue drop.

"This is the bathhouse in my home," Kate said. "I don't get to spend a lot of time there, but this is where I like to relax, and think."

Finally, she looked up. Her breath caught. Even in the darkness, he could see the flush that crept up her neck and spilled onto her cheeks. He wanted her all the more, with her blood rushing to the surface at the sight of him.

His broad chest extended to powerful shoulders and lean, muscular arms. His abdomen was trim, but firm. His skin was perfectly smooth, free of the scars and aging common to his line of work. His pale flesh shone in the near darkness enrobed in shadow by his raven hair, floating all around him.

She passed a hand over her face. It was all she seemed to need to break free from his hypnotic gaze, even when he put some effort into it. Being able to shake him off was not something easily done. It made him wonder just how strong her own mental powers were.

He let their battle of the minds go unheeded as Kate picked up a large round sponge and knelt on the rim of the tub. She let out a deep sigh and ran her fingers through her hair.

"Is something wrong?" Luca asked.

"I'll be fine, I just...did you ever have so many other people to worry about, that you didn't know what *you* wanted?"

Luca tilted his head. Kate's confidence was cracking. It caught him off guard.

"I'm sorry, I don't mean to burden you with this. But I haven't been able to think. I've just kept them moving." Her gaze fell to the floor. "Things aren't going well."

She couldn't express her doubts in front of her crew. Luca understood that. But she needed to talk to *someone*. It felt like a great privilege to be taken into her confidence. But it didn't stop him from asking the questions that nagged him.

"Why are you really here?" he asked.

"Quartz is our main energy source," Kate said. "Icarya didn't have electricity, or running water, when my brothers and I first arrived. My brother had been studying to become an engineer, so he knew how to build a circuit. When he lit up Castelmor for the first time, it was like a miracle. He was working on a big initiative to bring electricity to the most rural places. That's when we realized that Icarya had a very limited supply of the thing we needed most."

"Can't you go home and recalibrate your search? Get some fresh bodies to help you?"

Kate's shoulders sagged. "This is *not* the first expedition. We've been at this for decades, but...we've got two years left. That's it." She paused and put her hand to her forehead. "It sounds so much worse when I say it out loud. Only my brother and I know. I can't let Icarya go dark. I just can't."

"It wouldn't be your fault if it did."

Kate pursed her lips.

"It *wouldn't*."

"If it were only that easy. Everything falls on my head," she said. Her eyes took on that doleful glaze again, staring into nothing as the surface of the pool reflected in her dark eyes.

Luca shifted in his seat. "You don't have to do this. I don't want to add to your trouble."

She placed her hand on his shoulder, staying him. His breath caught in his throat at the feel of her warm fingertips pressing into his muscle. He met her warm, open gaze.

"You're not. You're not expecting anything, so I can tell you everything. Thank you for listening." Kate plunged the sponge into the water and squeezed it out gently over Luca's shoulder. He tried to grab the sponge from her, but she didn't let him.

"I'm capable of washing myself," he protested.

"No one said you weren't. Could you just let me pamper you?"

Luca didn't resist after that. Kate took Luca's flowing hair in her hands and pushed it over his right shoulder as she worked on the left. She gingerly scrubbed his skin, trailing down to his arms and fingers. Very slowly, she washed away the dirt, the exhaustion, and the emotional scars that Luca had allowed to build up over the course of ages. Every droplet of water that ran down his skin echoed into the bath quietly. Luca's flesh came alive, feeling each individual stream of sweet stimulation.

"What about your brother?" Luca asked, his voice hushed and dreamy. With every caress, his submerged flesh hardened.

Keep her talking. She might not notice.

"What about him?" she asked, running her fingers across his open palm.

Her skin is so soft. If it tastes even half as sweet as I dreamt...

She leaned forward. Luca's eyes gravitated to the shadow between her breasts. A shudder ran through him, prolonging the silence.

"Hmm?" she asked.

It's only water. How mad would she be if I just—

"Umm wouldn't he help you, if you were to return unsuccessful?" he stammered.

Get a grip.

His distraction was obvious. She smiled at him through thick lashes. "If I disappoint him again, I don't know if he'll even look at me anymore."

"Again?"

"His wife Cyrene came with us, once. I promised to keep it short and keep her safe." Kate shifted Luca's hair to his other shoulder, soaking the sponge again. When she resumed speaking, Luca heard her voice crack.

"Of all the people to die on me, I lost my brother's wife. I did everything I could, but I couldn't save her."

Luca said nothing. He had seen death, caused death, and had died himself so many times, that death had lost its edge.

"He thinks I was being careless. I didn't realize she was in danger until it was too late. And she was gone, just like that." She sat up to focus on Luca's back. "My relationship with him has been very tense, to say the least. I think he resents me."

"For what?"

"For coming home. If given the choice, he would have preferred his wife. I can't blame him, I would have made the same choice if I could have."

"You weren't given that choice."

"I know. But that doesn't make it hurt any less." Kate sighed. "Families are complicated."

You have no idea.

She moved on to washing Luca's collarbone and upper chest, which caused her to lean forward, bringing her face within inches of his. Luca noticed the tips of her hair as they dipped into the water in front of him. Kate was whispering now.

"Let's change the subject."

It was exactly the opening Luca had been waiting for.

"You said before that you were born in the year 1884," he started.

"Yes."

"That was ten thousand years ago."

Her hand stopped midair, but she recovered just as quickly.

"I see."

"I'm interested in the world you left behind," Luca said.

"What do you want to know?"

"To what extent did vampires and humans interact?"

"People didn't believe vampires existed at all, not unless you lived in some backwater. That must have changed at some point, I imagine."

Luca tried not to reveal his hand, but if he was going to ask, the time was now.

"You mentioned a book…"

"You mean, the one we both seem to know of?"

Careful.

"Yes. Do you know what it's about?"

"A powerful vampire who tries to take over the world and is beaten back by a group of stalwart men. He kills a few people in the process and victimizes the females of the story."

Sounds about right, thought Luca.

"I only mentioned it because *Dracula* was viewed as the quintessential definition of a vampire. Or the vampire myth, I should say," said Kate.

She put the sponge down on the ledge of the bath and went to work on Luca's shoulders. Her fingers were soft and caring but exerted enough pressure on his muscles to tenderize them. Luca closed his eyes in relaxation and let out a low sigh.

"Which is?" he asked.

"Let's see. Nocturnal, needs blood to survive, exceedingly strong and cunning, can take on animal forms, or mist, control the weather, and is vulnerable to garlic, stakes through the heart, and crosses. I'm sure I'm leaving things out. Are any of them right so far?"

"Most of them. But not all vampires are the same. Different vampires have varying levels of ability, no one possesses all those traits," Luca explained.

Except one. And a half.

"What causes the variation?" Kate inquired as dug her thumb into the flesh beneath his shoulder blade and held it there for a long minute.

"Genetics," he finally ground out when she released him.

"Oh. Vampires reproduce?"

"Of course."

"Sexually?"

"How else?"

He kept his gaze trained forward, away from her.

"I don't know, by taking victims?"

"That *does* increase the vampire population, but they are not as powerful as vampires created though mating."

"I see. It makes sense, I suppose, with so many human cultures, it would be odd for vampires to be completely uniform."

Kate spread her hands outward, reaching down Luca's arms to massage his hands and fingers. Luca wrapped her arms around his shoulders, giving her a momentary break. He could hear her heart pounding wildly in her chest. It made his own flutter in response.

"Why did you leave?" he asked.

"I can be so much more than someone's personal housekeeper, when given the choice. My whole world was defined by rules. Someone somewhere decided what every perfect woman should be, and I just did *not* fit that mold. Living in Icarya has made me free."

He tilted his head forward at her hands' request.

"It's funny though," she continued. "All the years I shunned the idea that my sole purpose in life was to get married and have children, I never expected to sacrifice companionship. Or love. Being on the road all the time can be very…"

"Lonely."

"Yes."

Luca paused for a moment. "That seems silly to me. Dividing humans up by what they can and can't do. All humans are still humans."

"Mmhmm." Kate looked at Luca, as if to say that's how she felt about vampires and humans, too. Cut from the same cloth.

"You shouldn't have to be alone," he said. A creature as lovely as Kate deserved more than the miserable lifestyle allotted to him.

"I'm not alone," she responded.

Luca's eyes questioned her.

"Not now."

A soft smile rose on his face. She leaned in again, resting her chin on his shoulder. He bent his elbow, placing his hand on the back of her head and wrapping red tendrils around his slender fingers.

"Do you feel better?" she whispered.

"Much better."

She lifted her face. Luca's gaze fell to her lips. They parted to let a subtle stream of air pass between them. He nudged her head closer to his and opened his mouth. He could almost feel her supple lips against his, when—

"Excuse me, Kate, but where should I put these?" The woman made of water had returned with a clean set of clothes for Luca.

Kate groaned and rested her forehead against his.

Damn.

"Just leave them outside." She turned back to Luca. "I'll wait for you outside, okay?"

He'd still been playing with her hair. He bit his tongue as he unfurled his fingers. But when she left, he noticed the full curve of her ass for the first time in delight.

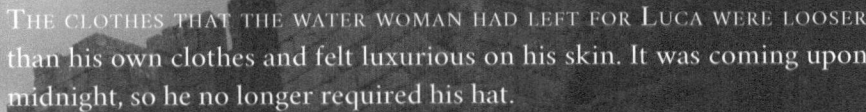

8

The clothes that the water woman had left for Luca were looser than his own clothes and felt luxurious on his skin. It was coming upon midnight, so he no longer required his hat.

He saw Kate sitting on a log next to Hercules, a bronze platter in her lap stacked with generously seasoned ribs, dripping in their own juices.

"I am about to get so messy, and I don't even care," Kate announced as she picked up one of the ribs. The intimacy of the bath had passed. It was time to sate another appetite.

Hercules motioned to Luca. "There's plenty of room here."

"Thanks," he said.

Hercules looked back at Kate, who was voraciously consuming her dinner.

"Are you planning to eat something other than ribs? You've got to stay balanced if you're gonna be on your game tomorrow."

"I'm busy," was all she cared to say between mouthfuls of meat.

Hercules just clucked his tongue. The woman with the bark of a tree for skin offered Luca a silver goblet. He looked down to find a liquid of deep crimson. Someone had liquified his pills.

His first instinct was to throw the cup away so he wouldn't be caught with it. But it had been *handed* to him. They knew what was in it.

Luca turned to Kate. "You didn't have to do that. I usually just swallow them dry."

"Where's the fun in that?" Kate said. She had finally swallowed enough of the ribs to speak. "Look around you. Everyone's enjoying a nice meal, having a good time. Why would we begrudge you a cup of sustenance?"

"Because it's not ale, or wine, or—"

"So what? I'm eating ribs. Hercules wants vegetables, the water nymphs only want water, Philip is having grass... No one cares what you're drinking. So drink up."

Luca had always treated his blood thirst like a dirty secret. Drinking in the open, around a crowd of people, was the most brazen thing he'd ever done. It was liberating.

It did not, however, improve the scent of the pills' contents, which smelled as sterile as the lab they'd come from. All around him, the smells were mouthwatering.

"It's rare to see such a feast out here. I think I'd like to have some."

Kate licked her fingers. "By all means. Have whatever you'd like."

Luca took a small plate with a rib and a couple of potatoes. Kate seemed to be enjoying the ribs thoroughly, so he tried that first.

"Huh."

"Like it?" Kate asked.

"Yeah. This is delicious." He dug his teeth in deeper. Kate smiled as she transferred some ribs from her plate onto his.

"Aren't you concerned about being out in the open this late at night?" he asked. "The forests around here are swarming with monsters."

"The camp is protected. See that spiral? It's not necessary for creating the camp itself, but it keeps things from getting in or out, monsters or no. Someone traveling through these woods would get turned around again and again. It would be next to impossible to find your way to this clearing," she explained.

"What about Cato? He wasn't in the circle when you made it," Luca observed.

"He's *a minotaur*. I'm pretty sure he can find his way through a maze."

"So Luca," Hercules jumped in, as he speared some grilled onions, "what do you do for a living?"

"I'm a hunter."

"What do you hunt?"

"Vampires."

Kate and Hercules looked at each other.

"Why would you do that?" Kate asked.

Luca just repeated her words from earlier. "Families are complicated."

Kate dipped her head in acknowledgement. "I had that coming."

"Yeah, I hear ya," Hercules said. "I fought my father all my life before joining up with Kate. Fat lotta good it did me. Is the pay good, at least? Me, I was stupid enough to help people for free, and live off their good graces."

"It's one of the highest paying jobs available, when I get paid."

"What do you mean, 'when you get paid'?" Kate interjected.

"My last employers decided that they didn't want to pay me, and would rather kill my horse and run me out of town."

"Oh, honey!" Kate blurted out. Luca looked at her. No one had ever called him *that* before. Hercules looked even more upset than she was.

"Figures. Nothing's changed. You work your ass off, and no one gives a damn that you risked your life to save theirs. All they care about is that you're different." He was turning bright red.

"Now who's getting hot under the collar?" Kate needled him.

"You wanna start something?!" Hercules cried.

"Oh grow up. Anyway...Luca, are you currently employed?" Kate asked.

"No."

"Would you like to be? I imagine that being a vampire hunter requires strength, speed, and brains?"

"Yes."

"Good. Because you're just the kind of man I'm looking for."

Am I?

Luca tilted his head. Hercules chuckled, and Kate smiled. There was that blush again. Oh how he liked making her blood race.

Luca still hadn't answered her, so Kate sweetened the deal.

"I'll pay you three times what you should have gotten for your last job. Plus, there will be fringe benefits."

"Such as?" he asked.

"You get us for company," Hercules joked. "What more could you ask for?"

"And," Kate added, "You don't have to kill anybody."

Luca considered Kate's offer. It was customary for vampire hunters to refuse any job other than hunting vampires. He had held especially true to this over the years, being a man on a mission. But her offer was very generous. And it kept him close to her. At least for a while.

"I'll accept, on one condition."

"Name it," she said.

"I won't take any more payment than the rest here."

Kate smile widened. "That's fine. You've got yourself a deal." She pulled a large handful of coins from her purse and gave them to Luca.

"What exactly are we doing?"

"Ever been spelunking?" Kate asked.

"What?"

"Cave diving. Granted, it's not the most efficient way to accumulate quartz, but an excavation would bring too much unwanted attention. There's a cave system that *should* have a decent amount of quartz ten minutes to the west of us. Tomorrow, we'll determine how much quartz is down there, and figure out how best to retrieve it. It should be a few days, at the most. Then we're off to some other godforsaken place."

So soon?

"Now that we're on the subject," Hercules cut in, "just how much longer is this going to take?"

"How should I know? Kate stuffed a potato in her mouth.

"It's just that...well..."

"Spit it out," Kate said.

"It's been several months since we've been home."

"I'm well aware of that." Kate's voice ran cold.

"And, we were only supposed to be gone for one month."

"I can't control that, Hercules. You know that the passage of time can be inconsistent when we travel. I thought it *would* be only one month."

"Yes, but—"

"But what?"

"These people have families, Kate. Families that miss them."

Kate's expression went blank. But Hercules just kept at it.

"You just don't understand, you don't have—" Hercules stopped himself mid-sentence.

Kate stood up. In a stony voice, she said: "You're right. I don't. Excuse me." She abruptly turned around and walked straight into her tent.

Hercules planted his face in his hands.

Luca got up to follow her.

"Can you tell her I'm sorry?" Hercules pleaded. "I really didn't mean that the way it sounded."

"Tell her yourself." After taking a few steps, Luca turned back around. "At least you have something to miss."

Luca pulled back the entrance to Kate's tent, and felt like he had walked into a cold spot. All the warmth had been sucked out of the room. The air was stifling. A light frost covered the grass at his feet. He saw Kate sitting upright on the bed, staring at the ground. She exhaled small puffs of white smoke. Luca noticed that the skin bordering her fingernails as she clasped the edge of the bed had turned a stark white. Her eyes were an empty, transparent gray. She hadn't noticed him.

He broke the silence.

"Hey."

Her head snapped in his direction and the room returned to normal. Her skin was as it had been before, her eyes once again a rich brown.

"Sorry, I didn't hear you come in," she said. "Let me just grab a few things and I'll be out of your way." She rummaged through her belongings, paying no mind to the dramatic change in the tent's climate.

Maybe she hadn't noticed. Maybe it wasn't worth talking about. Or she didn't *want* to talk about it. And everything was fine again, just like that. Luca brushed it off.

He stretched out on the bed and kicked off his boots. When she went to move past him, he caught her by the wrist and gave a gentle pull. She fell backward onto the bed next to him.

"This is big enough for both of us," he observed.

"Just a minute," Kate said, but her smile suggested she wasn't going anywhere. "I don't normally go to bed with people I just met. Besides, I promised you your own bed. I'll be fine outside." She echoed what he'd been saying all day. "I'm used to it."

Luca narrowed his eyes, and felt a grin creeping up the corners of his mouth.

"You promised me a *warm* bed. It will be warmer if you stay. And I'm not about to sleep in here with you on the cold ground outside. We're either both in here, or both out there. Your choice."

Kate accepted the challenge in Luca's eyes. She let the tension in her body melt away and snuggled up to him, squirming to get comfortable.

"Then I guess it's both of us in here. We *are* both grownups, I suppose."

"Mmhmm." He put his arm around her and stroked her hair. It had quickly become one of his favorite features.

"I don't see what all the fuss is about. Dhampirs don't seem so scary to me," she said.

"You're one of a kind in that regard," he replied.

Kate placed her hand on his chest. Luca tried to check the rhythm of his breathing as it ticked upward.

"Is there anything else I should know?" she murmured.

"The townsfolk would probably tell you not to trust me, that being with me is worse than being taken by a vampire, and that I have a heart of ice."

A few seconds passed. Kate lowered her head onto his chest and closed her eyes.

A moment's silence, she said, "That's silly. I can hear your heart beating just as much as my own."

Luca's eyes became glassy. He swallowed hard. With one hand in her hair and the other around her waist, he squeezed her in a tight embrace. His voice was shredded when it came out.

"Thank you."

"For what?"

"For unearthing me. For knowing what I am, and not caring."

"I care about *who* you are, not *what*," she answered.

He craned his neck and pressed his lips to her forehead. She laid her head down on his chest again and listened to his heartbeat while his fingers tangled themselves in her hair. Luca stared up at the night sky through the opening in the tent's ceiling. So much had changed since he had last laid down to rest. *He* had changed.

They remained quiet, just living in each other's arms. After a time, Luca's heart began beating so hard and so fast, he couldn't stop it. Her muscles had tensed, like she was preparing to move. Every inch of him coiled in attention.

His breathing rattled around his ribcage as Kate lifted her head. She let her lips graze his chest, then his neck as she rose. His heart hammered so hard it hurt when her lips brushed against his chin. Her gaze met his for a second before she descended on him and gave his lower lip a gentle tug. She pulled back, just a hair's breadth, but he followed her, cupping her face in his hands and pulling her to his mouth again. He ran his fingers through her hair, and sighed softly between kisses as she parted his lips with his tongue. What she took, he gave back. He wrapped his arm around her waist, pressing her to him, and cradled the back of her head with his other hand to taste the full sweetness of her mouth. When she nipped at him with her teeth, and slipped her tongue into his mouth to tease his, a low moan escaped him, and he lost it.

In one swift, graceful movement, he was on top of her. His hand traced the path of her throat, feeling electrified as his fingertips traveled along the protruding veins down to the curve of her breast. His exploration stopped at her hips, where he grabbed hold of her tight. He growled as she raked her nails ran through his dark locks and bent her knees to trap him there between her legs.

He needed to be nearer, to feel her closer to him. She sank into the cushion of the bed as he pressed down on her. His cock was straining against his pants and sent a jolt through him at the sensation of her body just on the other side. She tilted her hips to meet him, inviting him to move with her in a way that had his mouth hanging open. Lust blazed in her eyes. There wasn't a hint of hesitation in her expression as he moved his hand from her thigh and pulled at her leggings. Only need.

Luca's fangs were coming in. He separated his mouth from hers, leaving her breathless. He nudged her chin with his nose and extended her neck. He caressed her throat, beckoning to the blood under her skin, right beneath the surface. He traced the path of her veins with his tongue, his taste buds leaping at the blood rushing underneath.

He could not linger here. He made to rise and kiss Kate again, but she clasped the back of his neck and held him in place. She arched her body toward him and extended her neck, daring him to do what he wanted.

His fangs throbbed against her veins. He held his mouth open, perched against her flesh for what seemed like an eternity. His breath failed him. He would die if he didn't drink.

Stop. STOP.

A deep tremor took hold of him as he fought the overpowering, soul-shattering urge to sink his teeth into her neck. Kate lay still beneath him, waiting, wanting, stroking his hair, urging him on. His resolve was hanging by a single fraying thread.

Do. Not. Do. This.

He dragged his tongue against her skin from the base of her throat to her chin and kissed her hard. His fangs had receded. He let his head fall onto her collarbone. He was covered in sweat, and still shaking.

He spoke softly into her neck.

"Forgive me." He wanted so badly to separate himself from his bloodlust, to banish it completely. But he couldn't. It was part of him. He looked at Kate, pleading with her to understand.

"I won't ever hurt you."

Just please, please don't leave.

God what a mess he was.

"I'm sorry," he muttered. "I'm so sorry."

He couldn't clamber off her fast enough. But she wouldn't let him. Their bodies were still so tangled. All she had to do was bend her knee and he was stuck.

She caught his face in her warm, soft hands, and forced him to face her.

"Promise me you won't hold back next time."

"But I—"

"I *want* this. I want *you*, just as you are."

He couldn't believe what he was hearing. She didn't give him much time to think, bringing him down to her again, where their mouths came together like magnets. He allowed his body to melt into hers once more, unable to resist her sweet, delicate mouth. He lunged for her, and let the sharp edge of one of his teeth graze the lush curve of her lip before resting his forehead on hers.

"Happy now?" he whispered.

"Immensely." She licked his parted lips, entering his mouth for a second, then nuzzled his nose.

He rolled over with a groan, and Kate resumed her place, with her head buried in the crook of his neck and his cheek resting on top of her head. He put his arms around her once more, and she tucked her leg between his.

They remained in a tangled embrace all night. Luca felt too alive to sleep, so he just lay staring at the stars.

9

LUCA OPENED HIS EYES, NOT REMEMBERING WHEN HE'D DOZED OFF. KATE breathed deep against his chest.

It hadn't been a dream.

He rubbed her shoulder until she squirmed.

Kate groaned and turned her head from one side to the other. She spoke into his chest, her voice groggy and muffled. "Did I mention how I feel about mornings?"

"No."

"Don't like 'em. Bad for you. Need sleep."

The corners of his lips ticked upward. "Fine. Then no 'good morning' kiss."

Kate's head shot up like a rocket. "I love mornings! They're the best part of my day!" She was smiling, but her eyes were still closed. Her playfulness and warm affection made her smile contagious.

"You have to open your eyes to be awake," Luca said.

"Why? If you kiss me like you promised, I'll have to close them again."

He decided to bribe her with a compliment.

"I want to see your pretty brown eyes."

She batted her eyes open. "You really think they're pretty?"

"I think they're beautiful."

She blushed and bent her head to kiss his chest. "I like your eyes too."

"Oh yeah?"

"Mmhmm. They're deep and mysterious. I could lose myself in your eyes."

"That frightens most people."

"Oh, I find your eyes incredibly sexy."

He sat up, taking her with him.

"I could look into your eyes forever," she continued.

He brought his face closer to hers. When it became hard to focus, he eyed her mouth hungrily and kissed her. Her tongue met his in greeting, then permitted him to explore. He plundered her mouth until the warm, sweet taste of her coated his tongue and lingered on his lips.

Kate pressed her forehead to his as they came apart.

"Hi," she whispered.

"Hi."

Pain stabbed him through the back. The sun was up.

Luca flinched, and tried to stay hidden behind the tent's folds as the day lightened.

A ray of light peeked through the clouds and past the rear flaps of the tent, shining right in Kate's eyes.

"Ah!" She hurled herself off the bed to hide from the ray that had caught her in the eye. Her open palms made contact with the intricately woven carpet that peeked out from underneath the bed. She pushed herself up on the weight of her arms, then came back down again. She did this repeatedly, putting one hand behind her back, letting one arm do all the work, then the other.

"What are you doing?" Luca asked.

"Exercising. Gets the muscles going." She sat up on her knees and looked at Luca. "We can't all be born perfect."

Luca shifted on the bed, flattered but, somewhat uncomfortable. "Perfect" was the last word he would ever use to describe himself.

Kate moved her hands from her lap to the floor and began scavenging for food on all fours. She seemed to enjoy his compliments. So he gave her another.

"Your ass is perfect."

"Why, thank you. Hmm, I know there's some breakfast around here somewhere." For a woman who managed a whole crew of creatures, her living space was a mess.

"Here we go!" She pulled out a wedge of semi-hard cheese and a couple of apples from a stone bowl that had found its way under her desk. She pulled a small knife out of one of the maps on the desktop and started on the cheese. She passed Luca a bright red apple. He picked it up, rolling it around in his hand.

"This is smaller than the apples around here." He took a bite, the juice flowing freely onto his lips. "Mmm, and sweeter."

Kate finally popped her head up and rejoined him on the bed, sitting with her legs crossed.

"Here, try this." She handed him a cube of cheese. The creamy texture melted in his mouth, leaving behind a complex, almost pungent flavor profile. They shared a cup of water, poured from a stone jug. Even that tasted sweeter and cleaner.

When they had both had their fill, Kate wrapped the remainder of the cheese in a scrap of linen and returned it to the bowl. She held onto the uneaten pieces of apple, and after strapping on her belt and her weapons, she brought the apple bits outside to Philip, who made a hearty meal of them.

"Is everyone else waking up?" Kate asked Philip.

"It seemed that way from the rustlings I heard. This place will be buzzing with activity in a few minutes," he answered.

"Good, I want to be down there before the sun really comes up."

So do I. The higher the sun rose, the more vicious it became.

Kate's band roused in a matter of minutes and began checking and positioning their equipment, which consisted mostly of long ropes, some hefty pickaxes, an oversized pulley on wheels, explosives, and burlap sacks for carrying the quartz.

"Normally," Kate explained, "a small group of maybe two or three check out the cave and map what they can of it. Look for tunnels, entrances and exits, and unstable places. This is very precarious, as it's too dark to see almost anything, and we have no idea whether the cave is living or not, or whether something's living *inside* the cave. We check for signs of quartz clusters, and when we find one, we report back. Depending on what we find, it might only be enough quartz to carry back by hand, or we may need to lower the pulley. If we get stuck up against a wall, or the cave is closed off, we blow an opening, *if* the cave can withstand the blast. But no one goes in alone. Any questions?"

"No."

"Okay. Where do you think your skills would be most useful?" Kate asked.

"In the reconnaissance."

"Okay...are you sure? Because—"

"I can see in the dark," Luca said.

"What?"

"My vision in darkness is just as good as in broad daylight. I'll be able to see the cave perfectly."

"Oh. Okay, you're with me then. Corbin, you coming?" Kate called out.

"It would be my pleasure," the rat responded.

"Hercules, that means you're in charge up here. Make sure we've got plenty of slack," Kate said.

"No problem," Hercules responded.

Hercules had secured three ropes onto the base of the pulley. He brought the opposite ends to the small scouting party, standing at a small, deep hole in the dirt. Kate grabbed hold of hers, wrapping it around her waist. Corbin claimed his own, looping the thin rope into his belt.

"Tie this around yourself as tightly as you can," Kate instructed Luca. "It helps them keep track of us up here and pull us back in case of an emergency. As you need more length, someone up here will add it. Tug once for more slack. When it's ready, they'll tug back. If you need help, tug twice quickly."

Hercules checked on the knots around each of them, pulling and tightening where necessary.

Kate let out a sharp breath. "I need air. This isn't a damn corset."

"You'll thank me later. Okay, ready. Be careful down there," Hercules said.

"Borias, can you give us a hand?" Kate asked.

"Sure thing." The centaur standing nearby reared up, and quickly brought all the weight of his powerful front legs down on the small hole. The sides of it sunk in, creating an opening big enough for Kate and Luca to slide through.

The mouth of the cave sloped immediately downward at a sharp angle. The ground was slick. Luca and Kate clawed at the walls to stop from slipping, with Corbin perched on Kate's shoulder. It continued like that for several miles. When the last flicker of light from the tunnel above disappeared, a soft red light emanated from under Kate's shirt. She pulled at a chain around her neck, revealing a gold circular medallion with strange markings on it. In the center of the medallion was a glowing red stone.

"At least we've got *some* light." Kate's voice echoed down the tunnel. The only other sounds audible were the falling of water drops from the ceiling, and the sound of Kate and Luca's feet as they trekked carefully through the slime.

After several miles, the ground finally leveled off.

"Oh my god, my *knees*," Kate groaned. "I thought this tunnel would never e—"

"Stop!" Luca shouted.

Kate had taken two steps forward as she was speaking. Her third step landed on air. Luca, seeing the precipice plainly, grabbed Kate's arm before she had a chance to stumble.

"Whoops! Thanks."

"What do we do now?" Luca asked.

"Leave it to me! Hold my rope, please," shouted Corbin, who went to work scaling the drop, creeping along the edge to find a proper foothold for his companions. Luca pinched Corbin's rope in his fingers, so that if Corbin slipped, he wouldn't plummet.

In the meantime, Kate picked up a small rock and dropped it, waiting to hear it fall on the ground below. It didn't make a sound.

"*Damn*, that's deep," she commented.

"There it is now." Luca's ears pricked up at the sound of the stone finally reaching its destination. Kate whistled. "There must be a less painful way to get down there."

"I'm afraid not." Corbin was back, with bad news. "The gap is too wide for you to jump, and there's not a decent ledge or foothold anywhere. Even I had a hard time getting across."

"Fantastic." Kate responded. It would take them twice as long to climb back up and search for another entry point. Kate stretched her neck upward, then cocked her head. "Luca, what's that?"

"What's what?"

"Why does the ceiling look like it's moving?"

Luca turned his eyes upward in the direction of Kate's stare. "It's a reflection of water."

"Water...like a river?"

"It's not moving fast enough. It looks more like a lake."

Kate removed a handheld pickaxe from her belt.

"What are you doing?" Luca asked.

"Going down."

"I don't think that's a good idea."

"Then you better follow me and make sure everything goes alright." Her tone was less than courteous. He wasn't sure what he had done wrong.

Just before Kate hung over the ledge to dig her blade in for a controlled fall, Luca grabbed it from her.

"C'mon. I'd feel a lot better if we traveled together." He gestured for her to climb onto his back.

"I'll be fine."

"Please, let *me* pamper *you*." He had her there.

"Alright." She climbed out to meet him, wrapping her legs around his hips and then letting go of the wall to cling to his shoulders. "I *can* do this myself you know," she whispered in his ear.

"I don't doubt that."

"You don't have to protect me."

"I want to," he whispered.

Kate planted a silent kiss at the base of Luca's neck. He kissed the part of her forearm that was wrapped around him.

"Ready, Corbin?" Luca asked.

He jumped onto Luca's shoulder in response.

"Hold on tight," Luca told his cargo as he plunged the pick into the wall and began his descent. When they landed safely several minutes later, Luca saw that she was panting, and was reluctant to release her grip on him.

"Are you alright?" he asked.

"It's the...low altitude," she ground out. We're pretty deep now," she said.

"That we are, and still no sign of quartz." Corbin said.

"Let's have a look around," Kate said. Her pendant gave off a red glow, allowing them to see the subtle undulating of the lake's surface. Kate examined the soil around the lake's bank, looking for even a speck of quartz dust to shine back at her. Nothing.

"Are you sure there's quartz down here? I don't see a thing. Perhaps Hercules was mistaken?" asked Corbin.

"That would be a pretty bad mistake to make. If he says there's quartz down here, there's quartz down here. We just have to find it. Luca?"

"Yes?"

"Can you scan the perimeter? Are there any other ways in or out of this space?" Kate asked.

Luca's eyes took in the cavern. "The ceiling is one entry point. There's a small alcove on the far right, with a crack in the wall. To the left there's just water for a mile or two, then a solid wall. I don't see any other tunnels or chasms."

"We're missing something. How deep does the water look?" she asked.

"The water is clear, but I can't see to the bottom. Hmm. That's odd."

"What is?"

"The wall to the left. It doesn't extend all the way to the ground. There's water underneath it."

Kate took her boots off and removed her weapons and belt.

"What now?" he asked.

"I'm going down there."

"You can't Kate, it's too deep."

"Nothing's too deep." She pointed at a piece of coral fashioned into a cuff at the tip of her ear. "With this, I can breathe underwater."

"There could be monsters," Luca warned.

"You said the water's clear. Do you *see* any monsters?"

Luca saw he wasn't going to win this one.

"Okay then." She kept one blade, and doubled up the chain on her neck so her pendant would cast its light more directly in front of her. "I'll try to be quick. Wait right here. If I don't come back in an hour, pull on my rope."

"Please be careful," Luca said in resignation.

"I will." She dove in. Luca followed her graceful form with his eyes as long as he could. When she disappeared, he sat down on the bank, with Corbin beside him.

Please come back.

10

LUCA AND CORBIN WAITED IN THE DARKNESS ON THE UNDERGROUND lake's bank. After a long stretch of silence, Corbin tried to strike up a conversation.

"Trust in our good friend, Luca," Corbin said reassuringly. "She may be a risk-taker, but only calculated risks. She's not impulsive, and she is certainly *not* defenseless."

Luca considered how she had handled herself back at the inn. She was fast and nimble, and he didn't doubt that she could have done some serious damage. But would she be able to kill to survive, if it came to that?

When Luca didn't answer, Corbin tried a different tack.

"Broke someone's face, did she?" Corbin asked.

Luca nodded.

"And without so much as a thought. Now what do you think she could do if she put her mind to it?" Corbin chuffed. "She's a force you don't get on the wrong side of, a warrior of the highest caliber. I have every confidence in her."

Luca nodded again. But his heart wouldn't rest easy until she returned. He knew how fragile human life could be, regardless of how much her comrades believed in her. And though he had seen so many perish, the thought of Kate dying seemed unbearable to him. He had to admit that he had become attached to her. He had known her for a day, and yet already he felt closer to her than he had ever felt to anyone, ever. Her mortality frightened him beyond words.

But she's been doing this for hundreds of years. That counts for something, doesn't it?

An hour passed. Luca tugged on Kate's line, anxious for some movement on her end. She responded by tugging for more slack.

How far away is she?

Luca reluctantly sent that message back up to the surface, and in a few minutes Luca watched as more rope was pulled into the unfathomable lake.

Another hour passed. It was now late in the afternoon. Trying to be patient, Luca planned to wait a few minutes more before tugging on Kate's line again, when he saw her rope go slack. In less than an instant he grabbed hold of the rope and tugged.

Please be alright.

She tugged back. Soon after he saw the faintest flicker of a red light in the water's depths. It got progressively stronger until Luca saw Kate swimming under the partial rock wall. She surfaced where Luca and Corbin had been sitting for a good part of the day. She was grinning from ear to ear. Luca couldn't hold himself together any longer.

"Where have you been?"

"Corbin, let Hercules pull you up, and give him a message. We're going home after all," said Kate. She didn't say a word to Luca.

"What do you mean? Did you find a big cluster?" Corbin asked.

"You're not going to believe this, but there's enough quartz down there to last us a million years."

"Hurrah!" Corbin did a back flip.

"Spread the word."

"It will be my absolute delight!" Corbin pulled twice on his cord and immediately found himself being dragged the way he had come.

Kate exited the lake and finally turned her attention to him. He hugged her the minute he had the chance, not caring that he was becoming as soaked as she was. From the moment she had surfaced, Luca had smelled blood.

"I told you I'd be fine. Here I am," she said.

At that moment, he had the strongest desire to scold her. But she wasn't his child. She wasn't a child at all. And she'd made it clear that she didn't tolerate being treated like one. He took a deep breath and tried to get a hold of himself.

"What happened?" he asked.

"I'm sorry it took so long. It took me a while to find my way, and I was detained."

"Detained?" he asked.

You've got the stench of some sea creature's blood all over you. That's a bit more than "detained."

"Some sort of fish monster tried to eat me. Today was just not his lucky day."

What was it that Corbin had said? That she only took calculated risks? That she wasn't reckless? None of that rang true, from where he was standing.

Though he didn't say anything, she spoke as if she could hear the thoughts turning over in his head.

"I'm okay, Luca. It didn't hurt me, and it's dead."

"How do you know there's only one?"

"Oh, it was too big to be a part of a group."

He raised an eyebrow. "How big was it?"

She tried to downplay the danger. "I'm not quite sure how big it was. It was very dark, and I only saw portions of it at a time. It moved really slowly, so it wasn't all that hard to kill."

His whole body was screaming at him, at how much danger she'd walked blindly into, just as she'd almost walked blindly over the cliff. But he knew continuing any further would make this worse.

"I'm glad you're back," Luca said at last.

"I'm glad to be back. That water's frigid."

"Oh. Here." Luca took his coat off and wrapped it around her shoulders. He rubbed her arms to warm her up.

"Thank you."

Luca bent down and kissed her lips. She *was* cold, on the outside. But her mouth was as warm and velvety as ever. Her kisses left him breathless.

When they parted again, Kate squeezed the excess water out of her hair and said, "I should do something about the darkness. Pretty soon there will be a lot of people down here." She walked along the perimeter of the lake, and pulled a chunk of wet earth out of the wall every few steps to create a small ledge where she placed a pile of tiny yellow beads. After dotting the entire space, she returned to Luca's side. She had one bead left, resting on the tip of her middle finger. She brought her thumb up to reach it, catching the bead between her fingers. The friction as she snapped her fingers set the small bead aflame. The beads she had placed around the cave caught fire in response, illuminating the subterranean lake.

"That's impressive. What did you do?" he asked. "It's a combination of things. The right materials, some words or gestures, and mental concentration. Not as much as last night though. And no blood this time."

"I like that part."

"Me too." Kate looked around. The lake shimmered. She took in the sight. "Wow, it's really beautiful, isn't it?"

"Yeah."

She turned to see that he was looking at her. He put his arm around her and pulled her to him. He kissed her again, more urgent this time. Kate's mouth was still wet from her swim in the lake, and it made their lips and tongues slide together effortlessly. It was exhilarating. Luca felt his loins stir. It would be at least an hour or two until anyone rejoined them. They had plenty of time. His hands and lips guided Kate gently to her knees.

Her skin tingled at the touch of his fingertips as they tucked underneath her dress and made their way toward her breasts. Luca had not given them the attention he thought they demanded before, and he meant to rectify it. He felt along her abdomen, still cold and soft from the water. He teased her flesh as he made his way to the base of her breast. She folded her fingers with his, trying to pull him upward and press his hands where she wanted them. He made her wait for it. The look of sweet torture on her face made his mouth water. He wanted to draw the sensation out as long as possible.

He leaned in, causing her to arch her back. Her breasts swelled upright, and found their way into the palm of his hand. He extended his fingers and had his hands full of her. He pulled his fingers back, barely touching her skin as his fingertips met her nipples and greeted them with a pinch. Kate cried out, and he went rock hard.

Her lips hung open, wanting for more. He planted his tongue deep in her mouth to stop her from screaming and echoing up for the others to hear. There would be time enough later when he could enjoy every exquisite sound of her pleasure. He pinched her again, then smoothed it over with a kiss. The stifled sigh that caught in her throat seared through his brain and had every hair standing on end. When he came up for air, his eyes bore through hers as he put one finger to her lips to silence her. She didn't acquiesce easy; she rounded her hips and grazed her body against his erection. The finger to her lips? She'd welcomed it into her mouth, tracking the length of the digit and raking her teeth across his knuckles.

Now *he* was the one who couldn't keep quiet. He brought his mouth to her ear.

"Take this off." His voice was begging and commanding at the same time. As he tried to pull her dress over her head, her fingers fiddled with his belt.

This is really happening.

"Hey! Are you two still down there?" Hercules's voice rang through the tunnel. Luca fell on top of Kate in a heap of fury.

Unbelievable.

Kate pulled her dress back over her midriff before Luca had been able to see her glorious shape.

"We're here!" she cried. Then, just to Luca, "I'm going to *kill* him."

"Not if I do it first," he grumbled. He nibbled at her ear, stealing the last few moments of privacy to caress her neck where he had buried his face.

"I want you *now*." His hot breath fell upon her throat. His eyes burned through her.

"I want *you* now. But I want satisfaction, not something quick and dirty."

Luca had to agree with that. He wanted to savor every moment. He had waited centuries to discover a suitable lover. To enjoy her fully, he could wait a few more hours. Knowing that they were both on the same page made the anticipation even sweeter. He gave her breast one final squeeze and groaned in disappointment.

Hercules's approach was heralded by the squish of his footsteps. Luca stood up, and immediately pulled Kate to her feet in front of him.

"Don't move," he murmured.

"Why? What's the matter?"

Luca jutted his hips forward so she could feel the cockstand threatening to split his pants.

"Rubbing against me like that *isn't* going to help," she said.

"I know. But I like it." Luca's eyes sparkled in the darkness. He cupped her butt in his hand and groaned with disappointment as he squeezed.

"Don't make me throw you in the lake!" she giggled.

Hercules finally made his appearance. Kate stood like a bulwark in front of Luca, with a silly girlish look on her face.

Hercules shifted his gaze from one of them to the other. "Everything okay? Am I…interrupting anything?"

Kate avoided the question. Luca kept his eyes trained on the ground directly in front of Kate, trying to get his blood to slow its raging flood.

"How did you get here so fast?" Kate asked through her teeth.

"I ran." Hercules turned around to get a look at the lake, revealing a dark streak of mud trailing down his back.

"On your ass?" Kate tried hard to suppress her laughter. Even Luca couldn't hold back a laugh. Hercules looked over his shoulder and realized what had given him away.

"Okay, so I fell. Fell, ran, same thing."

"Right," said Kate.

"Point is, I'm here," Hercules said. "And I heard you found some quartz."

11

THE EXTRACTION WAS ARDUOUS. THEY HAD TO LOWER THE PULLEY DOWN to the lake. The water nymphs loaded up sacks of quartz underwater, then Hercules and the others used the pulley to bring the sacks to the surface of the lake. Once they had what they intended to take with them on dry ground, they would have to return the pulley back up to the forest floor and repeat the same procedure to get the quartz back to camp.

Kate and Luca had done their part. They reclined by the edge of the lake, their fingers entwined.

"We'll probably work through the night and have everything loaded up and ready to go tomorrow afternoon," Kate said. "We'll get a full night's rest in the camp, then we're gone."

"Where will you go?" Luca asked.

"Home. I had a half dozen more places lined up, but all that is unnecessary now." Kate had a sad look in her eyes. Luca knew what that meant. She was leaving. Leaving him behind. Once she did that, he could almost be sure never to see her again.

KATE COULD NOT THINK OF A SINGLE GOOD REASON NOT TO RETURN HOME the minute their task was completed. Except that she wanted to spend more time with Luca.

She had left Earth behind in search of adventure, in search of a life that she could be proud of. And she'd found it. But it had come at a higher price than she had ever expected or had even consciously agreed to pay. She was responsible for the lives of so many that any possible suitor found her too distracted, too preoccupied with the wellbeing of others for their liking. Those who had courted her gave up when she refused to stay in one place. Men wanted a home and stability. A throne next to hers. Everything that she could never give. She just couldn't do it, no matter how deep each rejection cut. She knew how important the role she played was. The only problem was how much of herself she had to sacrifice in the bargain.

But Luca was different. He was used to wandering and could more than keep up with her. The question was, would he be willing to leave this world behind for her? They had only known each other for a day. Kate had no idea what sort of ties he had keeping him bound to this place, whether he'd be willing to break them. Whether his feelings were as strong as her own. Given his age, which had to be a lot, she suspected that she was not the first woman he had shown affection for, and would not be the last. It was with these thoughts haunting her mind that she broached the subject.

"How did you like having a different job for a change? Less perilous than you're used to?" she asked.

"Still perilous, but in a different way. This was more stressful," Luca answered.

"Really?"

"When I'm alone, I don't worry as much." He turned to face her, seeming to try out his words before committing to them. "It was hard waiting for you, not being able to help you. I felt distracted."

Not exactly what Kate wanted to hear. "I'm sorry I distract you. I don't mean to."

"It's a welcome change."

"From what?" she asked.

"From not caring at all."

Maybe she could salvage this after all.

"Luca," Kate continued, "when we leave, would—"

Her sentence was broken by a thundering crash to the right. They both snapped turned their heads in the direction of the chaos. The low ceiling of the alcove had suddenly collapsed. Under the heap of rubble, Kate spied an arm.

She sprang up, and everyone rushed to gather around, working fast to remove the fallen ceiling. Torrence was trapped underneath. As soon as they were able, Kate and Hercules dragged the faun out from underneath the rock and laid him on his back. He made an ominous whistling sound as he struggled to breathe and spat blood. His chest was badly bruised and misshapen. Smashed. His ribs had caved in and were threatening to puncture the organs they were built to house.

Kate remembered how Luca had healed her hand.

"Can you help him?" she cried.

"Not fast enough," Luca said.

Luca's answer made her heart leap into her throat. She turned back to the faun. His eyes had rolled to the back of his head.

No. No no no no

Kate took Torrence's head in her hands, passing it from one to the other to keep him from losing consciousness.

"Come on, Torrence, don't do this…" she pleaded.

"Kate." Hercules's voice was low, and final.

Luca said nothing. He knew what was happening as well as Kate did, and no one could stop it. No one but her. But only if she…

"Goddamn it all!" She grabbed a purple orb from her belt. The minute Hercules saw it, he tried to steal it from her.

"Kate don't!"

She managed to wrestle her arm free and fling the orb into the wall. As it shattered into a fine purple powder, a thin stream of violet smoke was released. It created a vertical column that remained stationary for a moment, seemingly waiting for a command. Kate slashed her forearm with her dagger.

"You idiot!" Hercules roared.

Kate ignored him.

The mist traveled through Torrence's nostrils and inflated his chest.

A wave of dizziness started at her head, and pushed all the way down to her toes like a raging sea.

Shit. She'd cut too deep. There was blood everywhere. Her veins gushed again, and her vision swam. She groaned.

Luca attempted to clamp down on her arm, but she yanked it out of his reach.

"Not yet," she managed to blurt out. She tried to shake her head free of the haze. She had to concentrate if this was going to work.

Breathe, Torrence. In. Out. In. Out.

She had to keep the rhythm going while she worked to rebuild his ribcage. Repairing his chest wouldn't matter if he wasn't breathing. And if she bled out, soon they might both be dead.

Torrence opened his eyes and exhaled a cloud of indigo.

Kate's brain was mush.

So...much...blood.

"Now!" she shouted at Luca. If he hadn't been there to stop the bleeding...

He clamped down on the wound with both hands. He felt so warm. A shiver took hold of her, and she just wanted to curl into him.

Kate blinked. She realized she couldn't feel her face. She watched Hercules help Torrence to his feet, then let her eyes droop. The numbness traveled down her limbs to the tips of her fingers. Hercules looked at her like she was dying. She was just cold and tired, that's all.

"Lecture me later, okay?" she told Hercules, and focused on getting her breathing to stop shuddering. All at once, a buzzing noise invaded her brain as if a swarm of bees and just come charging through her ear. She swatted at the side of her head.

The wound in her arm was closed, at last.

She put her weight on Luca's shoulder and stood. Her limbs were a bit shaky, but they held. She blinked, once, then twice more. It wasn't going away. Everything she saw was purple. She took a few steps backward. She had meant to walk forward. Something was terribly wrong.

"Selucreh…"

Her muscles drew taught. She had to try again, try to have it come out right. Both Hercules and Luca turned in her direction. Their eyes went wide. From their expressions, she looked as poorly as she felt. Not a good sign.

"Kate!" Luca started. The edges of him were dark and blurry. She had to think, had to figure it all out backward so that it would make sense.

"Hercules, I don't feel…"

Then the whole world went dark. She collapsed, but instead of falling forward, her body tilted back, into the lake. The minute her body made contact with the water, the lake froze over, with her stuck underneath.

Luca and Hercules screamed and came running, but she couldn't hear them. Sinking deeper into the lake, her ears were assailed by the constant hissing of thick sheets of rain. Her mind regressed to a cold November day in 1898. She was fourteen, sitting on the steps that led from her parents' cramped London flat out onto the street. Her hair lay over her shoulder in a single braid. Thick-rimmed spectacles covered her face. She crouched in the cold, her arms wrapped around themselves. Water dripped from her eyebrows and the tip of her nose. Her clothes were soaked through. Her father had put her out without an umbrella. He was arguing with her mother. About her. Again.

A tall young man in a dark woolen coat walked down the street, approaching on Kate's left. His shoes clacked on the sidewalk despite the rain. His hands were tucked deep into his pockets. He too had no umbrella. He covered his head with a plaid scarf woven with vibrant blue fibers and the smallest hint of gold thread. Dusty brown hair that just barely touched his shoulders peaked out from underneath. Kate didn't protest when he sat down next to her.

"Whatchya doin' out here in this fine weather?" he asked her in a heavy Scottish brogue.

"My parents are arguing. I'm not allowed in."

"What's it about today?" he asked.

"Me."

"Did ya do somethin'?"

"No."

"What, then?"

She hugged herself closer. "He thinks I'm not his."

The man shifted on the step, tucking his long legs in and mimicking Kate's own posture. "What does your mother have to say about that?"

Kate didn't answer.

"I see. Well, your mother likes to pretend she's not from the Highlands."

Kate didn't understand what the man had said, but she was only half paying attention. He took the scarf off his head and placed it on hers.

"It looks like you need this more than me."

"Thank you. It's beautiful."

"Ya think so? My mother made me that."

"Are you Scottish?" Kate asked out of nowhere.

"Aye," he answered. "What do you know of Scotland?"

"I'm reading about Robert the Bruce."

"Are ya now? We're related ya know. I'm quite proud of him."

"Really?"

"Aye. He's my cousin's cousin's cousin on my great grandmother's side. Twice removed. We practically brothers," he joked, jostling her arm. Kate laughed.

"There ya go, lass. You're a mite prettier when you smile."

"I'd like to go there someday," Kate said. "I've heard it's full of magic."

"That it is," he said.

"Have you ever seen a faerie?" Kate queried.

"No."

She scoffed. "How can you believe in magic if you've never seen it?"

"That's the way i'is with faeries," he answered. "Ya may never see them, but they're always there."

"I wish I knew magic," Kate admitted. It felt childish, but what did it matter?

The man didn't chuckle the way she expected him to, but took her comment seriously.

"What would ya do with it?" he asked.

She didn't have to think of an answer. "Go somewhere far away. I hate it here," she said. She kept her eyes trained on the ground. She didn't need this stranger's sympathy. If he was out and about in the rain, he had his own problems.

"It's turning to snow," she said as the rain rushed together into slush at her feet.

The man followed her gaze and saw snow accumulating on her shoes. He put his hand out to test the weather, like he didn't believe what was right in front of his eyes. When she looked up, though, she saw raindrops hitting his palm. Not snowflakes. But flurries were gathering on the tops of her shoes, and the scarf he had draped over her. He looked up to the heavens.

Then he said something queer.

"Your magic will emerge in time. Be patient, and it will find you."

What did he mean by that? She didn't understand. She opened her mouth to ask a question, but there were footsteps coming from inside, getting louder. Someone was coming to the door.

The man crouched down again, his face inches from hers.

"Katelyn, listen to me. The reason your father thinks he's not your father...is because he's not. He's not yours, he's not your brother's, and he's not the bairn's growing in your mother's belly now."

"What? I don't understand." Kate paused. "I didn't tell you my name was Katelyn."

"Aye, ya didn't."

A jolt of alarm ran through her.

"Who are you?"

He stood up. "I've got to go."

Kate took the scarf from her head and held it out to him.

"Keep it," he said.

"But your mother made it," Kate insisted.

"She'd be happy to know ya have it," the man answered. He bent over and kissed her cheek. "She always wanted a granddaughter."

Kate smiled.

"What's going on out there?" the man she had until now called father shouted from beyond the door.

"Remember what I told ya, about the faeries," the man in the coat continued, whispering in her ear. "Ya may not see me, but I'll always be there..."

"Who in God's name are you talkin' to?" her mother's husband demanded.

She knew he was drunk, but was he also blind? Kate spun around to face the stranger. The street was empty. She clutched the scarf in her hand. It was real.

"No one," she said, brushing past her stepfather and reentering the house.

"Kate? Kate!" a voice reached her through the ages as the door slammed behind her. But she was unable to respond, or even move.

LUCA AND HERCULES RAN OUT ONTO THE ICE, LOOKING FOR KATE'S shadow. After a few interminable minutes, Hercules plunged his burly arm into the lake, breaking through a foot of solid ice. He grabbed onto Kate by the back of the neck and pulled her out onto the shore. She wasn't breathing. Luca laid her on his lap and covered her ears with his hands.

He had no idea what was wrong with her. He'd stopped the bleeding, and there were no other wounds on her, but she had swatted at her ear right before things went horrifically wrong. That was all he had to go on.

Her body began to jerk. She opened her eyes, flipped over onto her stomach, and choked out a small purple orb, a miniature copy of the one she had smashed. Her arms gave out underneath her, and she landed in the mud of the underground bank. Luca pulled her back onto his lap and turned her face to the sky. Every breath she took sounded like an effort.

"I'm fine," she croaked in between coughs. "I'm fine."

Was she insane?

"You're not fine, you almost drowned yourself in ice!" Luca shouted as he wrapped her with blankets provided by those nearby. "Why?"

Why had she been so reckless with her own life? It made no sense.

"Not again," she stammered. "Never again…" Kate let out a sigh, and blacked out again. His hands flew to her ears but, this time, he realized, she was still breathing. She'd simply fainted.

She had to get dry. It was no good for her to be so cold, and so wet. He grabbed the fabrics that her companions had heaped upon her and tried to chase the damp away. Luca's brain pulled his eyes down, directing his attention toward his hands. They were covered in Kate's blood. Gods, he could smell her, especially down here, where her scent bounced off the walls and doubled back on him that much stronger. He watched his fingers twitch as he beat back his desire to bring them to his mouth and suck them clean.

Don't......d...

Luca held his breath and wiped his hands on one of the blankets surrounding Kate. He wrapped his arms around her once more as she rested in his lap. When he looked up, Luca saw that Hercules was staring at him. He had seen Luca's struggle. Neither man said a word. After looking Luca straight in the eye, Hercules turned to help Torrence without saying anything.

Everyone did what they could to keep Kate warm and comfortable. They decided not to remove her from the cave until she had gotten some solid rest. Slowly, the ice covering the surface of the lake dissipated, and they resumed their work. Kate lay asleep in Luca's lap.

When everything was working smoothly again, Hercules came to sit beside him.

"Luca," Hercules said after a long while, "I saw what you did. You saved her life."

"I did what I could to help her. It was you who pulled her out of the ice."

"When I pulled her out of the lake, she wasn't breathing. That wasn't enough. You removed the magic. If you hadn't been here, that would have been it."

Luca remained silent, gazing at Kate, and stroking her hair. No matter how hard he tried, he couldn't get it completely dry. It kept her from getting warm.

"You've earned my respect, Luca, and my eternal gratitude. I don't know if Kate said anything to you yet, but I hope that you'll consider staying with us," Hercules said.

Luca had considered it, but what had just happened gave him pause. He knew Kate wasn't going to die that day. But he knew that day *would* come. No matter how long she lived, or how careful she was, she was mortal. His heart, which Kate had just opened and was already breaking.

If this is how I feel now, he wondered, *how much worse would it be then?*

Knowing that he would eventually lose her, he wondered if it might not be better to save himself the added agony.

"You know, I'm only half human too," Hercules said.

Luca turned his head in Hercules's direction.

What's the other half?

He said nothing.

"My father is the king of the ancient gods," Hercules continued. "Or, he was. I inherited his strength."

Luca nodded. So that was how he'd been able to crack through the frozen lake.

"I used that strength to fight the gods. They were cruel, manipulating humans and their emotions as if they were playthings."

That sounds familiar, Luca thought.

"My father was the worst of all. He resided over the relentless misery his family inflicted upon humans, and allowed it to happen."

Really familiar.

"I spent my entire life fighting them, fighting him. But, on my travels, I was fortunate enough to find a wife. She was a lot like Kate, actually. Smart, beautiful, and she didn't see me as a god, or a half-breed. She saw me as a man. We had four wonderful children together. I was truly happy." Tears welled up in his eyes. "I killed them all. I couldn't stop it. But I had to watch. I destroyed the only thing that ever mattered to me, all because of my fight with the gods."

"I'm sorry." It seemed like the right thing to say, but he wasn't quite sure what Hercules was getting at. Had the thoughts running through Luca's mind occur to him too? Would they all be better off if he just wasn't there when Kate woke up?

"Eventually, I killed all the gods, including my father, in revenge," Hercules said.

"And?" Luca was interested in this part. This story was so much like his own. He needed to know how it ended.

"And it changed nothing. I chased after them with every fiber of my being, for nothing. If I could do it again, I would take back all that wasted time and spend it with my family, who loved me, and who might have lived longer if not for me. The pain of missing them will never end for me. I am immortal, like you. I'll never get to rejoin them in the afterlife."

But was it worth *it?*

"And, if you could change it," Luca asked, "if you could do it *all* over again, would you?"

The answer came without hesitation. "In a heartbeat. Megara wouldn't have it any other way. Being together was not just *my* choice to make. It was hers, too."

Maybe, then—

Hercules chuckled, and broke Luca's train of thought. "About fifty years ago, Kate found me wandering around, doing nothing. She took one look at me, and she knew me. She knew my name, the details of my life, even my family. She knew all about me. Said I was some kind of legend, that my life had been a story told throughout the ages. She convinced me to go with her, to do something with my immortality. And I've never regretted it. Icarya is a paradise. I only wish my children would have been so lucky to see it. And by pretending not to fall apart without them, by picking up the pieces of my ruined life here with Kate, I honor their memory."

Luca continued to stroke Kate's hair, quietly absorbing all that Hercules had told him.

"Thank you for telling me this," he said.

"I've seen the way Kate looks at you," Hercules said. "I remember how that felt. Yesterday, you said you wouldn't hurt her."

"I wouldn't."

"Prove it. Stay."

Hercules pressed his hand on Luca's shoulder, then got up to help the others, who were moving the pulley into the tunnel for the final phase of retrieval. Luca turned his gaze back toward Kate, restless in her sleep.

Wake up, Kate, Luca thought.

~

KATE SLIPPED IN AND OUT OF CONSCIOUSNESS. AT ONE POINT, SHE regained consciousness while strapped onto Luca's back as he climbed back up the tunnel with his bare hands, heading for the surface. Luca heard her muffled words at his back.

"What time is it?"

"About three in the afternoon."

"Why didn't you wait? The sun will be hot now."

"That's not important. You need fresh air and sunlight, and that's where I'm taking you."

Her voice sounded far away, and then faded out again. "I don't want you to hurt anymore."

Luca blinked back tears. He struggled to make sense of emotions crashing over him like a tsunami. If he left, he'd be leaving his father free to do as he pleased. But did that even matter anymore? If it didn't, what did that mean for *him*?

Luca just didn't know. But he couldn't help caring for a woman who cared so much for him.

"Just hang on, Kate, we're almost there."

But she was already gone again, back into an unshakeable slumber.

He emerged from the cave with the sun staring right at him. He grimaced at the sight of his familiar foe and bared his teeth.

Go fuck yourself.

Luca laid Kate down on her bed and covered her with the blankets.

"Julian?" she asked.

"I'm here," Luca responded. He didn't want to confuse her. He tested her skin with his palm. She wasn't feverish; just delirious.

"I've missed you."

Luca didn't know what to say. She thought she was talking to someone else. A knot coiled in the pit of his stomach.

"That's not fair, Julian, you can't ask me to quit."

Was she reliving a conversation she had had with this "Julian?" Or were they just the incoherent ramblings of her overworked brain? Her eyes still closed, she looked troubled. Deep sadness etched itself across the lines of her face.

"Why didn't you love me, Julian?"

A single tear fell from her eye, crossing over the bridge of her nose before sinking into the weave of her pillow. Hearing the pain in her voice formed a lump in Luca's throat. He broke his silence.

"I *do* love you," he said, curling his fingers around hers and leaning in close, placing his lips on her forehead. He knew it was a strong word, but he had strong feelings for her. And she needed comforting.

I'll love you for as long as you'll have me.

She quieted down, and didn't speak again.

12

KATE OPENED HER EYES AND FOUND HERSELF IN HER TENT. SHE SAT UP, and tried to remember what she was doing there. It always took a while for her memory to come back to her once it slipped.

The air inside the tent was sultry, like the edge of a hot day. Her back was stiff, and her knees felt like she'd scaled a mountain.

She must have been traveling for a reason…*what was it?*

Kate groaned, rubbed her hands over her face, and craned her neck from one side to the other to banish the stiffness. Then she saw him.

The man who had soaked into her dreams.

Dhampir, she corrected herself. His sleek face and finely sculpted features robed in shadow, were more perfect than any dream. He was dark and paralyzingly beautiful. Her breath caught as he smiled at her, and everything came rushing back—the expedition, the extraction, the cave-in.

Luca was using a heavy trunk as a chair, watching her. How long had he been sitting there?

"How are you feeling?" he asked.

"I've been better. What time is it?"

"After sunset."

"You didn't have to stay cooped up inside here with me. You could have left."

"I'm where I want to be."

That made Kate smile.

But Luca's face became solemn. "What happened back there?" he asked. "Why did the lake turn to ice?"

The whole lake?

It was getting worse. Now, of all times. With her crew depending on her, and...and this reserved, sensuous man waiting for an explanation. She wished she had one.

"As far as I can figure, it's a side effect," Kate started. "A negative reaction to the magic I'm using, as a form of evening out the changes I've made to the natural order of things. And when I cast in emotional distress like I did, those side effects are amplified."

It was the best she could do. But it didn't really explain anything.

"Why ice? When I entered your tent last night, after you'd stormed off, you looked as if you were about to freeze over."

"I did?"

"Your eyes turned a clear gray. I could see right through them."

Had that ever happened before? Maybe when there was no one around to tell her?

"God, it scares me when I don't notice those things. I think I lose a little bit of my mind when that happens."

She tried her best to shake it off. There was no use worrying about something that was over and done. Whatever change Luca had observed in her, it wasn't permanent, and didn't have any lasting effects. Not that she could discern.

He was still listening. He was so good at that. It was so nice to be able to tell someone the things she always kept buried. He wasn't her responsibility, so she didn't have to worry about what her strange behavior would mean for *him*.

"The truth is," Kate continued, "I'm not quite sure. The nearest I can guess is because most of the spells I cast happen to be fire based. I suppose it's nature's way of balancing out. It's not clear cut, but then, magic rarely is."

"Kate?"

She felt a talking-to coming on. She wasn't sure she was up for it.

"Why did you do it?"

"To save Torrence. I don't want anyone else to die on my watch."

"I can understand that, but—"

"But?"

"At what cost?"

Kate tilted her head. What did he mean by that?

"Torrence is only one, Kate. How many more would die if you were not there to watch over them?"

In all the times that Hercules had warned her against casting her spells, Luca's point struck home.

"How can I face the families of those I've lost?"

"The same way you face everything else. With kindness and bravery. It's part of your job, isn't it?"

Her gaze drifted down to the bed. Yes, it was. That was the problem. She couldn't accept it.

"But it shouldn't just be *your* burden to bear."

He moved from his perch on the trunk and sat opposite her on the bed. The brush of his knuckles against her cheek, the press of his fingertips against the base of her skull, made her heart flutter like a girl.

"Seeing you like that was not fun for me either," Luca said. His voice was so low, and so soft, he sounded like he was purring.

"I'm sorry. It's just that, well..." Kate tried to escape his gaze, searching for the right words as embarrassment rushed to her cheeks. But it was obvious, wasn't it?

"I've never had someone who would fall apart if *I* didn't come back."

He tucked a curled finger under her chin and ensnared her in his stare again. "You do now."

If she looked long enough, she felt like she was falling. It made her heart race. The way he looked at her, she felt like the only woman in the world.

Maybe he would say yes. Maybe he *would* come with them. If she ever got around to asking him. But her stomach was a cruel tyrant.

"I'm...I'm a little hungry."

"There's plenty of food outside." He stood up and helped her to her feet.

They were almost immediately surrounded by the entire camp. Half a dozen voices asked at once:

"Kate, are you alright? How are you feeling?"

"I'm okay," she assured everyone, "I'm okay." She tried to put them more at ease by sounding energetic, but it was a bit much for her at the moment. "What do we have to eat around here?"

They disbursed to amass a banquet of food that they laid in her lap. Luca led her to a log close to the fire.

"I can't eat all of this. Do you want some?" she offered.

"Just water for me, thanks."

Kate took her time, letting her appetite gradually build. By the time she was full, she had cleared more off her plate than she had expected to. Torrence was the first to approach her. He looked sheepish, even for a faun.

"Kate, what can I say? Is there anything I can do, to—"

She reached out and grabbed his hands to stop him from wringing them.

"Torrence. What I did, I would have done for any of you. That's why I'm here. Say nothing. When you get home, kiss those kids for me," she said.

"I will." He began to walk away, then turned back to hug her. "Thank you!" he sobbed.

"It's alright, Torrence, it's alright." She patted him on the back.

Hercules was next in line. She really didn't have enough energy to deal with him.

"I suppose you're here to say I told you so. Go on, you can say it. You were right. It was dangerous, and foolish, and a little bit selfish. It won't happen again."

Hercules paused. "I came over to ask you how the food was."

"Uh huh." Kate tried to get her foot out of her mouth.

"But I *did* tell you so." His gaze drifted to Luca. He smiled. There was something in that, she was sure.

"Good to have you back, Kate," he said.

Once she was sure she had conversed with everyone who wanted to talk to her, she took Luca by the hand. If she was going to do it, the time was now.

"Will you come with me? I want to show you something," Kate said.

Luca followed her back to the tent they had shared.

"Open the back door, please," she asked.

"I think you've had enough water for one day." She'd been soaked to the bone for so many hours. She couldn't possibly want a bath now. But she insisted.

"Just open the door, please," she replied.

Luca did as she asked of him, and pulled back the flap at the rear of the tent. It did not lead to the bath. It opened up onto a hill overlooking a sprawling vista and a night sky of deepest indigo. The glittering stars didn't resemble any Luca had ever seen. They were entirely different constellations.

He drank in the view. He had never seen so much green. And the sounds—everywhere, both near to him and far, were sounds of life. Of creatures shifting in their nests, of wings flapping before tucking in for the night. Of crickets singing, and dancing through the grass to escape larger animals that would make a feast of them.

To his left stood an enormous tree. A thick branch stretched out like an arm, low enough for them to sit on. He turned back to look at her.

"Welcome to Icarya. Or at least, this small part of it. Please, sit with me."

They sat down together, Luca hugging her waist. She rested her head on his shoulder.

"This is my home," she said in a quiet voice. "Of all the places I have seen, this is the one where my heart stills." She closed her eyes and let the cool, clean night air fill her lungs.

Luca noticed that it was much later here, on the other side of the tent, than it was where they had been but moments before. The sky was lightening.

"I want you to watch the sunrise with me," she said.

Luca sat up and furrowed his brow. She knew full well that being exposed to the sun as it appeared over the horizon would be excruciating for him. She knew that. Only a few hours before, she had expressed her concern over his vulnerability to the sun. But she looked straight at him. Her eyes didn't falter, and she didn't give any excuses or reasons.

"Alright."

There was an awkward pause, and then—

"Luca," she started, "do you like being a vampire hunter?"

He guessed what was really on her mind, but he answered her question all the same.

"It's all I can do," he said.

"It might be all you can do here. Is there anything holding you here? I mean, would you consider…well, I was wondering if…" she closed her eyes, took a deep breath, and tried again.

"I want you to come back with me. I know we only just met, but I don't want to say goodbye. And before you decide, I need you to know something."

The sun came up. Its rays lit up the sky and the valley below. It shone directly on their faces.

On instinct, Luca closed his eyes to brace himself for the onslaught of torture. But he quickly opened them again in disbelief. He felt nothing but the warm breeze caressing his skin. He felt no pain. He breathed easy. The air was cool, and sweet, and felt exhilarating as it filled his lungs. He felt as light as a feather.

Luca stared at the sun for the first time, and found it glorious. A single tear ran down his cheek. He turned to Kate.

"How?"

"Icarya provides for those who live there, Luca." Her voice became more animated.

"Our sun will never burn you. Our food will sustain you. Icarya is a peaceful place, you don't have to be at war anymore. You could live out your days doing anything you want. Come with me," she pleaded. "There's nothing for you here. I'm offering you a chance at a real life."

"With you?"

She flinched.

"Oh, Luca, it doesn't have to be. There are no strings attached here. I just want you to be happy." She stretched out a tentative hand, and wiped the liquid joy from his face with the pad of her thumb.

"And if being with you...if that's what makes me happy?" he asked.

Her whole face brightened.

"Then you've made me happier than I've ever been."

"Kate..."

He held her cheek in the palm of his hand. She lunged for him, trying to bind him to her with every swipe of her tongue, every tug on his lips.

Silly little thing. Didn't she know?

He wrapped his arms around her, and let her finish her pleading. He couldn't bring himself to tell her it was all unnecessary, for her affection felt like the most necessary thing in the all the world.

When she pulled away to see if she would have her way, he pecked the tip of her nose.

"When do we leave?"

13

THE ONLY REMNANTS OF KATE'S CAMP WERE THE PILE OF FIREWOOD, STILL smoking from the water used to douse it, and the spiral she had drawn in the dirt to keep out interlopers.

Out of the forest stepped a tall, brooding figure. With broad shoulders, an aquiline nose, and a long dark complexion, he looked like an older, more dignified version of Luca. His face was stern and cold.

He entered the clearing and walked straight to the center, stepping over the lines of the magical spiral, ignoring the resistance nipping at his ankles. He bent over the burnt-out fire and ran his long pale fingers through the ashes. Out of the ashes he pulled out the blue orb that Kate had dropped into the fire. It was caked with her blood. He popped it into his mouth, and sucked it clean.

"Mmm."

The dark shadow swirled it around in his mouth for a minute, then spit it back out and rolled it around in his palm. The once blue sphere was now clear. Ice crystals filled the little curiosity.

To his left, the sun was rising. The man darted off into the shadows, taking the sphere with him.

14

KATE CHOSE THE TUNNEL AS THE PLACE TO OPEN THE GATE BACK TO Icarya. No one was likely to follow them there.

"Is everyone ready?" she asked. They all answered in the positive.

"Are *you* ready?" she asked Luca. She gripped his hand so hard, it was as if she thought that he would disappear into thin air if she let go.

"Ready," he smiled.

"Okay. Here we go." She threw a green orb at the wall. It lodged itself into the side of the cave. As it burrowed, it should have created an opening big enough for everyone to simply walk through. But that's not what happened. The orb began to melt, and flowed down onto the floor like water. The stream pouring from the wall quickly turned into a ferocious gush. It wasn't stopping.

"That's odd," Kate commented, nonplussed.

"What's going on?" Hercules asked.

He'd traveled back and forth with her many times, but it had never been quite like this.

"I don't know. Maybe we struck a river or something," she suggested. In a few minutes, the water was at knee level. Kate bent down and brought a small pool of water to her lips. She closed her eyes in the sudden realization and exhaled:

"Oh, great."

"What?" asked Hercules.

"Did you taste it?" she asked. Hercules followed after Kate, and had the same reaction.

"Crap. This is just what we needed," he replied.

The higher the water level rose, the more uncomfortable Luca became. The flooding of the cave made his muscles feel heavy and languid. His feet were heavy as lead, fixing him to the ground.

"What is it?" Luca queried.

"The water." Kate and Hercules answered at the same time: "It's sweet."

"What does that mean?"

"It means," Kate sighed, "that we're in the Great Sea."

Not good. Very not good.

Kate read the worry on Luca's face, but couldn't place it. And then it dawned on her.

"Luca, *can you swim?*"

He shook his head.

"Oh god. Alright, don't worry." She put her hand to the coral wrapped around her ear, and snapped it in half. "Here, put this on. It may not completely negate your problem, but it should help."

Luca affixed the coral to his ear. He didn't feel any different, but he wanted to be patient. He could still breathe, so far. And he didn't want Kate worrying for his sake.

"Are we going to drown?" Torrence asked. It seemed he and the other hoofed members of Kate's party were in a similar predicament to Luca's.

"No," Kate answered.

Torrence breathed a sigh of relief.

"The pressure of the water pushing us into the ceiling will probably crush us first," she said.

Hercules let out a nervous laugh.

"Well," Kate clapped her hands, "we'd best rip apart the pulley. We're going to need that wood." She shook her head. "These things are never easy."

Minutes later, the water level was at Kate's chest. The pulley had been broken down into a collection of wooden planks. The plan was to use the boards as flotation devices. The tree nymphs had taken refuge inside the grain of the boards. The ropes were tied around each member of the party and their crates of quartz, kept buoyant by the water women. As they were tying off the last pieces of rope, the floor of the cave became less tangible. The sea was taking over, and soon they would all be treading water. The ceiling got darker. There was a low rumble of thunder, followed soon after by a crack of lightning. The water churned.

"A storm. How appropriate!" Kate laughed.

The fact that she didn't seem worried was the only thing stopping Luca from giving into the dread panic that gripped his slowing heart.

The ceiling bowed tentatively to the sky. The water was up to their necks. Luca had hooked a plank under his arms, and the rest crouched, balancing their feet on tiny platforms. Philip was anxiously awaiting the dissolution of the ceiling, so he could take flight and look for help.

The water rushed into Kate's lips. "This is it. Hold your breath, Luca."

He could barely *take* a breath, let alone hold it. He didn't know how Kate planned on saving them all, but whatever was going to happen, it had to happen fast. He needed to get out of the water. Now. But there was no escape.

The sea stretched to the ceiling, and Kate dunked her head into the sea as a wave completely overtook them.

Luca tried to resist it, to keep his head above water. He flailed, but his limbs were so weak, he had to focus all his strength on holding onto the scrap of wood that stopped him from sinking.

The sea was indifferent. The waves kept coming, and flooded his nose and his mouth. His lungs burned for air. When his head resurfaced, it was out into the open sea air. The sea was all around them with no shore in sight.

Kate was right there with him, wiping the hair out of his eyes.

"Don't worry. Help will come," she assured him.

"Hu-hurry," he panted. He was using all his strength to fight his nature, but he was losing the battle.

"Okay, okay, I will."

The waves churned his stomach. His head spun as the stars above him bobbed and swayed. The cold and the wet threatened to pull him under. He *had to* stay awake. He lowered his lids so they were only half open, blocking out the worst of his whirling vision, and fixing his attention on Kate, the only solid thing.

She looked up for some sign of salvation. She must have seen something in the distance, but Luca was too afraid to tilt his head to look up. There was a good chance he would lose his grip and be lost to the sea if he craned his neck in that direction.

"Phil!" she shouted.

The pegasus was off like a shot.

"Just a little while longer," Kate said. She gripped him by the forearm and hauled him over the board, making sure he didn't slip under the surface.

Luca didn't answer. He couldn't pull air into his lungs and talk at the same time. His heart was beating so fast, he thought it might burst.

"There's a ship coming right toward us. They can help."

Luca couldn't see very well, but he could still hear. The waves thrashing them about didn't show any mercy to the ship. Men were shouting and scrambling about on deck, doing their best to brave the storm and keep the vessel upright.

"Hallo!" Philip called.

"Hallo there!" the lookout bellowed back.

"I have Icaryans stranded at sea, in need of assistance now!"

"Aye Aye!"

The nose of the ship tore through the waves, and knocked those stranded aside by the force of its momentum.

"Hercules, I need you here!" Kate yelled.

The two of them hoisted the creatures aboard. The crew lent what assistance they could as they balanced rescuing the party and securing the ship's sails.

It hurt to breathe. Air came in shallow fits and starts. His limbs were numb, and completely useless. Kate swam behind him and hooked him under the armpits, hoisting him up the ladder one step at a time until she could pass him into the outstretched arms of the sailors on deck.

"Get him dry!" she commanded. She gave Luca a peck on the cheek, and left him to the crew members to go help the others.

"Yes, yoor 'ighness!" the crewman shouted. In the darkness, the crew had recognized her.

The well-muscled man who held Luca by the shoulders led him into the captain's quarters, lit by a small hearth in the center of the room and a series of tapered candles strewn about. Between blinking, Luca realized that it was decorated very much like Kate's tent back at the camp. And he'd heard something…

The sailor wrapped Luca in warm thick blankets and laid him on the bed. He stoked the fire at the heart of the cabin.

"When yoor up to it, get outta those clothes and 'op into bed. The faster ya' do that, the faster yoo'll be dry. Nice and cozy-like."

"Your…your highness?" Luca repeated.

"Aye, lad! Or did ya not *know* yoor travelin' with the Queen of Icarya?"

15

THE SHADOWY MAN WHO HAD TRACKED LUCA TO KATE'S ABANDONED camp stifled the groan rising in his throat. The echo of waves crashed on all sides of him as he crouched in the darkness. That he had called forth the storm that now battered the ship was irrelevant. He had known the thrashing of the lower decks would nauseate him, but it kept the crew occupied. The bowels of the ship pitched back and forth in uninterrupted night. The shadow tilted his head forward to regain his center of gravity, but was knocked violently back as the stern heaved over an enormous crest. The back of his head landed against a barrel of gunpowder, sending his vision spinning.

He tucked himself into the deepest, darkest corner of the hold, and extended his legs. From his pocket he drew a small linen pouch, filled with earth. He pulled the drawstring open, and allowed rainwater dripping from the hull to soak the contents. He extracted the mud and smeared it over his forehead. The salve calmed his feverish brain. His vision stabilized, and his stomach ceased to churn in time with the storm. After several undetected hours, he allowed the gale to abate, relinquishing the savage winds, but sustaining the downpour. He retrieved the small orb he had acquired from the campfire out of his coat pocket, and held it in front of his face. The cloudy, crystalline matter inhabiting the orb was unchanged. He rotated it between his fingers to examine it closer, but watching it turn set his eyes whirling again. He promptly restored the mysterious object to his pocket. He closed his eyes and slid some of the mud downward over his lids. Then he crossed his hands over his chest and lay deathly still.

16

Luca regained enough of his strength to find a change of clothes and bury himself under the bedcovers. He watched the water rush past the small circular window on the cabin door, and saw people scurrying outside to protect the sails as they were clapped with wind and waves, on top of heavy rain. Kate was still out there, helping. Luca was comfortable, warmed by the fire. The solitude gave him time to think.

Kate was the queen. That part didn't surprise him. Looking back at how she had carried herself, how everyone had treated her—with love, but deference—it all came together. What bothered him was that she hadn't told him she was the queen. On purpose. That stung.

He couldn't figure out *why* she hadn't told him. Queen or not, *she* was the siren who had woken him out of a wonderful dream, just so she could offer him one he didn't have to wake up from. That she hadn't trusted him with that information, after he'd made clear his dual nature and wretched place in society knowing full well that it should have spelled the end of their interaction—that's what hurt.

Kate entered the cabin, dripping water everywhere, down to the tips of her hair. The storm had quieted down.

"Luca," she called out. He didn't answer. She walked over to the bed.

"Luca." His eyes were closed with his head turned to the side, his breathing calm. He did not feel like talking.

She brushed his brow with her hand. He wanted to lean in to her caress, wanted to pretend that it didn't matter. But it did. She'd lied. She moved as silently as she could to the far side of the room. Confident that he would not disturb her, she discarded her wet clothing. Luca opened his eyes, facing the wall that adjoined the bed. All he heard was the creaking of the ship, the crackling of the fire, and the occasional rustling of fabric.

Luca lay in bed listening as Kate disrobed, leaving her boots, stockings, and dress by the fire. She laid out all her armor and weapons, and squeezed her hair out. The water fell into the fire with a sizzle. She opened a dresser drawer and pulled out a clean, lightweight tunic dress in hunter green. She left her legs bare. She padded over to bed and slipped in behind him. Kate put her arm around his waist and her bent leg on top of his hip. She kissed the back of his shoulder and bade him goodnight before resting her head on the pillow, touching his back with her forehead. Luca didn't move a muscle. He just stared at the wall.

Kate was awoken the following morning by the sound of birds flying around the ship, and the captain issuing orders. She sat up in bed, and stretched. She turned to Luca, trying to rouse him from his sleep with caresses. He couldn't pretend to be asleep any longer. When he didn't respond to her affections, she thought he might still not be feeling well, and paused.

He rolled over onto his back, and stared up at her. He couldn't help but notice how lovely she looked in the morning sunlight.

"Good morning," she said.

"Good morning. Your Highness."

Kate closed her eyes in acknowledgement, and licked her lips.

"Call me Kate," she replied.

He fought hard to stop his face from forming a scowl. She drew back all the same, and bit her lip.

"Sorry. I'm no good at these things," she apologized.

Luca threw back the covers and stood up.

"Why didn't you tell me?" he demanded.

"Please, try to understand, Luca. Every time I've gotten close to someone, my title has always gotten in the way. I didn't want it to be like that with you. It's not who I am. I mean, it is, but it isn't."

"I told you everything. I came here because I felt *free* to tell you, free to be myself. You told me that it didn't matter, what—" He stopped himself, and tried to push that awful twisting sensation in his stomach away. "It didn't matter what I am, but *who*. Did you really think I would care?"

Kate sat up, swinging her legs to the side of the bed. She kept her voice down, tried to stay calm. Tried to encourage him to do the same. It was infuriating.

"I know you did," she said. "And I was going to tell you. I'm sorry you found out the way you did. But it *has* mattered to others."

"I'm not like the others, Kate. I'm not going to be like Julian. I would never ask you to be anything other than what you are."

That got a rise out of her, which was somehow infinitely worse.

"Wait—how did you know about Julian?"

"You talked about him in your sleep. Who is he?"

She looked offended, that he should ask about something else that he had learned about without her telling him. He hadn't pried deliberately, hadn't rooted around in her brain against her will.

So why did he feel like he'd made a wrong step?

Her eyes flashed in challenge. "You really want to know?"

"I do."

"He's my best friend. We grew up together, him, Lilla, and me. I had always hoped that Julian and I would end up together."

Of course you did. How could a woman like her live hundreds of years and *not* have a string of men trailing along behind her? He was just one more.

Now he really scowled. But she wasn't finished.

"He wouldn't come with me on my travels, and I never stayed home with him. One day I came back from a trip, thinking it was my last one, and I finally told him how I felt, only to find out he'd been sleeping with Lilla."

What kind of an idiot *chose another woman over her? How could anyone*

say no to her, with her looking like that, and the way she...the way she must
have treated him, the way she treated everyone...

It struck him that she hadn't paused for breath when she'd admitted
that the person she cared about had chosen someone else. She said it
like she'd expected it. Like she'd deserved it.

His anger dissipated. Suddenly, everything looked different from
where she was standing; from the place where he had always stood with
others. With everyone...except Kate.

This was a mistake.

But he couldn't take it back. She was the one yelling now.

"I poured my heart out. The feeling was mutual, but it didn't matter.
Know *why?*"

Her words crashed down on him like a sledgehammer.

"Because I'm the goddamned queen of Icarya! *Everyone's* business is
my business. The wants, the needs, the *lives* of all Icaryans have to come
before my own. I never asked for this, it just happened. But you know
what? I'm really good at it. We've been at peace for hundreds of years.
There's plenty of food, and plenty of work, and *everybody's* happy." She
plopped down on the bed and stared up at the ceiling.

"Everybody except you."

She pinched her nose, trying to regain her composure. Or...was
she—?

"It's *always* the same thing. Every man wants from me what I can't
give. And what I can, just isn't enough." She sat up again, and buried her
face in her hands. "I screwed up Luca. I admit it. I just...I just wanted it
to be different this time. I thought maybe if you got to know me first...
oh, never mind what I thought. You're right. You were open with me,
and I *should* have been open with you. I was scared, and stupid, and I've
just ruined it. When we get to shore, we can go our separate ways. Or, I
can take you back, if you want."

Luca started. Is that what *she* wanted?

No. I didn't mean it. I want—

"I don't want you to think I brought you here under false pretenses. I
just wanted so much to be with you," Kate said. As she brushed past him

and headed through the door, Luca saw the shimmer of tears in her eyes.

How stupid. He'd felt the same way his whole existence. Unlovable because of the things he couldn't change. He'd betrayed his own heart. She would have told him in her own time, he knew that. But he had been impatient and impulsive, and let jealousy cloud his judgment. By bringing up Julian, he'd made matters worse. Now, knowing the truth behind her feverish ravings, he regretted saying anything at all.

He couldn't let her send him away. Not with her thinking that he didn't want her.

OUTSIDE THE CABIN, MEN AND CREATURES ALIKE SCURRIED ABOUT, BUSY AT their work. Luca spotted the familiar faces of Kate's mining crew down the way, reassembling the pulley.

"Good morning, lad! Ya look a mite better today." The sailor who'd assisted him last night greeted him.

"Thank you for your help last night," Luca said.

"Not at all, lad! Anytime yoor needin' anything, just call on Brahm, and you can be sure it'll all turn out aright!"

Luca took his leave and searched for Kate. Her red hair gave her away. She was leaning her elbows over the starboard side, her soft waves blowing in the breeze. She was staring into the sea, hiding her face from the others. Luca saw ice crystals fall from her cheeks into the blue waters below. He approached quietly, and slipped his arms around her waist. When she didn't pull away, he clutched her tight.

"You *are* enough, Kate," he whispered in her ear.

She sniffed.

"I was hurt because I want you to trust me. I want all of you." He turned her to face him, and dried the tears staining her cheek. He brushed her lips with his thumb, and bent over her, bringing their mouths closer together.

"Don't send me away," he whispered.

When she still didn't answer, he took hold of her lips in his, and didn't let go for the longest time. It was his turn to beg.

Her rigid stance softened, and she melted against him. She reached her arms around his back, locking him in a close embrace even after their lips had parted.

"No more secrets, I promise," Kate said. "I'm sorry Luca."

"No secrets. Kate?"

She looked up into his eyes.

"I'm really happy to be here."

"Me too."

Luca let out a puff of air. "Queen."

She nodded. "Yeah."

"This is going to take some getting used to."

Kate shrugged. "Every relationship has its quirks."

They both smiled.

Luca's stomach rumbled. Kate laughed. "Hungry?"

"That's *never* happened before," Luca said.

"You might notice a few changes. Like an increased appetite for Icaryan food. But it probably won't get rid of...your other appetite." She looked up at him through veiled lids, but he just hung his head. Kate forced him to look at her.

"Luca, I told you before. When the time comes... don't hold back." He stared back at her, hungry for more than breakfast. He had a mind to pick her up and rush her back to the cabin, but his stomach grumbled again.

"Oh, quiet down," Kate said, looking at his belly. Then, to Luca, "Let's eat."

"Sure."

Can't make love on an empty stomach.

17

KATE AND LUCA REJOINED HER CREW, WHO HAD REASSEMBLED THE PULLEY.

"Guys, you didn't have to do that," Kate said.

"We wanted to," Cato declared. "We felt guilty having to take it apart."

"Nonsense, it got the job done. But thanks all the same. Well, welcome to the *Demeter*. Be sure to thank the captain for scooping us up when you see him."

"You're seeing him now," a polite voice said behind her.

Kate turned around and embraced the captain.

"Ah, Rene, there you are. I was wondering when you were going to make your entrance." Rene was a tall svelte man, dressed in a pale blue coat and white breeches.

"Here I am." He was very haughty, and put on airs when he spoke.

"Thank you so much for helping us, we would have had a rough go of it without you," Kate said.

"Oh, not at all. For letting me be captain of *your* ship, stopping you from drowning is the least I could do." The right side of his mouth quirked upward.

"I think I have a rough idea of where we are, but where might we be headed?"

"Home to Icarya, my dear. We should hit shore about twenty-four hours from now."

"Perfect, perfect, and how much time, pray tell, has it been since we left Icarya?"

"You've been absent for nigh on six months now. Start of summer, this is."

"Very good. Is there anything I or my companions can do to assist you?"

The captain tipped his hat in her direction.

"No, my lady. We're all the crew you need. Just relax, and we'll have you safely home in no time."

"Many thanks."

"My pleasure. Oh, and if you please?" he said as he made to leave.

"Yes?" Kate asked.

"Be mindful that, though you may be queen, I am the master and commander of this ship, and her crew."

Kate smiled. "Understood, Captain."

"Very good."

When Rene walked away, Kate turned around to see a bunch of amused faces.

"What? What did I miss?"

They were not used to Kate conversing with someone so formally, and they found it funny. She threw her hands in the air.

"I give up. Alright you numbskulls, did you happen to find breakfast?"

Kate's band spent the rest of the morning sharing a hearty meal.

Between bites of rustic bread and slices of orange, Luca asked, "What is Icarya like? I don't know anything about its government, or economy…"

"You don't know *anything* about its government? Really?" Kate said.

"I know their leader is a red-headed goddess, but that's about it," he quipped.

Kate blushed at the compliment. "I'm actually one of three monarchs. There's my older brother, Allistair, Lord of Castelmor, the surrounding village. My younger brother Ted manages all the administrative details, royal events, things of that nature. He's traveled with us plenty of times."

"He's a great guy," Hercules chimed in.

"Yeah. Dependable, funny, he keeps me sane," Kate replied.

"Not to mention handsome!" the woman made of leaves added.

"I wouldn't know about that," Kate said awkwardly.

"He may be handsome, but good luck keeping him interested!" another nymph harrumphed.

"Umm, yeah," Kate acknowledged. "You have my sympathy."

Hercules chuckled. "Ted never met a girl he didn't like. I remember one time, for my birthday, he took me to this—"

"Nope!" Kate shouted. "Stop right there! I simply will *not* have that image floating around in my head. My brother is a scoundrel, and I love him dearly. End of discussion."

"And you?" Luca asked, changing the subject.

"I'm the problem solver," Kate answered. "I procure energy supplies, settle disputes, conduct foreign relations, wage war, when there *is* a war, I fix bridges, build houses, monitor crops…"

Her crew began to snicker as she continued with the laundry list of duties she was responsible for.

"That doesn't sound very balanced," Luca commented.

"I know, but it keeps my life interesting. However I want to be clear about one thing. *All* Icaryans are free. And the choices we make are always with the full consent of the governed. We do not rule. We serve."

Luca nodded. He had seen first-hand that Kate was not exaggerating her approach to leadership. And it worked beautifully.

"And economy? What can I do for a living?" he asked.

Kate shrugged. "We work primarily on the barter system. Most of Icarya is either rural or thickly forested. We've been at peace for so long because we provide most of the world's food. There are no big Icaryan cities. The most you'll see is Castelmor. We're the only ones with electricity and running water. In terms of governance, most places are self-run. I wouldn't worry about a job."

"What do you mean?"

"If you're going to be with me all the time, then you'll be traveling with me and helping out that way. You don't need *another* job on top of that. Everything you could ever need or want will be provided."

"I want to feel useful. You've done so much for me already."

"You *will* be useful. You were useful on this last trip. Think you can handle it?"

He nodded.

"Good, because I'm going to start you off with a vacation."

"What?"

"This last trip took a lot out of me. I just want to relax a little. Right now, there is nothing pressing on my agenda. When we reach Icarya tomorrow, we can stay at my cottage at the base of the Northern Mountains. It's nice and quiet."

"Sounds good to me."

"You'll like it there. So, what do you want to do?"

"Just sit here."

"That's it?"

"I'm not used to being in the sun as much, Kate. I want to enjoy it."

Kate smiled at him. "Okay. Then we'll sit here."

When twilight came, they retired to Kate's cabin while the others danced to some music on deck, and burned through the last few bottles of liquor onboard.

Kate pulled the small red curtain covering the cabin window closed and discarded her gear. She sat down at her desk, and pulled a piece of parchment from her satchel. She laid it out on the table, weighing down the edges, removed a quill from an inkwell, and began scratching away.

"What are you working on?" Luca asked as he surveyed the furnishings of the room. The cabin was adorned with masks, tapestries, weapons, and the like, all of differing materials and styles.

"It's a treasure map. A gift for my nephew, Kaspar. He likes adventure, like me. So I'm contriving a way for him to explore Castelmor. It's huge."

"How old is he?"

"In earth time, about six or seven I should think. In Icaryan years, almost a hundred. People and things age much more slowly here."

"What is all this?"

"Hmm?" Kate looked up at Luca, still staring at the walls. "They're from some of the places I've visited. Sometimes I receive gifts as part of a treaty, or as a welcome, or in thanks. Some are the weapons of enemies. I usually bring back something to hang on my walls." she said as she took off her boots and stockings, stretching her feet and legs.

"Was this trip more stressful than normal?" Luca asked.

"In some ways, yes. I don't use magic on every trip. It took a lot out of me. As for the side effects, suffice it to say this past year has been unusually intense." She sighed. "Two blood spells. I've never cast them so close together before. I can't cast for a long time, or this last episode will look like a dream. I have to be careful now."

She gave Luca a gentle smile, and turned back to the parchment laid out in front of her.

Luca moved silently across the room, casting a tall shadow over her desk. Kate closed her eyes as he bent over, and pressed his cheek against hers. He curled his fingers around her shoulders, and let them travel down her arms where they intertwined with her fingers. His deep, velvety voice resounded in her head.

"Are you almost finished?"

A faint utterance was her only response.

"Good," he purred. "I'm still waiting on your promise."

They smiled at each other. It was late. They were alone. And no one would disturb them. The night was theirs.

He opened his mouth against her throat. Luca disentangled his right hand from hers and caressed her neck, tilting her toward him and sucking on her flesh. He allowed his lips to brush against her open mouth, and then stood. He released his grip on her, and sauntered over to the bed.

Luca watched with smug satisfaction as Kate struggled to catch her breath. The quill was still poised in her hand, but it hadn't moved since he left her side.

He felt a door open in his psyche. His inexperience with seduction faded away, and his thoughts came into sharp focus. It felt inherent, natural, instinctual.

Drop the pen.

Kate's grip on the quill loosened, and it fell to the parchment in one quick motion. His heartbeat quickened. He tried his luck again.

Come to me.

Her movements were languid and dreamlike as she joined him on the far side of the room and reclined on the bed. She blinked, and tried to focus.

Luca brushed his knuckles against her cheek, her neck. He released his grip. Not all the way, not enough to sever the connection, but enough for him to watch Kate's pupils come into focus and her mind to clear. His gaze stayed locked with hers.

Is this okay? he asked.

She nodded, and wormed her way further into his arms as he opened the door again between his mind and hers, and stepped through.

Open your mouth.

His mouth descended on her, exploring her recesses with his tongue. He reached between her legs. She arched toward him, but it wasn't enough. He skimmed her leg with his hand and pushed her knees into the bed, spreading her legs. He returned his hand in between them, and pulled away a thin layer of lace. He kept his lust-filled eyes locked on her as he caressed her thigh, then her tight flesh. Kate closed her eyes and moaned. Her muscles went limp, and her hips opened for him as he slipped a finger inside her. His cock twitched. She was so warm and wet, and her muscles squeezed against him, drawing him in. He let his mouth hang open as his fangs began to poke out of his lips. Luca danced on the edge of sanity as he nipped at her neck.

"Please," she moaned. Luca propped himself up, and used his other hand to tear open her dress. He drank in the bare sight of her. Her skin was soft and pink and luscious.

Oh gods. He was going to devour her.

He sucked, licked, and raked his teeth across her nipples before kissing them tender and causing a fierce blush to take hold of her skin.

Luca's lust snapped his concentration. A frenzied urgency overcame them as Kate regained her senses. She ran her fingers through Luca's hair, pulled his shirt over his head, and spread her hands over his smooth, pale skin. He inhaled a sharp, unsteady breath at the feel of her hands against his skin. She lunged for his pants, which hit the floor in less than a minute. As Luca's fingers glided smoothly in and out of her, she stroked him until he couldn't bear it.

Luca's fangs had fully extended. He was dying of thirst. He tempted himself by climbing on top of Kate, his mouth hovering around her neck and breasts, his ragged breath collecting on the curve of her shoulder. His beautiful dark tresses spilled over her, tickling her nipples. Kate pulled him closer, trapping him between her knees and pressing their abdomens together, urging him forward. Luca ground against her in torturous fashion. He couldn't stop himself from growling. It rose from a place so deep and powerful, the room shook with it.

Kate took Luca's head in her hands, and raised his face to hers. But he didn't open his eyes; he'd shut out the world, and explored by touch and smell alone. He hoped it would be enough.

He tried to burrow himself in her breasts, distracting her with his tongue so she wouldn't notice.

He should have known that Kate would never let him get away with it.

"Look at me," Kate panted.

"No." He tried to pull her mind away to somewhere else, like that spot right under her chin where blood was pooling under the surface as he sucked…

"Open your eyes, Luca. No secrets."

Luca took a deep breath, and opened his eyes. The outer edge of his irises flared a brilliant red. He knew they had turned, just as he knew his fangs were sharper than ever, waiting to drink.

"I'm sorry," he sighed, beyond embarrassed. "I can't help it."

"Luca…"

He tried to dip his head, to avert his gaze away from her, but there was no escaping her. She brought her lips to his. When she was close enough to close her eyes, she didn't. Her gaze didn't waver from him as she pressed a kiss to his mouth, and licked the seam of his lips with hers, beckoning him to follow after.

"Kate, I—"

She pressed him into silence with a kiss that made him forget everything, except how badly he needed to be inside her.

"I just see you," she whispered. "I want *you*. Don't ever hide your face from me again. Do you hear me? Never."

She wrapped her arm around his waist, and moved underneath him, taunting him.

Every muscle coiled tight in anticipation. It went beyond *want*. Loving Kate was a need, something he couldn't live without.

What if she regretted it? What if he *did* hurt her, even if he didn't mean to? What if—

"I'll kill you if you don't."

He'd lost himself at the doorway to her body, almost drowned in doubt. But she pulled him free again.

They remained lost in each other's eyes as Luca swallowed hard and pushed himself into her. Pleasure soaked his brain as Kate's warm flesh enveloped him. He removed Kate's hands from his face and planted them onto the bed. They became entangled in Kate's wild hair, splayed across the pillow. Luca folded their fingers together and used their palms as a platform to support his weight as he bore down on her.

His first thrusts were tentative. Luca was unsure of himself, and he sensed Kate quiver underneath him as her body stretched and strained to accommodate him. They slowly found their rhythm, and Luca throbbed harder with every thrust. He detected the scent of her blood intensify as he tore through her virginity. The fragrance, combined with their sweat, surrounded him in a lustful haze.

THE CANDLES THAT LIT THE ROOM FLICKERED OUT, LEAVING THEM IN complete darkness. Kate saw nothing except Luca's eyes, two bright crimson orbs enrapt by the thrill of bedding her. The darkness heightened her body's response to Luca's touch as he filled her, their stomachs grazing each other. She opened her hips wider, and dug into his sides with her knees, yearning for more. She unfurled her fingers from his and clung to his finely sculpted back, grabbing his ass and pulling him closer to her, pushing him in deeper and feeling his hips press against hers as his instincts drove him. She bit into his shoulder to muffle her cries of passion.

LUCA LOST CONTROL. HE DROVE INTO HER WITH ABANDON, HIS BLOOD RAN hot. He cried out in ecstasy, and the last shred of his restraint fizzled away. He arched his back, and brought his fangs down on top of her breast, breaking her skin. Kate screamed. Luca drank in the first few gushes of her sweet elixir like a starved beast. His body shuddered at the touch of his tongue against the fresh flow, quickly reduced to a trickle. His breathing sounded like a whine as the blood dripping from her breasts ebbed. Luca didn't waste a single drop, licking his lips and tonguing her breasts, desperate to discover any remnants of her blood while the wounds began to heal.

The taste of her blood brought new fervor to his hips. He swelled inside her, and she screamed again, from deep within her soul. Luca sighed in sweet satisfaction as wave after wave of pleasure gripped him in her body's aftershock.

He slipped his hands underneath her shoulders and pulled her closer as his hot seed spilled inside her. He held onto her for an eternity, his intake of breath sounding almost like a sob as guilt rushed over him. Kate buried her face in the crook of his neck and dissipated his fear.

He locked his eyes with Kate again as they recovered from their shared madness, sweating and panting. His lips lunged for hers one final time before he collapsed on top of her. Her breasts pushed against him with every rise and fall of her chest.

Luca groaned as he separated himself from her and rolled onto his back, utterly spent. She placed her hand on his lower abdomen, laid her head on his chest, and the two of them just laid there, gasping for air. In the absence of light, conversation, and energy, they were soon both sound asleep.

18

LUCA WAS AWAKENED BY THE SPICED FRAGRANCE OF KATE'S HAIR. WHEN she'd turned over, it had spread itself over his face. He brushed it aside, slowly bringing Kate off his shoulder and onto her stomach. She looked so sweet and peaceful when she was sleeping. Luca kissed her back, her neck.

"Kate," he whispered.

He wrapped his arm underneath her waist and gave her a little squeeze. She moaned.

"I could get used to waking up like this." She turned over, basking in their sweet afterglow. She twisted his hair, draping over her like a dark curtain, between her fingers.

Luca gazed at her body in admiration, his tracing a path with his index finger between her breasts, down the length of her abdomen.

"You are exquisite," he sighed.

She cradled his chin, bringing his lips to meet hers.

He reached for the puncture marks on her breast with a featherlight touch. "Did I hurt you?"

It was torture having to face her and ask this question. He'd given in to every whim and desire he had, in a way he had never even come close to doing before. The taste of her blood still coated his tongue. He'd done the thing he swore to himself he would never do. But that's what she'd wanted from him. She said so. Everything hinged on whether that still held true this morning.

"I feel wonderful. Don't apologize for life-altering sex."

Luca almost blushed. Being a novice love maker, he took it as a great compliment.

"Luca?" Kate's voice sounded tentative.

"Yes, love?"

"I'm a little afraid to ask this question, but…how many women have you been with?"

"Excuse me?"

"I don't *really* care, but, given your age, and what I just experienced last night, I'm curious. How often have you done this?"

"Kate," Luca smiled at her unwitting praise, "you're the only one."

Her mouth hung open. "Are you serious? I mean, I know you weren't winning any popularity contests, but with your looks, and what you did last night, the trance you put me in, surely you could've easily—"

Luca shook his head. "I never met anyone I wanted to be with." They were both all smiles. He nuzzled her nose, and pressed a gentle kiss to her lips.

"Since we're talking about this," Kate said, "it was my first time too. Doing *that*, anyway."

Luca bent his head toward her in question.

"It's not exactly a pleasant memory for me," Kate started. "It was a one-time thing, and I—"

Luca put one finger to her lips. "It doesn't matter."

She let out a sigh. "Thank you."

After spending the entire morning in bed, Kate brought them back to reality.

"We should probably get up," she said.

"I don't want to." Luca's voice dragged.

"I know, but we have to face everyone sooner or later."

"Oh, alright." He let out a groan as he stretched.

"There's a washroom in that corner," Kate said, "you can freshen up."

Luca hopped out of bed, picking up the clothes he had discarded the night before. He walked over to the water closet behind the bed, looking like a dark angel.

"You really *are* perfect," Kate swooned.

"Be right out," Luca said with a smirk.

Kate stood up, taking the bedcover with her. She found some bread and a few jams in the cupboard on the far side of the room, and laid everything out on a pedestal style table near the fire, which had died out. She opened the windows on either side of the hearth, looking out over the sea, and let in the warm summer breeze.

Luca reentered the room, switching places with Kate. "Feels like a beautiful day," he remarked.

"It sure does. Icaryan summers are quite pleasant."

"Hey, come here." Luca pulled Kate to him, and threw the cover back to the bed, leaving her standing nude in front of him. "That's much better." He kissed her neck and gave her butt a gentle pat as she flitted away into the water chamber. Luca looked at the food set out on his left. He heard Kate turn on the shower to his right. His smile turned mischievous.

KATE HAD ONLY WALKED INTO THE FLOWING STREAM A MOMENT AGO, JUST long enough to drench her body. She pushed a warm current through her hair. Her skin tingled when she felt Luca's hands caressing her arms, tracing the path made by her bent elbows. His cock beckoned at her thigh.

"I missed you," Luca said, his voice luxurious as silk against her ear. She reached behind her to grasp his neck. Water sluiced through her hair, sending shimmering waterfalls down her breasts as he bent his head forward, caressing her hips. His hands travelled south, feeling her skin grow taut as he brushed against wet hair. Her heart patted out a rapid beat as he fondled her. She reached behind her, groping for him in the steam. Turning her to face him, Luca's warm body pressed her back against the cold stone wall, and she cried out. He wrapped her left thigh around his waist as he drove into her. She clung to his shoulders, leaning her face against his strong chest. As he pumped into her, the ship pitched to the side unexpectedly. Luca slid in even deeper. His eyes flashed at her as their bodies pressed together. She bit his earlobe, and begged.

"More."

Her desperate plea hardened him, and he pushed himself in to the hilt. Oh, the sounds he made were enough to unravel her. He grabbed at her right thigh, pushing his abdomen against her and pressing her deeper into the wall. She tensed her legs, wary of being lifted off the floor, but he held her in his firm, caring grip.

"I've got you," he whispered, barely having the breath to speak. Her body melted into his hands, and her legs enveloped him. He drove even deeper, his powerful thrusts almost too much to bear. But anything less wouldn't have been enough.

Through the hiss of steam, Kate heard the faint sound of the wall cracking behind her from the pressure. She clung to him, her nipples rubbing against his chest, their hips colliding. She kissed him like a ravenous beast, heart hammering as she felt his heat flashing inside her and down her thigh. Her whole body shuddered against him in bliss. His tantalizing fangs rested on her throat as he climaxed. She ached for that exquisite pain, that all-consuming pinch that would open her flesh and feed his desire. Kate extended her neck, offering, tempting him. He growled, and she almost came again, her body pliant in his arms. She clasped at his hair, raking those sharp, hungry points against her skin. She wasn't sure which one of them wanted it more. Still he resisted.

"If I do that," he panted, eyes blazing, "there's no going back."

She bit her lower lip. Her hair soaked his chest as she leaned her forehead on his shoulder.

"Don't make me beg," she whispered.

~

WHEN THEY FINALLY SAT DOWN TO BREAKFAST, KATE PICKED UP THE medallion she had discarded the previous night and returned it to its normal place around her neck.

"That's an interesting piece," Luca commented. "Where did you get it?"

"The woman who was queen before me gave it to me," Kate answered. Her expression turned pensive at his question, which in turn made him curious.

"How *did* you come to be queen?" Luca asked.

"I still ask myself that question sometimes, and I still don't really know the answer. When my brothers and I first set foot in Icarya, we stumbled right into a civil war between the queen, Meryn, and her father." Kate squinted as she tried to remember details that were fuzzy to her even when she had first heard them. "I think that her father tried to claim that she wasn't his heir." Kate paused to munch on a piece of jam-covered toast, resuming her tale as Luca poured her a second cup of tea.

"Thank you. Anyway, the king had us locked up, but Meryn and her bodyguard came to the dungeon in the middle of the night and let us out. I think," Kate said, "there was something going on between the two of them."

"What makes you say that?" Luca asked, buttering another piece of bread.

"The way her bodyguard looked at her," Kate answered. "It's the way you're looking at me now." Her eyes rose to meet his tender expression, and she smiled.

Seeing the warmth suffuse her cheeks was just as tantalizing as ever. That was when he realized:

I'll never not be hungry for her.

"Before parting ways," Kate continued, "she gave me this, for safekeeping. I'll never forget what she said: 'It's yours anyway. One day, you'll need it.' No one ever saw her again. Or her father. The next day, I was summoned back to the castle by the royal guard, for my coronation. I barely had time to blink, and I'd been crowned Queen of Icarya. I was nineteen and terrified. My first order was to split the crown into three. I wanted my brother's help. I made Ted a king too, but...when we were little, it was just Allistair and me for a long time. I've always craved his counsel." She swallowed hard. "We are not as close as we once were, but, whenever I leave, I know the world is in good hands. I don't know what Meryn was thinking," Kate pondered, "giving me such a prized possession. She was strong, and smart, and so brave. She didn't look that much older than me at the time, but from the few minutes I knew her, I could tell that she was capable of things I'd only ever dreamed of. She made a great impression on me. I don't know what she saw in a quiet, bookish little girl like me." Kate stared into her lap, reflecting on how much her life had changed in three hundred years.

"I do," Luca said with a gentle smile.

Kate grinned in response. "It took me a long time to step out of her shadow." She sighed deeply. "I'm glad to be home."

After breakfast, Kate stood before a full-length mirror and took a quick look at the two marks that Luca's bite had left as she dressed. She was figuring out how to conceal them to preserve her modesty, and inhaled sharply when her fingers touched them. Guilt stabbed through him. Luca walked up behind her, looking at her reflection. His impression was far lighter than hers, making him appear almost transparent. He brought his hands to her hips.

"Are you alright?" he asked.

"I'm fine, just a bit tender."

When Luca raised his hand, she covered her wound, protecting it.

"What are you doing?" she protested.

"I don't want you to be in pain."

"I told you, I'm only a little sore." She smiled at him seductively. "If *something* wasn't a little sore after a night like that, I'd feel like we did something wrong."

Luca chuckled.

"Leave it, I like it."

"You *like* it?" How could that be?

"It's a little reminder that I'm yours."

"But you were covering it up," Luca said.

"Of course. What we do isn't anyone's business. But I know it's there. And so do you."

He didn't really understand. All the same, it made his blood simmer in his veins. "Okay, I'll leave it. No matter *where* it happens to be," he said.

Kate raised an eyebrow at him.

The couple heard the lookout's cry of land approaching and joined the congregation of Icaryans waiting at the ship's stern. A thick blanket of fog obscured the view far into the distance. All Luca could see were magnificent creatures diving through the clouds. The wind created by an approaching griffon's golden wingspan as he treaded the air almost knocked Kate and Luca off their feet. He flew close to them, hovering overhead.

"Welcome home, Your Majesty," he addressed Kate.

"Hi, Gideon. How goes it?"

"All is well," he answered, dropping a parchment into her hands. "From King Allistair."

"Of course," she murmured, and thanked the griffon. "I bring great news. Do you think you could round up some friends? I've got a few things onboard that won't quite fit in the rowboat."

"With pleasure," he replied, and disappeared back into the mist. The clouds parted, and cheers erupted on deck as a luscious green landscape came into sight. In the distance to the right, Luca spied a towering castle complex built into a steep cliff. As the overcast sky darkened, Luca saw the soft glow of lampposts flickering on inside the stone walls of the town attached to the castle's base. At the leftmost edge of his vision was a harbor, with little houses dotting the climbing hills behind. Straight ahead, a majestic, snow-capped mountain range stretched into the horizon. Most of the land was thickly forested, with clearings in the canopy shining light on the small villages, marketplaces, and expansive fields. Far from the parched fields and wastelands of steel and rubble that Luca had wandered for ages, this place was lush, and vibrant, and alive.

"Wow," Luca whispered, wrapping his arm around Kate's waist and folding their hands together.

She turned her head to kiss his cheek, and took in a deep breath of fresh sea air.

"Aren't we all going ashore?" Luca asked as the hoofed members of

Kate's band, along with crates of quartz, were hoisted off the ship by griffons, firebirds, and giant birds of prey.

"Yes, but the *ship* isn't coming ashore. Rene is just dropping us off. He's got to bring her around and moor her in Cathair," she explained, indicating the port on the western shore. "Alright, let's see what he wants now," she grumbled, unfurling the parchment in her hands.

Luca read over her shoulder. The king's missive to his sister made them both see red:

Kate,

As I write this, Ted is planning a gala to celebrate your return. In a day's time Castelmor will be overflowing with eligible and eager bachelors. Before scampering off into the wilderness, consider carefully. If you can manage to impress even one with some newfound maturity, you just might have one last chance to exchange the chaos of your condition with some stability, and perhaps cater to the duties of your sex. I'll see you tonight.

Your brother and king,
Allistair

"You're not going to go, are you?" Luca asked. He had no desire to meet this brother of hers if this was how he treated her.

"I'm sorry, Luca, I couldn't hear you. The blood is still ringing in my ears," Kate remarked. She took her rage out on the letter, creating a pile of parchment dust in front of her feet. "I don't go for him," she said. "I go for them." She gestured toward the crowd that had gathered on the shore, now dancing in jubilant circles around their precious cargo.

The water women said their goodbyes before dissolving into the thinning fog. As the rest boarded a smaller boat, Rene bid Kate farewell.

"Thanks again Rene, you're a lifesaver," Kate said, clasping his hands.

Rene kissed her on the cheek. "My pleasure, dear. Do come and see me soon. The missus has been begging for a visit. You are welcome too, of course," he said to Luca.

It was the first time he'd been invited anywhere. "You can count on it," he said.

Corbin sat on Kate's shoulder as their boat neared the shore.

"Look at Philip, he's so anxious to get moving, he doesn't know what to do with himself," Corbin mused, observing him trotting in place on the shore.

"He's sorely missed. We should all be so lucky," Kate replied. "Me, I get *ordered* to show up someplace."

Luca grasped her hand as he sat hunched next to her at the edge of the little boat.

"The loss of his wife still feels fresh," Corbin answered.

"And it always will," Hercules said.

"That doesn't mean he can speak to her that way," Corbin retorted.

"Be patient with him," Hercules counseled.

Kate sighed, lightening the mood by changing the subject.

"I don't have to get my feet wet *again*, do I?" she asked Hercules as the boat was carried to the beach by a gentle wave.

"Nope," he said, hopping out and pulling the party onto the sand by himself. The pebbles scraped against the floor of the boat as he brought it to a stop. He stood up and lent Kate his hand, bowing his head.

"Welcome home, Your Persnicketyness. Ooph!"

"Thank you," she said, putting all her weight in her hand as she used the top of his head to steady herself.

"I guess I deserve that," he said, smiling as he rubbed his nick. He held his arms open and squeezed Kate in a gargantuan hug. He took Luca's arm firmly in his.

"Don't make me wait too long for the next adventure," Hercules said to Kate. "You know how I get bored."

"Always a pleasure, Herc. And Herc?" Kate said.

"Yeah?"

"Thanks."

"Anytime." He turned to Luca. "Take good care of yourself. And her."

"I will," Luca said.

"Until next time." With that, Hercules started off along a path in the sand that led to one of the smaller villages.

"I have to check on Cara," Philip insisted as Kate and Luca approached. "She's pretty far along now," Philip answered.

"Yes, I would imagine so," Kate replied.

"My mare is pregnant," Philip explained when Luca cocked his head.

"Congratulations," Luca replied.

"Thank you, thank you. I just hope she's feeling better. She was under the weather when I left. That's normal though, isn't it?" he turned to Kate, as if her female anatomy came with expertise about childbearing. For that of a horse, no less.

"She's probably fine. But," Kate said in a hopeful tone, "we may have another pegasus on our hands soon."

"Do you really think so?" he asked.

"It could be. Might explain the trouble she's been having," Corbin suggested.

"Yeah, maybe. *She* will be alright though, won't she?"

"She's a war horse, Philip. She can handle it," Corbin reassured him.

"You're right, of course. Shall we?" Philip asked Kate.

19

PHILIP SOARED ABOVE THE CLOUDS, CARRYING LUCA AND KATE ON HIS back. The altitude took Luca's breath away and made his head swim. They flew over rivers and valleys before reaching the castle. It was an enormous white structure with endless towers and turrets, topped with deep indigo roofs. It was surrounded on every side by lush, well-maintained gardens and populated with alabaster statues and mosaic fountains.

"It's magnificent," Luca commented.

"Wait until you see the inside," replied Kate.

Philip landed near the stone wall that marked the outer edges of Castelmor. The villagers were hustling and bustling every which way in hurried preparation for the reception of their beloved queen. Philip flew to the western side of the castle complex, towards his own patch of garden.

Luca took in his surroundings. The villagers were dressed simply but cleanly, carrying carts of bread, fish, and hay, buckets of water, barrels of wine, and piles of freshly washed linens in every direction. The unpaved street was littered with vendors, selling everything from shoes and jewelry to pots and pans to every spice and herb. This section of the marketplace let off an overpowering fragrance, so the whole town smelled like a savory stew. The townsfolk hurried to complete their preparations before twilight turned to night, and the dim lights from the elegant lampposts fashioned out of brass became insufficient. As the trio entered the village walls, all eyes turned to them.

Corbin jumped off Kate's shoulder as she approached a young boy holding a stack of papers in his hand.

"Good evening. May I?" she lifted a sheet of parchment from the top of the pile and brought it to the edge of her nose. She squinted. "I can't read this, it hurts my eyes. No no no," she said, giving the boy back his paper and scaling the lamppost. "That won't do." She fiddled with the bulb inside the glass case. "What you need is...more light!" She turned the post up as bright as it would go. All the lampposts throughout the village responded to Kate's fingers, lighting up the entire town.

Corbin laughed out loud as the population exploded in joy. The sound of their exultation was deafening. Luca kept his eyes on Kate's face. She beamed with pride.

"What's all this racket?"

A deep voice rang out from a window high above them. The man leaning out his balcony was a little taller than Kate, with short chestnut brown hair, hazel eyes, and a slender frame.

"Hallo, brother!" Kate shouted. "Just brightening up the place."

"Yes, I see," he said. A gleaming smile spread across his lips. "By all means, as you were!" His head disappeared back into the tower as cheers crescendoed again, and the villagers continued in their work, their steps lighter than before.

"Which one was that?" Luca asked in Kate's ear as she hopped down. He smiled in smug satisfaction as she crumpled against him at the sound of his voice, made deliberately sultry.

"Ted. Younger brother."

"Got it," he answered, kissing the skin behind her ear and inhaling her hair's perfume.

"Can you at least wait until we're inside?" she asked, but she only stepped further into his embrace.

"Not hardly," he said, raking the tips of his teeth against her throat.

Her knees buckled. "At this rate, I'll never get anything done again." She spun around, escaping his clutches. "Would you like a short tour?"

Luca crooked his elbow, and Kate slipped hers in. "Lead the way."

Luca was introduced to a flurry of different people and their occupations, none of which he would remember. What struck him the most were their expressions as he walked through town. He was used to being the new face, but their reactions to him ranged from polite interest to warm hugs. He'd never met a village so friendly, or so welcoming to outsiders.

Kate led Luca by the hand to an enclosed stall selling clothing. The fabrics hanging everywhere were woven with the finest silks and cottons in the most luxurious shades, and embellished with fine brocade and lacework. Toward the back, an array of armored breastplates, greaves, helmets, shields, and leather vests and skirts were on display. The proprietor of the stall rushed to greet them with open arms.

"Welcome back, Your Majesty! Oh how I have missed my number one customer!"

"Hello, Taelus, it *has* been too long!" Kate hugged the man, then introduced him to Luca.

"Luca, this is Taelus, the best dressmaker in Icarya, and my personal tailor."

"Pleased to meet you," Luca responded.

"It is *I* who am pleased to meet *you*! *Any* friend of Kate's is a friend of mine. To what do I owe the honor of this visit?"

Kate pulled the green dress she had worn the night before out of a leather satchel bag she wore over her shoulder. "I'm going to need a replacement for this," she explained.

Taelus held it up. The front had been completely torn open, the size and width of the marks Luca had left as he hungrily clawed at her skin lending it the appearance that Kate had almost been mauled to death.

"Oh my word, what sort of beast attacked you?"

"A wild animal," she answered, her smile just for him. Luca licked his lips and turned his head to the side, attempting not to give himself away by revealing the satisfied look on his face.

"You're lucky it didn't break your skin!"

Kate blinked, and her smile widened. She didn't know what to say.

"Rest assured, My Queen, I'll have a new one for you by week's end, and it will be even better than this one!"

"Thank you. One more thing, Taelus."

"Name it."

"My friend here and I are expected tomorrow evening. I'm well prepared, but might you have something suitable for Luca, that can be made ready quickly?"

"Oh, not to worry, not to worry! I have several exquisite garments I am working on now. Luca, you may have your pick, and I'll have it finished to your measurements in a few hours."

"You're very kind," Luca said.

"Not at all. It is my dear queen who is most kind and most generous to me, but a humble dressmaker. Kell!" Taelus shouted to his assistant and disappeared behind a curtain.

"He's certainly glad to see you," Luca said.

"That's because I always pay him three times his asking price," Kate replied under her breath.

"Three times the price?"

"I do it with everyone. A little cash injection every once in a while keeps money flowing smoothly."

"Hmm. Not a bad idea."

"It's worked for me so far."

"Ah, here we are!" Taelus returned, followed by Kell, waddling toward them carrying a bundle of partially finished clothes that they laid out for Luca to inspect.

Luca had never chosen his clothes before. On Earth he had simply picked up his shirt from a pile of shirts, and his pants from a pile of them at a rundown general store.

"Get whatever you like, Luca," said Kate, gesturing toward the table. "Get them all, if the mood strikes you. I've got you covered."

Taelus laughed nervously and wrung his hands at the prospect of clearing out his most expensive inventory at a triple profit. Luca walked over to the clothing, and immediately gravitated to a set of black vest and pants trimmed in black braiding around the shoulders. It had an accompanying set of ebony outer robes embellished with a subtle, masculine design and deep red lining.

"Black. I like black," Luca said.

"Black it is then! Sir, when I am finished with you, you will be the night itself!"

"He *already* looks like that," Kate muttered.

"Stand up here, please," Kell gestured to a raised part of the floor, positioned in front of a tall looking glass. Luca followed his lead, and Kell removed a long piece of tape from around his neck and began to mark Luca's measurements, starting with the width of his neck and shoulders, and the length of his arms. When he got to the waist, Kell measured several times, to make sure the small number he'd written down was accurate. Kate snickered at the scene, but kept herself collected.

Kell went for the inseam. Luca went from slightly confused and embarrassed to insulted in less than half a second. He slapped Kell's hand away from his thigh and cried out:

"Watch where you're going."

Kate lost it, covering her face with her hands, making every effort to stifle the uncontrollable laughter that was bubbling up in her throat.

Kell attempted to get the measurement twice more, with the same result. He turned to Kate for assistance, but it took a minute for her to open her mouth without becoming hysterical. Luca shot barbs at her with his eyes, demanding to know why she had taken him to this place to be molested.

"Luca," she said as evenly as possible, "he's measuring you for your pants, so they fit right. He's a professional, just let him do his job."

"Nothing feels better than pants that fit like a glove," Taelus chimed in.

Luca wasn't satisfied, and was two seconds away from lifting Kell off the floor with one hand by the scruff of his neck.

"Okay Kell," Kate interceded, "just leave him plenty of room." She flashed a toothy smile at Luca.

Luca pursed his lips and raised an eyebrow at Kate, who held his stare. He gave in, and relaxed. Kell, trying to put Luca at ease, suggested that he try on the robes for length. He looked at his faint reflection with the robes, tilting his head.

"These *are* quite nice."

"Oh, thank you sir, thank you! I hope you will remember us for all your clothing needs," said Taelus.

Kate agreed. "Yes, they're very flattering. Are you sure you won't take more?"

Luca hesitated. "How many fancy outfits do I need? Maybe if there were something simpler."

"If you like," Taelus suggested, "I can outfit you with a small collection of well-coordinated garments, fit for your travels with our fair queen."

Luca considered how well-dressed he thought Kate was.

"That sounds fine."

"All in black, sir?"

"All dark tones, at least."

"What, no pink?" Kate joked. "Taelus, give him clothes that fit his personality, as well as his physique."

"You can count on me! All will be ready in a month's time. This one I shall have delivered later on."

"Have them sent to my chambers."

"Excellent. And here, Luca, take a pair of boots with you."

Kell had finished pinning the bottom and sleeves of the robe, and had taken it from Luca to begin finishing the garment. Luca stepped down from the pedestal, and selected sturdy leather boots, good for all occasions.

Kate pulled several large coins out of her hefty purse string. She tucked the coins into her belt, and left her purse on the table. Taelus's eyes went wide. Kell reached for the bag, but Taelus quickly shoved him back, almost pushing him over.

"Oh, Kate once again you are so very generous, how I *do* miss you when you're away."

"I bet," Luca murmured under his breath.

"Thank you, Taelus, for your wonderful clothes, and Kell, for your exemplary service," she said.

The men waved as Kate and Luca exited the stall. When Kate turned back to release the flap, she caught a glimpse of the two tailors inside, wrestling over her purse. She laughed to herself and shook her head, leaving them to their tomfoolery.

"Everything in one piece?" Kate asked Luca, her grin impossible to miss.

"You might have warned me."

"And spoil the fun? There's no harm done, is there?"

He shook his head. "Thanks, by the way."

"You're quite welcome. I think we're ready for the castle now. I want to slip in through the kitchen, find out what's for dinner."

As they approached a small wooden door fitted with wrought-iron hinges, Luca got a whiff of game meat being cooked to perfection.

"Mmmm, fine by me," he declared as he inhaled the delicious aroma.

20

Just behind the heavy wooden door, clusters of people were hard at work. Several long wooden tables were manned by people peeling carrots, chopping onions, and rolling out bread dough. The sound of searing meat sizzled on rustic stoves, and huge pots of broth were stirred and tasted for seasoning. The table to the left of Kate and Luca was covered in flour and eggs. The head chef was kneading pastry dough, dividing it into small portions the size of a fist and stuffing them with fresh berries. He was covered in flour. The young assistant to his right was mixing more dough, and added a sprinkle of salt.

The chef smacked him on the back of the head, sending flour everywhere. The assistant's face nearly fell into the dough.

"Whaddya doin, addin' salt to the dough? This is pastry dough, ya blockhead! You're gonna give the king a heart attack, with all this salt!"

Kate laughed at the scene. She motioned to Luca to be quiet as she snuck up behind the chef. A tray of freshly baked pastries was on his right, and one by one he sprinkled them with sugar and placed them on a silver platter to his left. As he placed a pastry, Kate popped one into her mouth. He looked at the tray as he went to place the next one and did a double take. Kate ducked deftly and silently behind him. The man counted them out with his fingers, shrugged, and then continued. Kate took another one. He turned back again, and threw his hands up in the air.

"That does it! If food's disappearin' from my kitchen, it can only mean one thing. Hiya Katie!" He turned around with his arms open wide.

"Hiya Georg!" She laughed and gave him a big hug. He got flour all over her.

"Oh, hello, my beautiful queen! Where you been?"

"On another adventure. Georg, this is Luca."

"Nice to meet ya Luca, have a pastry." He held a doughy ball in his hand.

"I'll wait until after dinner, thank you," Luca replied.

"Suit yourself!" Kate took the pastry.

"Always had a good appetite, this one!" Georg laughed.

"That's because I work hard for it," Kate said in between bites.

"You're the only one I let into my kitchen. You and the kiddo, that is."

"Aunt Kate!!" Just then, a little boy ran up to Kate and jumped into her arms.

"Hello, my little prince! How have you been?" she asked, ruffling his short, dusky brown hair.

"Have a pastry!" Georg offered.

"I'm good Aunt Kate. Did you bring me something?"

Kaspar started picking at Kate's clothes with his tiny fingers, looking for hidden pockets. She put him down and placed her hands on her hips.

"Do I have something for you? Is that the only reason you're happy to see me?" she asked. Kaspar got a guilty look on his face, almost immediately replaced by a mischievous one.

"No. But you *did* bring me something, right?" The smile on Kate's face told him she was holding out on him.

"I didn't buy you anything, but I *did* find this map..."

"Is it a treasure map?" he asked, jumping up and down.

"I'm not sure. It's full of riddles, and I can't really make them out. Maybe you could help me with it?"

"Sure! I'm really good at puzzles!"

"I know!" Kate said, trying to match the young boy's eager enthusiasm.

"We can look at it in my room!"

"Okay! Hey Kaspar, I want you to meet somebody. This is my friend Luca. Luca, this is my nephew, Kaspar."

Luca smiled. "It's nice to meet you, Kaspar."

"Nice to meet you too. Wow, your sword is really big! Can I hold it?"

"Only if your dad says it's okay."

"It's okay. My dad doesn't care what I do."

Luca and Kate exchanged glances. Before either could question him further, Kaspar grabbed them both by the hand.

"Let's go guys! We've got puzzles to solve!"

The couple was dragged to Kaspar's chamber, which was the size of a small cottage. He had toys, dolls, maps, and wooden weapons strewn everywhere. The room was in complete disarray. He cleared a space on the floor and took the rolled-up parchment that Kate had lovingly prepared for him over the last several months.

"Let's see, it looks like a map of a castle. Is it our castle?" Kaspar asked.

"I think so," Kate played along.

"So the treasure is in this castle! And it says here, that if you find this secret room, you can have one wish granted." He looked up at Kate. "Can it be *any* wish?"

It was written plain on his small face, in his glassy eyes, that the little boy's mind was on his mother.

"Anything's possible, Kaspar," Kate answered, stifling her own emotion.

"I'm gonna give it my best shot then!"

"You better!"

"Where do we start?"

"I don't know, let's take a look." Kate sat down and folded her legs, and he sat in her lap. Luca watched her with him as she pointed out different features on the map and teasingly provided tidbits of information on how to use it.

Luca looked on, musing at the complex nature of the woman who had taken him as a lover. She was smart, cunning, and brutal when necessary. In that moment, he felt content. He had found in Kate all he had ever hoped for in a partner, and more.

Luca's reverie was broken by Kaspar's outburst of gratitude. Both he and Kate noticed a change in Kaspar's mood as he seemed to hold on a little too long and a little too tight. Kate pulled herself away from Kaspar, and saw his eyes were wet with tears.

"Kaspar, what's the matter sweetheart?" she asked.

"Can I come live with you?"

"What? Oh, honey, you can't come live with me. Your daddy would miss you too much."

"My daddy wouldn't miss me at all. He doesn't love me anymore," Kaspar sobbed. Kate looked at Luca, who moved closer to them.

"Of course your dad loves you, Kaspar. What would make you think he didn't?" Kate asked.

"He never plays with me, he's always yelling at me and says he doesn't have time for me."

"He said that?" Kate asked.

"Mmhmm," Kaspar whimpered, burying his face in the crook of Kate's neck.

"Shh, shh," she tried to comfort him. She looked at Luca again, livid. Luca looked the same. He did not take kindly to distant or cold fathers.

He had already decided that he did not like Allistair at all.

Kate continued to rub Kaspar's back, and Luca patted him on the head.

"Do you want me to talk to him?" Kate asked.

Kaspar rubbed his eyes and nodded.

"Okay, I'm going to go right now, but you've got to promise not to cry, okay? It breaks my heart to see you like that."

He sniffled. "Okay, I promise."

"Everything will be alright, I swear."

"Do you think," Kaspar asked, "that he'll play chess with me? I don't have anyone to play with."

"What about Uncle Ted? Doesn't he play with you sometimes?" Kate asked.

"Yes, but I think he lets me win, because he always makes stupid moves."

Kate laughed. "You're probably right. I'll talk to him too, so you can wipe the floor with him nice and proper."

"Okay. Thanks Aunt Kate, you're my favorite."

She hugged him again. "And you're mine," she said as she kissed the top of his head. "I'll see you in a little bit, okay?"

"Okay. I'm gonna get started on the map!" He plopped himself down on the floor again, poring over the clues Kate had written out for him.

Kate grabbed Luca's hand on the way out. Once she had closed the door, she leaned her head back against the hallway with a thud and closed her eyes.

"First that fucking letter, and now this. I am going to *kill* Allistair," she said in a voice so low Kaspar wouldn't hear.

21

Kate's determined steps echoed through the hallway leading to Allistair's quarters. As she and Luca passed through the dark stone hallway lined with suits of armor and flags bearing a golden crest rife with woodland creatures, Kate began grumbling to herself. By the time they were halfway down the hallway, her voice was bouncing off the walls.

"He must have lost his bloody mind. What is he thinking, treating that sweet little boy like that? What I wouldn't give to have a hundred just like him!"

"A hundred?" Luca tried to break her concentration and keep her mood light.

"Okay, maybe not a hundred, but a good few dozen!"

Luca smirked. Kate continued ranting. Two thirds of the way down the hall, she and Luca were met by her younger brother. After a warm welcome, Kate made the introductions.

"Ted, this is Luca. Luca, my brother Ted."

"What brings you to our humble abode?" Ted asked.

"I'm here with Kate."

"You're *with* Kate?" Ted clarified.

"I am," Luca said proudly.

"Splendid! Good for you Kate!" Ted shook Luca's hand. Luca suspected he was going to like Ted far better than Allistair.

Then Ted grew serious. "I'm glad you're back. I arrested someone I really think you should see."

Kate brushed past him. "I don't have time to talk to prisoners. I need to talk to Allistair."

Ted grabbed her arm. "It can wait."

Kate sighed. "Who is he?"

"At first, I thought it was *him*, because he wouldn't give me a name. He didn't say *anything*, actually."

Kate froze.

"Him who?" Luca asked, put on edge by Kate's rapid change in mood.

"An assassin. The best. He's like a phantom, no one knows who he is or where he came from," Ted answered. "Though, I think his more serious crimes are quite out of our jurisdiction."

"What do you mean?" Luca asked.

"He hasn't operated in Icarya for the past century, as far as anyone knows."

Kate swallowed hard.

"Anyway," Ted addressed Kate, "he finally spoke, after two months of complete silence. He asked for you, refuses to speak to anyone but you. Said his name was Alaric. Kate, you've blanched. Are you alright?"

She backed away from her brother, her eyes a glassy haze. "What the fuck were you thinking, letting him in here?!" she cried.

"Letting him in??" Ted asked, astonished by his sister's response. "I told you I *arrested* him. Kate? Kate!"

"You damned fool. If he's here, it's because he *wants* to be!" Without another word, Kate raced down the hallway, headed for the dungeon. Luca remained at her side, but she said nothing to him as she descended a dark, spiraled stone staircase as fast as she could without tumbling down it.

"Wait a minute," Luca said, grabbing her arm and forcing her to stop. "Tell me what this is about."

"There's no time, he's probably out already," Kate said, and tried to break away from Luca's grip.

He refused to relinquish her arm. He stared at her, waiting for an answer. Kate had no choice but to give Luca what he wanted.

"If he let himself be arrested, it's because he has a mark, someone inside the castle."

"So it *is* the assassin. And he's asking for you."

"Yeah," she said, her voice not even a whisper.

Luca had never seen her so uneasy. "Are you sure?"

"I know him," Kate insisted.

Something in her eyes made Luca suspicious. "What is he to you?"

"An unpleasant memory." She rubbed at her throat.

Luca's head throbbed as he recalled those same words from that morning. "Kate," he asked, lowering his voice, "did he hurt you?"

When she blinked, a small tear ran down her cheek. "It's not as simple as that."

Luca pressed his lips to her forehead and pulled her close. This man had gotten inside her head.

"Did he hurt you?" he repeated.

She closed her eyes and nodded.

He could feel the heat rising to his irises, ready to flash crimson. Luca swallowed hard. All of Icarya would know him for a monster if he unleashed his rage. Yet he asked without having to think about it.

"Do you want me to deal with him?"

She straightened up in his arms. "No."

Luca nodded. "I didn't think so."

22

ALARIC SAT ON THE WOODEN BENCH IN HIS CELL IN THE BOWELS OF THE castle, resting the back of his head against the wall slick with moisture buried deep within the stones. He was tall and well-built. His broad chest was cloaked in a leather vest lined with animal fur, his wild hair falling past his shoulders. His feet were planted firmly on the ground, his hands folded in his lap. Eyes closed, he savored the memory, a century old now, of his last meeting with the Queen of Icarya.

~

HE HAD HEARD HER ASCENDING THE WALL LEADING TO HIS BEDROOM window the minute she took her first step. He chose not to get dressed, but remained splayed out on his stomach, eyes shut, his hand resting on the dagger underneath his pillow. His breath was calm as he heard her climb through his window and approach him. She grabbed the knife she had in her teeth and raised it above her head.

He sprang on her, grabbing her by the wrist and pinning her underneath him. The young queen gasped in surprise, but kept her tenacious grip on her knife. It was still pointed at the assassin's throat.

His dark piercing eyes stared at hers. Her eyes were full of fearfear, but she tried, badly, to hide it.

"You'll have to be a lot faster and quieter to kill me. But, by the gods," he said, taking in the rest of her face, "you are *beautiful*."

Kate said nothing, but he could feel her whole body shaking underneath him. With one look, he knew that she had never killed anyone before. An arrogant grin spread across his face.

"Come on," he chided her. "Do what you came for." He pressed his powerful frame closer to her. The tip of her blade embedded itself in his throat. He didn't blink as it drew blood, but Kate flinched as it dripped down onto her neck. He scoffed at her and grabbed the knife out of her hand in one swift movement, tossing it to his left. It clattered on the floor near the door.

"Tell your brother not to send a little girl to do his job," he sneered as he began to rise off her. "Son of a—!" He had intended to let her go, not wanting to kill a girl just for being young and impulsive. But Kate was enraged by his comment, and kneed him between his legs as hard as she could. Without a single scrap of clothing for protection, he took the blow hard. He shrank back from her with a grunt. Kate leapt out of the bed and bounded for the door.

Losing only seconds, the assassin reached for the knife under his pillow and raced Kate to the door. Before she could kneel to recover her weapon, he wrapped his right arm around her, ramming her into the wall and threatening to slit her throat. In his rage, he hurriedly jammed his free hand up her shirt and twisted her breast until she cried out in pain.

"It's only fair," he snarled. She tried to wriggle herself away from his rough grasp, but he overpowered her. He craned his neck close to hers, smelling her hair. His lust was intensifying by the minute. Her bold spirit excited him. He brushed his lips against her ear.

"Take your clothes off," he said in a deep voice. "Then maybe we can talk about making a deal."

"Fuck you!" she shouted.

"That's the general idea, yes," he countered. She fought hard to free herself, but his strength was no match for her.

"Save your energy," he huffed as he kept his hold on her. "You're not coming out of this unscathed." After several minutes of struggling, he felt her body go limp in his arms. His knife was still in position at her neck. As she turned to face him, a thin line of red welled up on her throat. What she said next took him by surprise.

"Kill me, fuck me, do whatever you want. But leave my nephew alone. He's only a little boy. He's all I have left." Tears filled her eyes.

"Don't you care which?" he inquired.

Kate's eyes went vacant. "No."

His eyes narrowed at her. He didn't know why, but she was starting to gain his sympathy.

"Something else is wrong. Tell me what it is."

"Why should you care?"

"I don't. Humor me."

"Forget it."

He clucked his tongue at her. "My god girl! You break into my room, try to kill me in my sleep, while I'm naked, and you don't want to give me some fucking *information*? Why don't you care what happens to you?" He threatened to deepen the hairline scratch she had inflicted.

She relented. In a quiet voice, she said, "My brother won't care what you do to me. Neither will anyone else. No matter where I go, I'm not wanted." She turned her face from him in her embarrassment.

"Get in line," he quipped. She continued to stare at the wall. To see someone so young and so beautiful look so dejected tugged on his heartstrings. He dropped his knife and turned her face to him, his gaze tender. "I've only known you about a minute, and *I* want you. Or hasn't that become obvious by now?"

Without giving herself time to think better of it, Kate looked down. She spied his burgeoning erection, and hurriedly looked away. She blushed. He released his grip on her. Her hand reached for the door. He grabbed her hand, and forced her arm downward. Under his guidance, she stroked his swollen flesh. When he released her, she did not pull her hand away.

With her back to him, he slipped his fingers underneath her belt. His fingertips grazed her abdomen first, which shrank back from him. He wandered below her navel and past a coarse patch of hair. He ran a single finger between the folds of her flesh and rubbed her. He was surprised to find her already damp. She sighed softly as his fingers penetrated her and leaned the back of her head against his chest. He spoke to her in hushed tones.

"Stay."

He turned her toward him, their faces inches from each other. She stared back at him as he closed the gap between them, pressing his lips against hers. He pulled away to look into her eyes once more, searching for her acceptance before kissing her again. Her lifeless mouth annoyed him, so he bit her lip, drawing blood.

"Ow!" she screamed, her eyes burning with fury. He slammed her against the wall again as she fought him. She bit back. He grabbed her hair, their kisses becoming more heated as he tore at her clothes. He lifted her off the ground by her hips and walked back to the bed, tossing her on the mattress.

They wrestled as Kate resisted being flung on top of him. But he remained in control and kept her above him. He separated his lips from hers and put his hand on top of her head. Gently but firmly, he guided her downwards, past a thin dusting of hair. He jutted his hips forward, invading her mouth. She tasted the salt of his sex as he pushed repeatedly past her lips. She acquiesced—hesitantly at first, but as the assassin's approval became more audible, she became more daring with her tongue, tasting more of his salt and sweat sliding down her throat. She didn't surface for what felt like forever.

On the verge of exploding, the assassin pulled on Kate's hair, lifting her head. She stared into his eyes and licked her lips. He rose off his back, rolling over on his side and bringing her with him, spooning her. He wrapped his muscular arms around her and yanked on her thigh, positioning her leg on top of his own as he thrust himself forward and entered her ass. He grabbed her by the throat with his left hand. He jammed his right thumb against her sensitive flesh as the rest of his digits groped her insides. His fingers were soaked. She interlaced the fingers of her right hand with his as they pushed into her. He moaned loudly in her ear. She could barely breathe, rapidly becoming light-headed. She winced in pain, and tried to disengage herself from him.

"Do you want me to stop?" he asked, slowing his brisk rhythm.

She turned to glare at him.

"Then shut up," he growled. He squeezed her tighter.

As the assassin's fervor increased, his thrusts swelled in their violence. Pain seared through Kate's inexperienced body. Her cries were smothered in her throat as his fingers crushed her neck. She rolled onto her stomach, tucking her knees underneath her as she tried to squirm away, searching for air and for relief. But the assassin was too foregone in his own pleasure, mindless to her desperation as he kept pace with her, not leaving her flesh for a second. He had better leverage on top of her crouched form, and clawed at her hips as he pounded harder. She couldn't breathe at all. Her already blurry vision started to darken. His moans crescendoed to a roar as he pulled on her neck, forcing her upright. His powerful haunches burned as he penetrated her while she sat on his lap. He screamed, and fell on top of her again as his flesh bulged expectantly. He relinquished his terrible grip on Kate, letting his hot surge spill onto her thigh as he rested his face on her skin. Their bodies were slick with sweat. He slid off her chest, heaving.

"Holy hell," he shouted in a ragged tone, "you can't buy sex like *that!*"

Kate remained silent as she scrambled to cover herself. She turned away from him, clutching the sheets close to her neck, her knees tucked into her stomach.

"It's a little late for that, don't you think?" he said. "Come here."

Kate's whole frame tensed. She couldn't take any more. To her surprise, his touch was gentle as he put his arm around her and encouraged her to lay her head on his chest.

"Come on. I'm not above cuddling," he chided. "I want to hold you. Come here."

She obeyed, turning her body toward him, pressing her cheek to his sprawling pectorals. He stroked her hair, kissing the top of her head.

After he regained his breath, and was sure that Kate was once again comfortable, he lifted her chin.

"Let me see," he said, turning her head from one side to the other. He inspected the deep bruising that was already showing on her neck and in her eyes, almost admiring his work.

"You'll be alright."

She kept her head down, averting his gaze.

"Are you going to look at me?" he asked.

"I...I don't even know your name," she stammered.

He smiled at her. Gazing into her eyes, he impulsively divulged a well-guarded secret.

"Alaric. My name is Alaric." He cradled her face in his hands, and kissed her.

She kissed him back. She rested her head against his shoulder and caressed the rough skin of his open palm.

"What's his name?" Alaric asked.

"Whose name?" Kate's voice was dreamy. The knot in her stomach was still drawn tight, but her pain was subsiding. For the moment, she felt safe in the arms of the murderer. One who now knew her more intimately than any other man alive.

"The guy who sent you running into the arms of a stranger. And a very dangerous one at that."

She sighed. She'd already bared her body. Where was the harm in baring her soul?

"He's my best friend. Or, he *was*. Until I found out he was fucking someone else."

Alaric laughed. "Is he some kind of an idiot, to give *you* up?"

"He doesn't know what he's missing."

The smile vanished from Alaric's face. "What are you saying? That you're a—"

"Not anymore."

She felt his solid flesh tremble under her cheek.

"I had no idea. If I'd known, I would've—"

"You would've what? Handled me with kid gloves, like everyone else?" she countered.

"Okay, but still. I would've done things differently."

"I'll live. If you'll let me."

"I can't kill you now. I'm too fond of you." He caressed her bare back. She let the sheet covering her slip, and settled deeper into his embrace.

"WHAT DID YOU LIKE ABOUT HIM SO MUCH, ANYWAY?" HE ASKED.

"He makes me laugh. When I'm with him, I forget about everything else."

Alaric licked his lips and stared blankly at the ceiling. She'd given up her secret, knowing deep down that this night was all they were going to get. He responded in kind.

"I was married once. We had a big house, one that I barely saw. I never told her what I did. I didn't want her to carry my sins. But that meant she never really knew me. I was gone for long stretches of time, and I wasn't faithful. I doubt she was either. The more secrets I kept, the more we were strangers. One night, she wrenched the truth from me. She didn't say a word. Not even the next day, when I left again. Five months later, I came home." He swallowed hard, remembering. "Her body was swinging from the tree in front of our house. The birds had gotten to her. They tore out her stomach…and what might have been my child. I don't even know how long she was hanging there," his voice broke off. He rubbed his face, pushing the image burned into his retinas back to the darkest parts of his soul. Kate continued to trace her fingers across his palms in silence. He relished her tender touch against his scarred, battered skin. When Alaric composed himself, he continued.

"You don't want someone to help you escape your life," he said. "People like us don't get to live a dream. The best you can do is find someone willing to stand *with* you. Even in the muck."

KATE WOKE BEFORE THE SUN. THE ASSASSIN CLUTCHED HER IN HIS SLEEP. She pried his hands open and left the bed, collecting her clothes from the opposite side of the room. He stirred.

"Leaving so soon, My Queen?" he asked. "You're welcome to stay."

"I'm no queen," she said, annoyed. "I always mess everything up. I can't even protect my own family."

"You were clever enough to find *me*, weren't you? That's a lot more than most. You'll learn." That didn't satisfy her. The assassin let out a deep sigh as he rolled onto his side, leaning on his elbow. "You don't have to worry about your nephew, alright? Now wipe that sour look off your face. It detracts from your beauty."

"I still need to know who hired you," she insisted as she sat on the edge of the bed opposite him, pulling up her leggings. "They will try again."

He sat up, and kissed the top of her shoulder before she donned her shirt. "I'll take care of it."

She considered what he said before asking, "How much?"

He shrugged, and offered her a wry smile. "What's one murder between bedfellows?"

"You're really not going to tell me who?"

"You'd have to rip me apart to get that," he commented.

She furrowed her brow in confusion, pausing to look at him as she laced up her boots.

"I have this dirty habit of swallowing my contracts," he explained.

Dressed again at last, she stood to face him, her hands at her hips. "So our business is concluded, then?"

His smile slipped. "Is that what this was?"

She took her hands off her hips, relinquishing her defiant stance. "No. Can I expect to see you again?"

He didn't answer. He didn't have to.

As she exited the window, preparing to retreat the way she had come, words poured from his mouth like water.

"Always carry more than one concealed weapon. Learn to fight with both hands. Strike quickly and quietly. When the kill is there, take it. *Don't* hesitate. And never—"

"Why are you telling me all this?" she interrupted.

"To keep you alive. I don't want to hear about you being slain on the side of the road by some stupid brigand."

Kate saw a sincerity in his eyes that surprised her. She let him finish.

"Never let them see you coming." He put his hand on her cheek and caressed her face. He put his lips to hers for the last time.

"Farewell, My Queen."

"Farewell—"

The assassin opened his eyes, coming back to his senses at the sound of hurried footsteps on the stairs. He guessed their owner.

WHEN KATE AND LUCA REACHED THE BOTTOM OF THE STAIRWAY, THEY met Corbin. He was coordinating the changing of the guard when Kate and Luca appeared unannounced.

"Kate, what's—"

She didn't give him time to finish. "Where?!" she demanded.

Confused by her sense of urgency, Corbin pointed to his right, indicating the end of the line of cells.

Kate slowed when she saw that Alaric was still in his small, hay-filled cell, sitting with this his hands folded in his lap. His dark eyes stared straight into Kate's. Neither spoke.

"He only had one weapon when he was brought in," Corbin said, approaching Kate from behind. "And believe me, we searched."

Kate held out her right hand. Corbin handed her the key to the prisoner's cell. She took a step forward, and just then heard the sound of two people clambering down the staircase. It was Allistair, with Ted close on his heels.

"Go away, Allistair," she said, without turning to look in his direction.

"Excuse me?" he replied, indignant. "When are you going to get it into your head that you can't do whatever you want?!"

"I'll deal with you later!!" she barked. She was in rare form, and it startled them. She turned back to face the assassin, who was grinning. He stood up as Kate approached his cell door.

"You're not the little girl I knew once," he said in an arrogant tone. "What have you done with her?"

"I'm not her anymore." She stood stone-faced, her eyes vacant and cold.

"I see. Care to make a deal?"

"Not this time," Kate replied quietly.

"You *know* him?" Allistair shouted, incredulous. His question went unanswered.

"That's a shame. I did *so* enjoy doing business with you last time." The assassin licked his lips.

Luca flinched at his insinuation. Kate didn't move a muscle. The reaction the prisoner was hoping for came instead from her brother.

"We don't do business with murderers!" Allistair shouted.

The assassin looked at Allistair, then back at Kate. "You never told him? Oh ho ho," he chuckled. "You should thank your sister, *sire*," the assassin snickered, "for all she has done for you. And she does it very, very well."

Luca's whole body quivered. All he had to do was reach through the metal bars and tear out the man's throat. Kate took hold of his wrist to calm him.

"Enough!" Allistair cried, stepping forward. Ted held him back.

"Shut up Allistair," Kate said as she unlocked the door. Once the cell was unlocked, she backed away, and gestured toward the stairs.

"Don't let the gate hit you on the way out," she said.

Her comment snapped Luca out of his jealous, indignant rage.

What is she up to? he wondered. Just a minute ago, he had practically flown down the stairs alongside her to make sure this man *didn't* get out. He exchanged glances with Kate, but couldn't read her expression.

"He's wanted for hundreds of murders all over the universe, Kate. You can't just release him!" Ted said.

"I just did."

The assassin was amused by her determination. "That's it?" he asked.

"That's it," Kate said. "Consider yourself pardoned. For sparing the life of the heir to Icarya. You know," Kate said, looking at Allistair, "the one you don't have time for?"

Allistair was stunned. "I've known you to do a lot of stupid things, Kate," he cried, "but don't tell me you *sold* yourself to this villain!"

Kate ignored him.

The prisoner exited his cell and stopped just inches in front of Kate.

Luca's heart raced. The murderous tension he sensed between Kate and Alaric hung thick in the air. As the assassin drew closer to Kate, he took her hand and raised it to his lips in gratitude. Luca felt her tighten up. For a fraction of a second, Luca detected the smell of sulfur and burnt almonds. Then, he understood.

The killer released Kate's hand, and looked her over. For a moment, they conversed with each other as if they were the only ones in the room.

"I've heard tales of your exploits far and wide. I would have liked to have been there," the assassin said. His expression was soft.

"You were. You kept me alive."

His eyes shined at her. "This job disgusts me. I want you to know that."

"Are we about through exchanging pleasantries?" Allistair screamed, infuriated that no one was paying attention to him.

"Shut up!" Kate and the assassin snapped at Allistair simultaneously, turning their heads in the same direction. When they turned back to look at each other, they both smiled. At that moment, the killer's saliva got caught in his throat, and he coughed. It caught him off-guard, and he backed away from Kate before she could strike. As he stepped backward, he lost his balance, and had to lean against the wall to his left to steady his vision. He put his fist up to his mouth and kept coughing. His hand was covered in blood. He looked to Kate.

"You just couldn't keep your hands to yourself, could you?" She waved her fingers at him.

Alaric groaned, spitting blood as Kate drew nearer. Her face was within inches of his. He started crying blood. They whispered quickly to each other, but Luca could still hear them. To him, the conversation lasted an eternity.

"Now that...I didn't see coming," Alaric croaked.

Kate pulled her hand into her shirt and passed him a small vial. "Take this and get lost."

Alaric turned his face from her and coughed.

"Don't be stupid, Alaric," Kate hissed. "Take it. Please. I don't want to do this..."

He wheezed horribly. Kate growled in frustration.

"I really hate you, you know."

Alaric took Kate's hands in his own.

"It's been almost a hundred years, and I *still* want you. I just wish you would have wanted *me*," he murmured, losing his voice entirely.

Kate grimaced, turning her head to the side as her eyes filled with tears.

"All you ever had to do was ask."

Alaric's face twisted up in pain. "Am I too late?"

Kate nodded. She shoved the vial into his hands.

"Take it goddamn it. That's an order."

The assassin let out a small laugh, putting his hand to Kate's face and patting her cheek. He smeared his blood on her face, dragging his crimson thumb against her lips.

"What for, if I can't have you?"

She couldn't force him. "Goodbye," she whispered.

He took in a sharp last breath. Genuine tears mingled with the blood streaming from his eyes.

"Goodbye, my beautiful queen." The man coughed blood all over her. He slumped to the ground, his hand trailing down Kate's body as he died.

She stepped over her expired lover and looked up at her audience. Her brothers stared in shock. Luca knit his brow. Under the veil of Alaric's blood, Kate's cheeks flushed a hot red.

Kate looked back in the corpse's direction. She returned to it for a moment and closed Alaric's eyes, covering them with two large coins from her belt. She walked past Luca and her brothers without saying a word. Before climbing the stairs, she returned the key back to Corbin and threw the few coins she had left at his feet.

"If it's not too much trouble, I would like him to be buried properly." Once she was beyond the first spiral and out of sight, her stony façade broke. She stopped and braced herself, smearing blood all over the walls. Veins of ice emanated from her hands, crawling along the wall and filling in the cracks in the stones. She had stopped breathing. Luca realized he couldn't hear the steady pounding of her heart. She nearly fell into his arms when he reached for her.

"Breathe."

The ice that had spread along the corridor dissipated. She buried her face in his chest, sobbing. He put his arms around her, stroking the back of her head. He raised her face to his, and wiped the tears from her eyes. They continued walking.

23

Tʜᴇ ʙᴀᴛʜʜᴏᴜsᴇ sᴀᴛ ᴀᴛ ᴛʜᴇ ᴇɴᴅ ᴏꜰ ᴀ ʟᴏɴɢ ʜᴀʟʟᴡᴀʏ. Lᴜᴄᴀ ʟᴇꜰᴛ Kᴀᴛᴇ alone to undress as he rummaged through the antechamber. He grabbed a plush towel from a large wooden chest. Hanging from the stone wall on little brass hooks was a series of garments in fine silks and cottons. He chose a flowing silk dress in sapphire blue, remembering how vibrant the color looked against her milky skin and dazzling red hair when he'd first met her.

When he reentered the bathhouse, she was already submerged up to her shoulders, with her hair pinned up. It showcased her long, graceful neck. Her arms were outstretched, lifting her chest out of the water just enough for Luca to see the tops of her nipples peeking out at him over the surface of the water. She'd already cleaned the blood off her face. The water lapped beckoningly at her porcelain skin, shining with moisture. Though it had only been a few hours since they'd been together aboard the *Demeter*, the vision he now saw made his heart skip a beat, and his blood drain downward.

Kate had a sad look in her eyes. She said nothing as Luca approached her. Dotting the surface of the water were several small clusters of ice, like little floating glaciers.

"Remember what you said, about not being able to help it Well," she said, her gaze focused on the bathwater turning to ice, "I can't help this."

Luca said as he walked around behind her. He laid himself out perpendicular to her, kissing her behind her ear before stretching his arm out on the floor.

"You offered him a way out, Kate. He made his choice." He tucked a loose strand of hair behind her ear. "You hold so much power, and yet you are the most compassionate creature I have ever met."

Kate wiped her face, not convinced that it was clean. "When I met Alaric, my whole world was collapsing. It wasn't long after Cyrene died, and I'd just found out about Julian and Lilla. I sought him out to kill him, but I was young and unskilled, and went after him half-cocked like an idiot. I was no match for him, and I knew it. I went there to die. That's just...not what happened."

Luca pressed a kiss to her temple. "Why is this affecting you so much if you didn't—" he paused, not knowing how to express himself delicately. But he didn't want to dance around it. "You were a virgin until yesterday, Kate. I could smell it."

She turned her head to the side, away from his inquisitive gaze. "That...is a shallow technicality. I let him do what he wanted." She turned to face Luca, her eyes wide. "*Whatever* he wanted. I just didn't care."

Luca closed his eyes, trying to blot out the image that wrenched in his gut.

"I never expected to...feel..."

Luca's gentle fingers silenced her. "You don't have to explain anything. You're with me now. And you make me feel like a prince. I've been undead forever. You gave me *life*. You're the only thing that matters to me. The only thing that has ever mattered."

Kate teared up.

"I don't want to see you like this." Luca's gestured toward the icy water, which had been steaming hot when she had first entered it. "Let me take you somewhere. We can go anywhere else you want. I want to keep you safe."

"Just, stay with me," Kate said. She turned around and brought her forehead to meet Luca's.

As Kate felt Luca's full lips tugging on hers, the bath steamed again. Kate moved to the right side of the bath's edge and faced Luca's bulging pants. She gently put her mouth around him, still covered in clothes. But she exerted enough pressure with her lips and her teeth to carry the sensation home. Luca's legs writhed, and he let out a breathy sigh. He did not need to be asked twice. In a minute's time, he was entering the pool alongside Kate. He put his back to the wall, and she straddled him, kneeling on the floor of the bath and bringing herself down on him. Their submersion in water made everything infinitely slicker. He unpinned her hair, surrounding them both in a tangle of red.

He moaned as she took her pleasure from him, and grabbed hold of her round, firm ass. Her breasts bobbed against him, creating whorls in the water separating their chests. Kate held onto the ledge behind Luca's head. She pulled herself up, arching her back and pressing her breasts against Luca. His mouth dove in almost by instinct, licking, sucking, and biting her. He nipped playfully at her with his protruding teeth, every now and again pressing down enough to make Kate cry out softly in a blend of pain and bliss. Kate's body was in complete control. Her breasts smothered him. He was at her mercy, and it felt heavenly.

"You should have done this," he panted, "the first time we were here."

"It took all I had not to," she sighed. She tried to bite back a scream, but he wrenched it out of her, driving himself in deeper. She was done talking.

Luca trailed his hands up her back and pulled her as close as possible, breathing her in as she filled his existence.

24

AN HOUR LATER, KATE AND LUCA WALKED DOWN THE MAIN HALL OF THE southern tower hand in hand. Their skin was still damp under their clothing, and the ends of Luca's hair clung together from excess moisture. The plan was to retrieve some dry clothes and head out quietly. When Kate pushed open the heavy double doors to her suite, a fire was already burning in the hearth. The room was spacious with high coffered ceilings, and wooden paneling on the walls. Her bed jutted out into the room from the right. The tailor had already delivered Luca's clothes. They were laid out over one of the two heavily gilded and upholstered chairs facing the hearth in the center of the space. In the far corner was a small alcove with a sitting area and an inset bookshelf.

Alaric, alive and well, reclined on her bed. He eyed Luca, then Kate. He saw the damp marks where their clothing clung to their wet bodies, and the droplets of water falling from Luca's hair, not to mention the deep purple bruise at the base of Kate's neck. He guessed the rest. Kate gasped at the sight of him, and nearly jumped out of her skin. He spoke in a deep, calm voice.

"Why didn't you tell me your bed was more comfortable than mine? I would have visited you much sooner."

Luca's blood boiled in his veins.

"What the hell's the matter with you, are you trying to give me a heart attack?" Kate shouted.

Alaric smiled. "I'd never defy a royal order." He tossed her the vial that used to house the poison's antidote, now empty.

"Get out of there," Luca growled.

"I don't think so," Alaric answered. He turned his attention to Kate. "Care to join me?"

Kate grabbed his ankle and dragged him from the bed with singular force, crashing the back of his head against the gilded chest at the foot of the bed before thudding on the floor. He groaned in response.

Luca grinned. But Alaric refused to relinquish his haughty façade.

"Did I do something to offend you?" he snapped.

"You tried to kill me!" Kate answered.

"Did I? You poisoned *me*!"

"I told you to get lost, not make your way to my bedchamber!"

Alaric laughed uncontrollably. In a low voice he said, "you *must* be joking."

Kate moved to stomp on his neck as he lay prone on the floor, but Luca saw the glint in Alaric's eyes, and held her back.

"Don't give him what he wants."

She walked toward the fireplace, breathing through her nose like a bull ready to charge. She turned to face the man she thought she had killed, and watched him rise to his feet.

"You are *not* my enemy. But Alaric—what are you doing here?"

Alaric walked over to her, the cocky grin gone. Luca kept pace with him. Alaric sneered at him as Luca came to stand behind Kate, glaring at him over her shoulder.

"I meant what I said before," Alaric said. "I'm disgusted with this job. I'm done. To the world, I *am* dead. I came to help. And I was hoping that you could help me."

"Alright," she spat out. "What?"

"Check your pocket again," he said.

Luca handed her the belt he had slung over his shoulder. The small pouch she had thought was empty contained a slip of paper. She unfolded it and read the name of her would-be murderer.

"Reza?" she said. "I don't understand."

Alaric shrugged. "Seems fairly simple to me."

"Who's Reza?" Luca asked, eager not to be excluded from the conversation, especially since it pertained to Kate's welfare.

"Where have *you* been?" Alaric asked.

"Reza's the Seht of Likhan, the biggest slaving city in the world," Kate answered.

"Seems our fair queen has gotten in his way more than once," Alaric said. "I took care of him, but—"

"Whoa, whoa wait—what do you mean, you took care of him?" Kate asked, suddenly on edge. She grabbed Alaric's wrists on impulse, but withdrew just as quickly.

Alaric answered without hesitation, reveling in the awkward tension Kate's reaction had created.

"He's dead, just like every other person who's ever hired me to kill you. But that's not the end of it, because when I was hired, I was told that I'd have two contacts, people who were already inside the castle. There were too many eyes in the dungeon. I didn't trust anyone but you."

Kate's eyes flared. She remained silent, clenching her fists. The fire burning to Kate's left blazed. It drew both men's attention as it threatened to overtake the hearth and climb up the walls.

The flames quieted down as Kate channeled her rage, striking Alaric's jaw with the broad side of her hand, nearly twisting his skull off its mooring. She roared at him.

"Don't you ever take another life in *my* name without my permission. Ever. Or it *will* be your head!"

Alaric steadied himself after Kate's unexpected, powerful blow. He spat a loosened tooth into the fire.

"I can't imagine *why* I've been doing that all this time," he snarled. "Oh, right. To protect you!"

Luca put his hand on Kate's shoulder. Her skin was hot to the touch.

"Kate, you're burning up," he said, struck with worry.

She simply looked at him. "So I am."

"*Calm down.*"

Luca helped her to a seat at the low round table at the edge of the room jutting out from Kate's reading alcove. The surface of the table was an alabaster relief of Icarya and its bordering countries. The men sat on either side of her. Luca pulled his chair in close, putting his knuckles on her cheek. Under his touch, her temperature returned to normal.

She clasped his fingertips. "I'm okay," she said, giving him a tender smile.

Alaric observed the couple's exchange, and knew his fate was sealed. Kate had found what she'd been looking for, and he couldn't compete with their obvious affection.

Kate turned to Alaric, looking to cool her head by focusing on his news.

"Reza is dead?"

"Yes," Alaric answered. "I would have thought someone like you would rejoice at the death of a slaver."

Kate shook her head. "Reza was a close ally. He swore never to buy or sell Icaryans, and he kept his word. He was a good friend. I can't see him doing something so underhanded."

"He was one of the biggest slavers in the world, and you call him your friend?" Alaric asked.

"Yes."

"Based on what?"

"Personal respect. His own servants held a place of honor in his house." She paused, deep in thought. "Are you *sure* Reza hired you?"

Alaric scoffed. "It's kind of hard to be mistaken about that."

"You talked to Reza yourself?"

"No, he was busy at the time, and couldn't see me, but his brother said—"

"You talked to *Mehmnet?*"

Alaric scrunched up his face. "Ohh, shit."

"Sounds like you were mistaken," Luca said.

Alaric shot him a rude glace.

"This is *bad*," Kate said, drawing both men's attention back to her. "If Mehmnet takes control, it'll be open season on Icaryans. That was probably his idea in the first place—to provoke a war by using *you* as a pawn."

"A pawn?" Alaric asked. "Killing you is no small move."

"You think you're the first he's sent?" Kate lowered her eyes, thinking through Mehmnet's motive. "He had no reason to expect you to succeed where others didn't. But if I thought Reza sent you, I'd break our alliance, and Reza would allow Mehmnet to capture Icaryans. And you wouldn't be here to say otherwise. That was his assumption. The circumstances are different, but the end result is the same. Mehmnet is in control."

"I had no idea of the position I was putting you in," Alaric said. "Forgive me, My Queen."

"Kate," she replied.

"What?"

"My name is Kate. Try using it sometime." She sighed. "It would have happened eventually. No one lives forever. Except you," she said to Luca.

He smirked.

She ran her fingers through her hair. "This is too big for just me. I need my brothers."

25

"LUCA, ON THE WALL TO THE RIGHT OF MY BED, THERE'S A PANEL. OPEN IT, and pull the rope on the right, please," Kate said.

Luca did as he was asked. After tugging on the rope, he heard Ted's voice echo down a hollow shaft.

"I'm in the middle of something," he said gruffly.

"Get in here now," Kate called out in a voice that brooked no excuses, "and fetch Allistair."

Before shutting the panel, Luca heard the faint sound of clothes rustling.

"You'll have to leave," Ted said to his female companion, who moaned in disappointment.

A few minutes later, Ted opened the door to Kate's suite. He stood petrified in the entryway at the sight of Alaric seated next to Kate.

"Come in, and close the door behind you," Kate said.

Ted sat across from Kate, next to Luca. She stared at her brother, strumming her fingers on the table. She kept quiet for longer than anyone expected.

"Next time you come here, take the extra minute to put your shirt back on correctly," Kate said.

Ted looked down. His shirt was on backwards. "Huh," he said as he righted himself, "I thought it felt funny."

Alaric snickered.

Kate did not look amused.

"You've got a little something on your neck there, miss high and mighty," Ted retorted. "It seems we're *both* having a good day."

Kate pulled at the provocative neckline of the dress Luca had chosen for her and pursed her lips. She returned to the reason she had called him.

"While we're waiting, it's your job to hire castle workers, is it not?"

"Yes," Ted answered.

Kate looked to Alaric. "Tell him what you told me."

Alaric repeated his story. Ted looked troubled.

"Any idea how that might have happened?" Kate asked.

"No," Ted responded. "No, I always take extra care when hiring people I don't know personally."

"How many times have you hired people since I've been away?" Kate asked.

Something suddenly dawned on Ted, and he covered his eyes with his hand.

"Oh, no…"

"What?" Kate asked.

"There was *one* group I didn't hire. I passed it to Allistair."

"Why the hell would you do that?" Kate asked. "What were you doing?"

Ted hesitated before answering. "The acting troupe."

Kate blinked as she caught his meaning. "The whole—*the whole* troupe??"

"They were in town for a couple of days. They did an acrobatic performance at the summer festival. It was quite a show, you would have enjoyed—"

"You couldn't contain yourself just this once?" Kate cried.

"Did you hear what I just said? They were *acrobats*."

Alaric laughed out loud. "Bravo, your highness."

"Shut up!" Kate snapped.

"What?" he asked. "*You've* got nothing to be jealous of."

"Hey, that's my sister you're talking about!" Ted shouted.

Her eyes flared at him, and she kicked Alaric under the table.

She had been tolerating his innuendo up to a point, but this crossed the line. Luca leapt across the table, grabbed him by the throat, and bared his fangs.

"She just saved your life. She deserves more than that from you," he growled.

Even though Alaric had visibly paled, he maintained his brash façade.

"Give me an excuse," Luca provoked him, seeing a sense of challenge in Alaric's eyes. Luca flashed a menacing smile.

"I can fix this," Ted said, getting up. He ran to the door and shouted to a guard down the hall to bring him the list of the latest batch of recruits.

Kate pinched the top of her nose in frustration. "Let's settle this right now. Alaric?"

"Yes?" He barely had room to turn his face in Luca's iron grip.

"*You* just happened. *Him*, I chose."

Luca released Alaric's collar with a smug grin. Alaric slumped in his chair. Shortly thereafter, there was a knock on the door.

"Enter," Kate said.

Her older brother walked with distracted steps through the door, focused on the note in his hand.

"Reza's dead," he said, waving the paper.

"We know, that's why we called you." Kate gestured for him to sit. He grabbed the open chair between Ted and Alaric.

"And who might you two be?" Allistair asked.

"Alaric, at your service."

"Luca."

"What are you doing in the queen's private chambers?"

Luca didn't get the chance to introduce himself properly. "They're here because I want them here," Kate answered.

Allistair shook his head.

"So, Reza's dead. What can we do about it?" Ted asked.

"Make sure that Mehmnet honors his brother's treaty with us," Allistair replied.

"That's not going to happen," Kate said. "Mehmnet is a weasel. He will take Icaryans the first chance he gets, with more exotic citizens fetching the highest prices. Anyone travelling abroad right now is at risk." She turned to Ted.

He nodded. "I'll double the naval guard."

"Triple it," Kate answered. "I don't want one of mine falling into his hands. Not one."

"That's an untenable solution, long-term. We can't be on high alert forever. But the minute an Icaryan is taken, it's an act of war," Allistair observed.

"Agreed," Kate replied. She opened the floor. "I'm tired, and not interested in making war. Any suggestions on how we avoid that?"

"Is war such a bad thing?" Alaric asked. "If you win, you can abolish slavery for everyone. Problem solved."

Kate shook her head. "It's not a question of 'if.' It's 'how much.' War costs lives."

"Doesn't slavery?" Ted asked, seeing the potential in Alaric's suggestion.

"Not Icaryan ones," Kate answered in a monotone.

"I'm surprised at you," Ted said.

"Those I am entrusted to protect come first. Unless you can think of some *other* means of bringing about a revolution."

Luca kept an awkward silence. He wanted to feel of use to Kate, but he had no experience with organized society beyond the local militia from town to town, which sometimes elected a mayor. He was reluctant to speak out of turn, but anxious to make the effort.

"Are there any alternatives to Mehmnet?" he asked. "I mean, someone else who might rule instead of him, one more willing to negotiate?"

Ted shifted in his chair.

"You have something to say?" Allistair asked.

"There is...*one* alternative."

Allistair and Kate exchanged glances.

"Let's have it then!" Allistair prodded him.

"Reza was working toward a new form of government. He was hoping to retire quietly, and leave ruling Likhan to his councilors. It's grown into quite a large group."

"So, dozens of sehts instead of one?" Kate asked.

"No, not kings, more like…"

"Roman senators?" Allistair suggested.

"Is that Earth history? I don't know that. Sorry."

Allistair and Kate spoke in unison and with an air of authority.

"Senators."

Neither of them seemed to notice that the only ones who understood what they were talking about were each other. She was right, Luca thought. As much as Kate had made about them no longer being close, they were very much the same.

"Fine. Anyway, there's one young man among them who grew up in Reza's household, raised as the son Reza never had," Ted said. "He was grooming him to lead this group. The Hi'dinn, they call it. He's very popular with the people. His name is Darien."

Kate strummed her fingers on the table.

"He respects our laws and holds them up as a model. I'm sure he'd be eager to forge a closer alliance." Ted's voice trailed off, his gaze boring a hole in the table.

Allistair breathed a sigh of relief. "Why didn't you say something sooner? He can take control, and we'll send our overtures to him."

"Mehmnet will murder that boy in his sleep," Kate answered.

Ted wrung his hands. "You can't let that happen. *All* our lives depend on it."

"Yours most of all?" Kate asked in a low tone. The rest of the table turned quickly to Kate, confused. She kept her eyes trained on her brother, tonguing the inside of her cheek.

Ted's stare at the table intensified.

"I don't quite understand what you're getting at," Allistair interjected.

"*He* does," Kate insisted. Ted didn't reply.

"Teddy, you said this Darien was raised in Reza's. household?" Allistair asked.

"The Likhanni won't install the son of a servant as their leader. It's against their nature," Alaric pointed out.

"Nefteri took him in," Ted answered. Luca watched him tremble.

At hearing the name, Alaric squeezed Kate's leg under the table. She looked quickly at him.

Luca growled. One more time. That's all it would take. He shot Alaric a murderous stare that lingered long after he had retracted his hand.

"Reza's first wife?" Allistair asked.

"Yes," Ted answered. "He was her orphaned nephew. She raised him to admire Icaryans." He licked his lips. "When Nefteri died, Reza...Reza swore to look after the boy. Now he's a fine young man."

Ted's words caught in his throat. The only one not curious about Ted's apparent turmoil was Kate.

Alaric whispered in her ear. Only Luca overheard him. "Hers was the name I wouldn't give you."

Kate stared at him.

"You seem to know quite a lot about this young man," Luca observed. Though he knew nothing of statecraft, he knew deception when he heard it.

"Well? Come on," Kate pushed again. "I want to hear you say it."

Ted looked with bleary-eyes at his siblings. They stared back at him, waiting. He swallowed hard. "Forgive me," he said.

Luca heard Kate's breath catch in her throat.

"Darien has a very peculiar complexion. He has one green eye...one blue." Ted looked through veiled eyelids at his family.

"Oh Lord in Heaven!" Allistair shouted. He slammed his hand down on the table and leapt from his seat. Then he turned his face to Kate, who was unmoved. After a moment's pause, his eyes widened. "You *knew*?" he cried.

"I did," she said. Before her elder brother could open his mouth in protest, she said, "It wasn't my secret to tell."

"Why didn't you say anything?" Ted asked. His cheeks had turned a bright pink.

She squeezed his knuckles, and answered him in a soft voice. "I didn't know if you remembered. I didn't want you to share my burden."

What difference did it make that his eyes didn't match? Luca snuck a glance at Alaric, hoping for a clue. He looked just as confused. Kate explained without being asked.

"Our mother had one green eye and one blue," she said.

"I loved Nefteri," Ted confessed. "He's her son. Our son. She hid the truth from Reza to save his life. Please, Kate," he begged. "Don't let Mehmnet kill him."

"This changes everything," Allistair said. "We can't support him."

"Why? Just because he's my son?" Ted cried. "He doesn't *know* he's my son. I've never told a soul. And Nefteri took that secret to her grave." Ted stood at his place, becoming more and more agitated.

"It doesn't matter that he doesn't know. *We* know. We're not imperialists!" Allistair shouted.

"Not what??"

"There's that damn Earth history eluding you again," Allistair cried in an acrid tone. He pointed squarely at Kate. "*She* knows what I mean, and I can tell from the look on her face that *she* doesn't like it, either!"

Kate stared blankly at the table, her fist covering her mouth.

The two brothers drifted away from the table, arguing. Kate pulled Luca and Alaric to her, huddling their heads.

"Now we know *why* Nefteri wanted Kaspar dead. She must have done it without telling Ted," she said to Alaric.

"Are you sure of that?" Luca asked.

"*Yes*. I trust my brother. He wouldn't dream of hurting Kaspar."

Alaric interjected. "She *was* particular about no one being around when we struck our bargain. More than most. It makes sense if she didn't want him to know."

"Why would she? All he had to do was out her to Reza, and she *and* her kid would've been burned to death," Kate reasoned. "Alaric—"

"I won't tell a soul. You have my word."

She nodded, and the trio leaned back in their seats as Allistar called out to his sister.

"It's out of the question, isn't it? How can we possibly put him in a place of power, knowing his connection to us?"

"He's still Nefteri's son!" Ted countered.

"He's *not* Reza's and that's what counts. It's not for us to extend our reach. That has *never* been who we are."

Ted stomped his feet. Kate rose from her chair, looking at him behind Allistair's back with a gesture of reassurance.

"Allistair, you're not thinking this through," she said.

"Not thinking it through? Have you lost your mind?!"

"No," she said, grabbing her elder brother by the arm and pulling him aside.

Alaric opened his mouth to say something to Ted, but Ted cut him off, staring after at his siblings.

"Not now. Mother and Father are talking."

His older siblings shot him a glance with the same hard face.

Indeed the same face.

Luca continued to listen to their conversation.

"Give Darien what he wants, and keep him in Likhan," Kate argued. Allistair turned his head from her, but she kept his attention, speaking in hushed tones. "I don't know this man, and I don't know what his mother might have told him. Regardless, *Kaspar* is the crown prince of Icarya. Give Darien what he believes is his now, and he won't look in our direction later."

Allistair remained silent, implacable.

"I will defend Kaspar to the death," she said.

Suddenly and without warning, Allistair slapped Kate hard across the face.

"What the fuck?!" Ted shouted from across the room.

"The last time you made a promise like that, I became a widower," Allistair snarled.

Luca jumped out of his seat and leveled his sword at Allistair's throat. "Put your hands on her again and you can join your wife," he barked. His eyes blazed red, and he didn't give a damn who saw.

"Threatening the king is high treason," Allistair retorted.

"Then I'll bet striking the queen is punishable by death," Alaric countered.

Kate held Luca back. "Don't. *Don't.* Please."

Ted pulled Allistair out of reach of the two killers intent on the same target.

"I am fed up of this," he cried. "Get your head out of your ass and stop blaming Kate. Cyrene's death was an accident, and you're damn lucky it was only Cyrene who didn't come back!"

"Ted." Kate tried to stop him, but he didn't hear her.

"Lucky?!" Allistair cried.

"That's right, lucky! When Cyrene fell and Kate couldn't catch her, she fell herself. I *happened* to be close enough to grab her sleeve, and all the while she's screaming at me to let her go. Why? Because she didn't want to face her big brother. 'Ally will hate me, he'll never forgive me!'" Ted cried, mimicking Kate.

"Ted!" Kate glared at him. Ted realized what he'd done, and his eyes begged Kate for forgiveness for betraying her confidence.

Luca sheathed his weapon.

Alaric closed his eyes in sudden realization. "That's why you came that night, isn't it?" he whispered, looking at her.

"Can we focus, please?" Kate responded, staying squarely in the present. She let the matter drop as if it had never been there at all. "Ted, we'll support Darien's claim to Likhan, and help him get the Hi'dinn off the ground."

Ted burst into a smile.

"But you can't tell him he's your son."

"Wait, what? Why the hell not? I want to be a part of his life!" Ted protested.

"I understand, Ted, I really do. I'm not saying you can't see him. And in time…maybe. But that's my condition."

Ted's eyes burned with resentment.

"It's for your own protection. And *his.*"

He sighed. "I guess I can live with that."

"Ted?"

He knew what she wanted. "I swear. What I've said does not leave this room."

"Okay," she said. "Okay?" she turned to Allistair, who was staring out the window.

"Do what you want," he said. "You always do anyway." With that, he stormed off.

Ted kissed her cheek. "There's no excuse for him," he said.

She swatted him away like a fly. "I've been hit harder than that."

Ted shrunk back. "Never by *family*."

Kate laughed, her voice bitter. It took her brother by surprise.

He clasped Kate's hands before taking his leave. "Protect him," he pleaded.

26

THE HEAVY DOOR ECHOED CLOSED BEHIND TED AS ALARIC SPOKE.

"Kate?"

"Yes?"

"If you'll permit me, I'd like to go. I feel like I've been part of this from the beginning. I want to help make it right."

Kate considered his offer.

"I wouldn't disappoint you."

She looked to Luca. He shrugged, having no objection to anything that kept Alaric as far from Kate as possible.

"Mehmnet *does* know your face, though," Luca commented.

"Dammit," Alaric cursed under his breath.

"That's alright," Kate said, fiddling with her pendant. "I'll give you a new one."

"Excuse me?"

She pulled both men into the far corner of the room. Kneeling on the floor, she pulled up the corner of the crimson embroidered rug, exposing two small black metal rings nailed into the mahogany floor, about a foot apart.

"Have a seat," she said, slipping both index fingers around the rings and pulling up a large wooden box. Luca and Alaric crouched beside her as she laid the case flat at her knees. Opening the lid, she searched through a series of small vials, each holding a measure of clear, viscous fluid.

"What is this?" Alaric asked.

"They're Masques. Each will give you a different appearance. I just need to pick something suitable." She pulled out a single vial, read the label, and returned it before moving on to the next one. The labels had words like *Cobbler*, *Merchant*, *Nobleman*, and *Pirate* scrawled across them.

"That's some collection. Where did you buy all of this?" Alaric pondered.

Kate gave him a wry smile and laughed under her breath.

"Oh."

"Wait a minute," Luca interjected. "If you made these—"

Kate answered the question rising in his throat. "Different kind of magic. And they're active. Using them now won't affect me."

He stared at her.

"I would *not* lie," she said. "Especially about this."

He nodded, satisfied. "Okay." He caressed her hair. Luca knew it wasn't the most appropriate time for open affection, but that was exactly why he was doing it. Kate did not flinch or falter, not for a moment. He was elated.

"I'm still here," Alaric interrupted them, annoyed.

"Yes. And I think this should fit you just right," Kate replied. The bottle in her hand read *Emissary*. "Let's do a test run, shall we?" She tensed her calves and rose to her feet. To the right of the hearth, there was a high window. Opposite that window and behind her ivory table, Kate reached into a tall slim closet. She pulled out a black hooded cloak, a pair of tall slender boots, and a corset in midnight green laced with emerald and black satin. Alaric spied the garments in Kate's hands, and looked at her face. She had a wicked smile on her face that was catching.

"No."

"It's going to be weird, but you'll live," Kate replied. "This body is much smaller than yours, but it's strong and extremely agile. It should serve your purpose very well. Now, take your clothes off."

"Like hell!"

Kate grabbed the fur-lined cowl from his neck, ripping it off him. "You're a fucking giant, Alaric! You'll tear these clothes otherwise, now do it!"

Alaric grunted. "For fuck's sake!" he cried, tearing at his shirt and pants.

"You volunteered," Luca said.

Kate arranged Alaric's clothes in a careful pile. Alaric muttered under his breath. He stood before them with just a loincloth for coverage. He began to untie it. Kate put her fingers on his hip to stop him.

"Leave that."

The trio exchanged awkward glances as she shrank back, but she just cleared her throat and stayed focused. She went to slip a thin layer of black cotton above Alaric's head, but he caught her by the wrist.

"I'm not wearing that unless I look like a girl."

"If you don't put this on now, you'll be a topless girl in just a minute," she argued.

"So?"

She clucked her tongue. "Put the damn thing on, stop being childish."

Alaric cursed to himself as he struggled to get the slip past his shoulders.

"Okay, now what?"

Kate descended into a peculiar focus. "Pay close attention, you will have to do all this yourself." She retrieved a petite dagger from the trunk, its point as fine as a needle. "Give me your left hand." Alaric extended his arm. She separated his middle fingers and made a small incision in the webbing. "It doesn't have to be here, but apply it somewhere that no one will notice. It just has to get under your skin."

Alaric remained quiet, attentive. At least he was taking it seriously.

She handed him the dagger. "Keep it clean. Do *not* use it for any other purpose." She opened the lid of the vial, which contained a small glass dropper. "Two full drops will give you twelve hours. It's important that you keep a working watch."

"What happens after twelve hours?" Alaric asked.

"You'll turn into a pumpkin."

Both men gave her a weird look. She rolled her eyes.

"It'll wear off," she said. "For God's sake, lighten up. This will last just a few minutes now." She touched the tip of the dropper to the minute cut in Alaric's hand without squeezing it and returned the dropper to the vial. Luca grabbed Kate by the hand and pulled her to him. He wanted to be sure that Kate wasn't affected. She was unchanged as Alaric shrank before their eyes. The rapidity of the transformation put him off balance. He reached out to the mantle to his right for support. A pale, petite hand extended from his unusually slender arm.

"Is it done?" he asked.

"See for yourself," Kate said, gesturing to the full-length mirror on the opposite side of the room. Alaric crossed the fireplace and stood in front of a tall pane of glass encased in ornate ironwork. Kate and Luca followed.

"What do you think?" she asked.

Alaric tilted his head, taking in the vision in the mirror. Staring back at him in disbelief was a girl who was shorter than Kate, with a tight, strong frame. She had sharp features, and vibrant blue eyes. Straight dark hair came past her shoulders. Alaric touched his small hand to high cheeks, then moved toward his flat stomach. He twisted his hips and looked at his ass.

"Don't even think about it. This body is modeled after a dear friend of mine," Kate warned. "Treat it with the utmost respect."

Alaric dropped his hands to his hips.

"I expect to get back whatever is not used when your mission is complete."

He looked down, glaring at the shadow between the two firm mounds of flesh on his chest.

"That is the most beautiful thing I have even seen," he said in a high voice, salivating.

Kate sighed as she held out the unlaced corset and a long stretch of black satin.

"My experience is limited to taking them *off*," Alaric quipped.

"You're useless, you know that? Hands up." A flustered Kate slipped the corset over his head. He held the front in place as Kate laced the back. "Your name is Christine. You've been my emissary for the past fifty years," she informed him.

"It's too tight," Alaric complained as she pulled the strings taut.

"It's supposed to be." She pulled even tighter, giving him great cleavage. "See that?"

"Wow. What a dirty trick," Alaric observed.

"You're to attend Reza's funeral. Darien's part of the household, right?"

Luca nodded. His attention at the moment was on making Alaric as uncomfortable as possible without getting in Kate's way, but he *had* been listening.

"Pay your respects to Reza's widow, and to Darien. Get him alone, let him know that we wish him to succeed, and he can rely on us to assist him with whatever he requires. Get him to take you into your confidence."

Alaric nodded.

"Stay close to him. Observe his habits. Find out if he has any wives or lovers. His relationship with his stepmother. Learn his plans for the government, his way of thinking. Familiarize yourself with the household, especially the servants, and the other members of the Hi'dinn. I want to be able to tell his friends from his enemies better than he can. And figure out what Mehmnet is planning."

"That's a big job," he said.

She turned him around to face her. "If you don't think you can handle it, tell me now."

He blinked. "I won't fail." He licked his lips. "Kate?"

She raised an eyebrow.

"About Mehmnet..."

Her mouth twitched.

"It would make what's coming easier," Alaric offered.

"We don't know that for sure." Kate looked at Alaric, stared past the masque. "You meant what you said in the dungeon? About wanting to start over?"

Alaric swallowed hard, cowed by her directness. "Every word."

Kate ignored the fact that that included how he felt about her. Luca was grateful for the complete lack of reaction on that front.

"I won't do that to you," she said.

His eyes were glassy. "Thank you," he whispered.

She nodded. "If it's in defense of yourself or of Darien, I trust your discretion."

"Understood."

Kate continued lacing the bodice, turning him to face Luca.

Luca noticed the sudden change in Alaric's demeanor. His eyes widened, and his lips parted. He seemed dazed. Luca had seen that look before. He raised an eyebrow. Alaric's pale cheek flushed bright red.

"You're not my type," Luca deadpanned.

Alaric turned his head away, ashamed. "Go to hell," he spat.

Kate grinned. She put her lips to Alaric's ears as she stood upright, finishing the bottom of the sash.

"Welcome to my world," she whispered. Luca turned a sultry gaze on her.

"I think I'm going to be sick," Alaric groaned.

"Be careful," Kate warned. "This spell can go to your head. I came on to a woman once, dressed like a guy. The evening did *not* end well."

"Oh yeah?" Alaric asked, desperate to cling to his fading sense of masculinity. "What did she look like?"

Kate's eyes darted toward his reflected image. "That's how we met." She untied just the bottom bow and loosened the ribbon. She rotated the bodice around Alaric's waist, so the ties faced the front.

"When you put it on again, just pull down on these to tighten it, then twist it around. Now take it off."

"How do you propose I do that?

"You're a woman. Figure it out."

After several false starts, Alaric was once again wearing only his loincloth. He ran his fingers reassuringly over his own muscles as Kate handed him back his clothes.

She went about the room, packing everything she could think of that Alaric might need for his journey. She stuffed Christine's clothing, weapons, a golden medallion with her personal crest, the vial and an extra dropper, a large quantity of gold, blank parchment rolls and a quill, and myriad other things in a heavy leather satchel. Then she grabbed the vial labeled *Merchant* and a second set of clothes.

"If you're compromised, this will get you out of the city."

"Are you going to pack some trinkets for me to sell too?" Alaric asked. Kate paused to look at him.

"Someone once told me not to rely on one weapon. Must have been yanking my chain," she smirked.

Alaric's eyes narrowed at her. "Pack it, minx," he hissed between his teeth.

"Watch it," Luca warned.

"Are you suggesting that she's *not*?"

Killing him would be so satisfying.

"Please," Kate interrupted. "I've never delegated something of this magnitude before. Just let me do it my way, okay?"

"Why *aren't* you going yourself, then?" Alaric asked.

Kate took a deep breath and looked at Luca. Ever since they'd crossed into her realm, she'd been mindful of him. "Because I have to stop, and let people help me."

Luca's heart melted. He stood behind her nuzzling her ear.She turned and touched her lips to his, then readied for Alaric's departure.

"One more thing. When you get there, I want you to start a rumor. If a single Icaryan is captured or sold, I'll cut off their food supply. If they think they can enslave us, they can starve to death."

"You didn't say anything about that to your brothers," Luca said. He didn't understand how either of them deserved their titles, when Kate clearly made all the decisions.

"No, I didn't."

Alaric sneered at him. "You're really *not* from around here, are you? She may have crowned her brothers, but power has always passed to women. All Icaryans know who their sovereign is."

"You're goddamn right," Kate agreed, grinning. She leaned her body out the open window to her right, calling out to the population of birds congregating on a nearby roof.

"Hallo there! I need a messenger for an extended period. Any volunteers?"

A hawk flew in, perching himself on the sill as he settled his massive wings. "At your service, My Queen."

"Much obliged. This is Alaric, you'll be traveling with him to Likhan. Alaric, I want a report as soon as you're settled."

"You can trust me."

"I know," Kate answered. "I appreciate this."

He bowed his head. "The pleasure, I fear, is entirely mine, My Queen. You *are* my queen, you know."

Kate nodded. "Cathair, right?"

Alaric was taken aback. "How did you—"

She held out his palms in front of him. "Rough hands. The rest was...elementary."

He smirked. "You never lacked for brains, did you?"

"It's a lifelong curse. Alaric, I can't allow you to work for me without payment any longer. Name your price."

His eyes turned downward, and he shrugged. "You can't give me what I want."

Her brow creased. "I *am* sorry, Alaric," she said, her voice barely a whisper.

He stepped closer to her, and placed the two large coins that she had used to cover his eyes in the dungeon in her hand.

"Save these for when it counts." He winked at her.

"Godspeed."

Luca pressed his hand to Kate's shoulder as Alaric disappeared out the window. She squeezed back.

27

"Now then," Kate said, "where were we?"

She pounced on Luca, causing him to fall backward onto her plush mattress.

"Ooh, this *is* nice," Luca purred. He chomped his teeth at her. Kate proved surprisingly strong as they each tried to trap the other, seeing who would be able to pin who to the mattress. Luca raked at her collarbone with his extended fangs, pulling her dress past her shoulders.

There was a knock at the door.

"Kate?"

Luca groaned as they rose from the bed, fixing their clothes. Kate adjusted her dress and fanned the hot flush from her face.

"Just a minute," she said, her voice wavering.

"Is there *anywhere* we can go where no one will bother us?" Luca asked in a tone so low only she could hear.

"I own a few desert islands," she suggested.

"Sounds perfect."

"Yes?" she answered, opening the door.

"Sorry." Ted recognized the hurried, disheveled nature of Kate's hair all too well. "One good turn deserves another. I came to see if I could interest you in a late supper."

"I am a little hungry," Luca said, popping his head over Kate's shoulder.

"Oh good. See you in the west dining hall in a few minutes."

KATE PULLED THE BRASS RINGS ON THE WOODEN DOUBLE DOORS OF THE dining hall apart to reveal a long narrow room. It was decorated with a golden green wallpaper depicting a mythical epic mural, buttressed by dark wooden wainscoting. The corners of the room were furnished with lush plants featuring exquisite blooms in vibrant purples and yellows. The hushed light came from round incandescent bulbs affixed to the wall in bronze sconces. A delicate ivory carpeted the floor, softening the sounds of the room and offering it a quiet, cozy ambiance. The long table at the center of the space was hewn from the bark of a single tree, its simple polish highlighting its knots and swirls. Atop it were silver platters overflowing with fruit, cheeses, and cured meats, accompanied by baskets of freshly baked breads. A hand-blown decanter housed a luxuriant red wine, and matching glass goblets with golden leaf finials waited to be filled.

Luca realized that there were four settings, but there was no time to warn Kate. Allistair stepped out from behind the door.

"Oh, come on," Kate cried, and turned to leave.

"No no, wait, please," Allistair pleaded, reaching for Kate's wrists. She wrenched herself free. A bashful Ted entered from a door at the back which led to the butler's station.

"I don't appreciate being ambushed," Kate said in a curt tone.

"I wanted to apologize, Kate, for behaving so badly," Allistair started.

Luca raised an eyebrow.

"Alright, abhorrently. It's truly disgraceful. I never should have struck you, Kate. Not ever. The fate of the last man who struck you should be my own."

Kate turned her head to the side, her eyes glassy. Allistair's words confused Luca and Ted, but both knew well enough to allow the siblings room to reconcile.

Luca took hold of Kate's hand, hanging at her side. Her fingers were limp and unresponsive. He squeezed a little harder, and she took a deep breath. She cared for her brother deeply and couldn't stand the way things were between them. Allistair stared at her stalwartly, his eyes shimmering with regret.

"I am most sorry for *why* I hit you. What happened to Cyrene wasn't your fault. It was mine."

"You weren't there," Kate said.

"I know. But I should have been. She wanted me to go with her. Did she tell you that?"

Surprise washed over Kate's face. She shook her head.

"We argued, and she left, with harsh words the last thing spoken between us."

Kate swallowed hard.

"I didn't even run after her," Allistair moaned, a silent tear racing down his cheek. "I just sulked like the boorish, stubborn fool that I am. And now, I'm pushing you away too. One day you'll stop putting up with me, and you won't ever come back again." Allistair's face broke in sorrow, and he lunged at his sister, squeezing her in his arms.

"I'm so sorry, Katie," he sobbed. "For everything."

Luca was just as taken aback as Kate was at her brother's sudden turnabout. After the initial shock wore off, she hugged him back. Ted approached them, and Allistair wrapped his long arm around his neck.

"Come here, you lug." Ted reached for his kin. They kept their heads pressed together for an extended moment, then parted, wiping their faces.

Luca didn't know what to make of the scene. He had never before having seen such an outpouring of emotion, and certainly not after such animus at first greeting. Kate's family dynamic was so dramatically different from his own, which was by any measure nonexistent.

Allistair turned to Luca and extended his hand. His normal sense of propriety took over.

"We've gotten off to a very rough start. Let's begin again. I'm Allistair, the king of Icarya, and Kate's older brother. You are?"

"Luca," he said, taking Allistair's hand in his own. Kate's face beamed.

"Luca. I'm pleased to meet you. Anyone Kate brings home is welcome here."

"Thank you."

"Daddy?" There was a small knock on the door. Kaspar appeared in a pair of silk green pajamas and bare feet. He was carrying an enamel chess set under his arm.

"What are you doing up, little man?" Ted asked.

"I couldn't sleep. I heard your voice," he said, looking up at his father. "I thought you were awake."

"I am," Allistair answered. "That doesn't mean you're supposed to be."

"Well, could we play chess now? No one else will come for you if they're all sleeping. Just one game? Please?"

"Oh, Kaspar," his father replied, "you don't have to beg. We can play. But just for tonight. Tomorrow, we'll play *before* your bedtime."

"Okay!" The jubilant boy scurried up one of the high-backed chairs at the end of the table, and set his box down. He pulled at a small knob underneath the checkered surface and went about carefully bringing the intricately carved pieces out of their velvet resting place and into position. The others took their seats around the table. Ted clasped Luca's hands again as he sat down.

"I can't tell you how happy I am that you're here with her. My sister deserves someone great, and you certainly seem to make her happy. That makes you great in my book." Ted was referring to the smile that Kate wore from ear to ear.

"I'm glad to be here," Luca said, pleased by Ted's warm welcome.

"So tell me, how did you come to cross paths?"

Luca related the story of how Kate had come to his rescue, and how they had traversed the cave and discovered the quartz. He left out the intimate details, as well as the details pertaining to him being a dhampir. He didn't deliberately hide his nature, but he had been put so much at ease that he no longer felt the compulsion to divulge it as a matter of course. Every Icaryan who knew didn't mind his being half-vampire, and he started to mind it less too. It was fading in his mind as one of the primary aspects of his identity, and sense of self. And that, for him, was the most liberating feeling of all.

Several kitchen workers came in at that moment, each carrying a plate loaded with fresh greens, fruit, and fried bits of cheese that oozed creamy goodness when bitten. Goblets were filled. Luca picked up his glass and went to drink from it. Kate whispered in his ear.

"Don't feel obligated to eat or drink anything you don't want to. No one is going to mind, and nothing will go to waste."

"I *do* drink wine, Kate."

"You do?"

"Occasionally."

"Oh," Kate shrugged. "Then, by all means, help yourself."

"I intend to, thank you." He was flattered by her attempt to make sure he was always comfortable in his surroundings, and his own skin. It was her warm kindness that Luca loved the most about her.

"Alright, alright," she said, placing her arm on his thigh. Luca looked down at her hand, then looked into her face, brimming with love for him. At that moment, he was happy.

Allistair barely touched his salad, thoroughly entrenched in his game. Ted looked on with envy written plain on his face. Kate took note of his sad look, and grasped his fingers.

"That's all I ever wanted," Ted said.

"I know Ted, I know. Are you *sure* Nefteri didn't tell him?"

"Yes," he said. "I've met him a few times, on social occasions. He didn't say anything to me. We chatted about the weather, his plans for the Hi'dinn. Nothing personal."

"All that means is that he didn't let on, if he does know," Luca observed.

"That's exactly what I was thinking," Kate chimed in. Luca was glad that his contributions to the conversation were appreciated.

Ted opened his mouth to protest, but she cut him off.

"Either way, we're going to help him, for now. Let's just hope he's as great as you think he is."

The empty plates around the table were cleared.

"That was really good," Luca said, satisfied.

Kate looked confused for a minute, then laughed a bit and shook her head.

"That was only the second course."

"What do you mean, 'second course'?"

"The second round of food. There's a lot more coming, we haven't had the main dish yet. That was just to whet your appetite."

"But I'm nearly full already. How many courses are left?"

"Tonight? Three."

"Three? We're not even halfway done yet."

"Tomorrow, probably ten."

"Ten different meals in one sitting? Who could eat all that food?"

"The portions are small, and it's only something you do on a special occasion. It's an indulgence."

"I can't eat all that."

"No one expects you to clear every plate. Just eat what you want and stop when you want."

"Where do *you* fit all that food?" Luca wondered. He couldn't fathom how Kate was able to keep her seductive figure.

"It's my lifestyle. I'm always active and eat next to nothing when I'm working. Don't worry," she said in a voice only he could hear, "my body will stay exactly the way it is for a long time." He licked his lips. He craved her body, and was grateful for her unabashed confidence in her own curves.

Kate held his seductive stare as she sidled over to Allistair and Kaspar, observing their game. She whispered in Kaspar's ear, making it seem as if she were giving him tips on how to beat his dad. What she really said was:

"Kaspar, you must do me one favor. Keep the map I gave you a secret, until you think you've found the hidden room. Don't tell anyone, not even your father. When you've found the treasure, call on me and I will come. I want to be there when you find it. Okay?"

"Okay," said Kaspar, trying to sound mysterious. While Kate had been whispering in his ear, his eyes had sparkled at the idea of being privy to a bit of intrigue. His uncle had told him tales of when the three monarchs were younger and all living in the castle, and how they used to invent ways to explore it by pretending it was three separate castles. They told of how they created imaginary alliances, fought pretend wars, and even had their caregivers act as make-believe spies. Kaspar was thrilled at the thought of being included in some grand game.

"Hey, no cheating," Allistair called out.

"I'm not cheating. I just beat you fair and square. Checkmate!" Kaspar called out, raising his hands in the air in triumph.

"What?" Allistair looked over the board, and his mouth gaped in surprise. He covered his face in his hands. Kate saw the look on his face and realized that it was no hoax. Allistair had been beaten by his own son.

"Hurray for you!" Kate laughed, tossing Kaspar in the air. He giggled in delight. Allistair sounded light and happy, like he'd shaved a hundred years off his life.

"No fair, I was distracted. I demand a rematch! In the morning. Now, a good prince keeps his word, Kaspar. March straight off to dreamland and don't stop until you get there."

The boy stood frozen in the doorway, trying to remember his mother's nightly sendoff.

"I don't know how to get there. I can't remember anymore." He looked at his toes, and rubbed his eyes.

Allistair knelt in front of him and picked up his chin. "Second star to the right, and straight on 'til morning."

Kaspar's face lit up, and he jumped into his father's arms. Kate dug her wet face into Luca's shoulder. She kissed the top of Kaspar's head.

"Sweet dreams, little one."

"Goodnight, Aunt Kate, 'night Luca. See you tomorrow...at the party!" He skipped along the hallway, his light steps echoing on the marble floor. The adult diners were each presented with fine porcelain plates adorned with strips of tender red meat and summer vegetables atop a hearty mound of wild grains.

"You know," Ted said in between bites, "I have to say, I'm actually relieved to have all this out in the open. It was quite the burden."

"One I'm still peeved about. You *could* have told us," Allistair remarked.

"Adultery is not really a forgivable crime in Likhan, especially for women. I feared for her safety."

"Yes, but we could have helped you—smuggled her out, something. It didn't have to be this way. Now we have a nephew we know nothing about."

"Mm." Kate nodded her assent, her mouth full. "That's not really fair to us," she said.

Ted shrugged. "It's better this way, I think. I loved that woman, but she could be downright cruel. Those eyes like emeralds could make you do anything."

Kate looked up from her plate, her appetite suddenly suspended. "Such as?"

"Uh, she suggested once that I kill Reza."

"Theodore!" Allistair shouted.

"I told her no, of course!" Ted cried. "She stormed off and didn't speak of it again. Anyway, it's done now. Let's just move forward."

Allistair swallowed. "Speaking of which, Kate, do you think your man will come through?"

"I think he'll do his best," she said. "But there's no telling what the future holds. We'll just have to wait and see."

"I did what you asked," Ted chimed in. "More guards will be posted on Icaryan ships. I've also increased the number of weapons available for private sale."

"Do most Icaryans know how to *use* them?" Luca inquired.

"Good point," Allistair replied. "We can offer instruction, can't we?"

"We already do, in the southern garden most mornings. Just increase awareness," Kate answered.

"That I can do," Ted said. "Oh, and I told Corbin about our two 'unwanted guests.' He promised speedy results."

"From him I expect nothing less," Kate said. "That's all we can do for now. We shouldn't let it damper tomorrow's festivities. Icarya is in desperate need of a celebration."

"No doubt. Tomorrow should be quite the event. You're not going to disappear into the night, are you?" Ted asked Kate. She deferred to Luca.

"We'll stay until tomorrow, at least," he answered.

"Splendid."

They were anxious to retire after several cups of tea.

"We'll see you in the morning. Breakfast by the pool?" Allistair asked.

"How can you even think about more food?" asked Luca, stretching his limbs and feeling the extra weight in his gut. "I won't eat again for a month."

"You'll be fine," said Kate, "just don't make a habit out of overeating." Luca gave Kate a wry look. "Can't have you out of breath on the job," she said, fully aware of her statement's double meaning. Allistair took that as his cue to depart.

Luca let himself fall face first into Kate's mattress, exhausted.

Kate stood behind him and crawled up his legs, laying on top of his back. Luca groaned as her weight pushed his overstuffed stomach into the bed.

"It's a good thing that I've already had my way with you today," she said in dulcet tones. Luca turned over underneath her, grabbing her and taking her by surprise.

"Who said *I've* had my way with *you*?"

She giggled. But after a full day, sleep called. Luca placed his hands on her shoulders and removed her dress. She reached for a sheer strip of fabric, meant as a light pajama, but Luca insisted.

"I want you just like this," he said as she discarded her last scrap of clothing. He was enamored of her form. To him, she was a work of perfection. They climbed under the covers and spooned, and let sleep come.

28

BEFORE THE SUN BROKE OVER THE HORIZON, LUCA SLOWLY REGAINED consciousness. He had been in the exact same position all night, pressing his bare flesh up against Kate. As he stretched, he became sensitive to how nice her ass felt as he pushed against it. He nurtured the feeling by rocking his hips. He reached his arm around her until his fingers found her breasts. She woke with a start as he pinched her nipples. She tried to turn around, but Luca grabbed hold of her arm and pinned her to the bed, her back facing him. He wanted to try something different. Kate was on her stomach, with her face turned to the side. He kissed her lips, then pushed her thighs open with his knee. He supported himself on his hands and knees as he drove into her from behind. Her touch sent waves of pleasure into him, seeping into his brain. Her flesh grew wet, and in no time at all he was gliding in and out of her with ease. He gripped her hips as they collided with his own. He felt her muscles tightening around him as she moaned into her pillow. He remained close to her, feeling his chest brush against her silky, graceful back.

The battle of wills made their intimacy that much more exciting. It felt glorious to have his way with her, grunting as he pushed himself deeper. He climaxed inside her with a raspy growl. When he was spent, he slumped on top of her, kissing her back.

Kate rolled to the side, and Luca slid back onto the mattress with a sigh of satisfaction. She laid on top of him.

"Good morning," Kate greeted him, the first words spoken between them.

"Great morning," Luca said. He was pleased with her. She knew when to fight back, and when to be quiet.

"Did you enjoy that?" she asked.

"Mmhmm."

"Good, because next time it's my turn."

"We'll see," he teased.

She leaned forward, slipping her tongue into his mouth. He grabbed a handful of her hair as he pulled her closer, deepening their kiss. As Kate pulled away, he dug the teeth from one corner of his mouth into her lower lip, causing her to bleed. She let out a little whimper. Sucking on it, he was aroused again by the taste of her blood. It was the most wonderful flavor he had tasted in all the world. Kate was delectable. Blood clouded his irises, and his countenance changed from one of blissful satisfaction to pure lust. Whatever enjoyment they had derived from her, he had only just begun. His whole being thirsted for her.

LUCA SAT UP, BRINGING KATE WITH HIM. HE CONTINUED TO STARE AT HER hungrily. The deeper she gazed into his eyes, the more her head swam. He was doing it again—hypnotizing her, but this time it was much stronger. She had never seen him look more vampiric than he did at that moment. The aura he created surrounded them both, its intensity threatening to shatter her consciousness. But Luca kept her awake, able to feel every sensation. He leaned in further, causing her to lay on her back near the foot of the bed. Everything else fell away. Kate felt as if she were sinking. She saw nothing beyond the deep red curtains, and the bed itself seemed to be falling deeper into darkness. He sucked at her neck, bringing the blood to the surface while trailing his hand down her torso and in between her legs, tracing the same path with his tongue and burying his face in her warm, wet sex.

She called out to him as she felt the delicate touch of his tongue. On hearing her desperation, Luca became ravenous. She pulled at her hair, going almost mad as he sucked and lapped at her flesh, still soft and pliable. The taste of her virgin blood lingered, mixing with the scent of her desire. The blood coursing through her veins concentrated itself between her legs. The fragrance was rich, threatening to overwhelm the power he exerted over her. His tongue explored her inner recesses as he kept her legs spread, searching desperately for a taste of her maidenhead, which belonged to him, and him alone. Her feet were planted into the mattress, with her knees bent. Every time he plunged his tongue further, or flicked at her outer skin, she felt a rush of adrenaline. Her knees reacted, threatening to crush him. He grabbed onto her hips and tugged at her, holding her firmly by her inner thighs and bringing her as close to him as possible.

Kate succumbed to Luca's skillful mouth. The tension in her legs melted as she was brought to heights of pleasure that were unimaginable. Her knees sank into the bed, leaving her legs wide open. She was at Luca's mercy. She sighed in ecstasy with every breath, and gave herself to him, body and soul.

After an eternity of worldly delight, she felt a rush of blood between her legs as all her muscles spasmed. In the same instant, Luca bit her hard. The blood from her inner thigh gushed into his mouth. She cried out, not sure if it was pain or pleasure she felt. She grasped at his hair, but Luca was undeterred, feeding wildly. Luca's spell overpowered her. After several full minutes of drinking, the blood flow slowed. He staunched the flood with his tongue, and looked up at Kate.

She looked as pale as Luca. Her head felt funny, and her legs tingled, numb. Through her still blurry vision, she saw Luca's face. His eyes burned brightly as her life force coursed through him, invigorating him. Her blood soaked his lips. He licked them clean, taking in every last drop of her. His mouth ached for hers, and she parted her lips in invitation as his tongue caressed them. She tasted her own coppery sweetness on his mouth. Seeing him like that, for the first time Kate was awed by his terrible power. But as terrifying as Luca was now, in his purest form, she was not terrified *of* him. She was safe inside his trance, could feel his emotional attachment to her as if it were a physical force binding her to him. Putting her so deep under his spell, he'd protected her from the pain of being fed upon. She had allowed herself to fall uninhibited under his power, and he had shown her the full extent of his nature with confidence. She was at his mercy, and he was at hers. At the realization, the cords pulling them together tightened.

Luca brought his forehead up to Kate's. She felt the pathways to their souls open between them. She could not determine where her mind ended and Luca's began. Luca curled his arms around her, wrapped her in undying love. Kate felt utterly surrounded by him, and clung to him as she slowly regained her senses. Luca's bloodlust subsided, sated in a way it had never been before. He felt whole.

Kate and Luca sat beneath her window swathed in each other's embrace and a single sheet from Kate's bed for hours. Neither had spoken a word in what seemed like forever. Nothing needed to be said. Luca knew that when he had bitten her, he had connected her life to his. As long as her blood flowed through his veins, they were bound together. Luca rested his head on top of Kate's, her cheek pressed against his chest.

As they were getting ready to finally leave Kate's room and head for the pool, Kate remembered something.

"I wanted to give you this last night, but I was so tired I forgot." She walked over to the far side of the room, and picked up a book from the alcove's shelf. "Here." She held a well-read copy of *Dracula* in her hands. "It's probably going to be a little strange, but I thought you might be interested."

He took the book from her, passing his thumb over the title as she headed for the door. He whispered to himself: "No secrets."

Behind her, Kate felt tension rising in Luca's heart. He stood in place, clasping the book she had given him. She turned.

"What?"

"Kate, there's something I've got to tell you."

"What is it, Luca?"

"Dracula," he corrected her.

"What?"

"My name is Dracula."

Kate said nothing. She didn't know what to say.

"My mother never gave me a name of my own. I haven't read this book, but from what you told me, I think it's based on my father."

Luca took one quick stride and caught Kate in his arms. Her consciousness was unloosed, falling back through millennia. Her psyche merged with Luca's memory.

A WOMAN WITH DARK FLOWING HAIR AND DARK EYES STARED IMPATIENTLY down at Luca. Her plain, tattered shirt lay open, her breast in his mouth. Her face had all the markers of beauty—round eyes, full lips, a slim nose and high cheeks. But heartache robbed her of her youthful countenance, as did the mean expression that was constant.

"Hurry up already," she said, shifting the weight of her knees underneath Luca's little body, splayed across her lap. "You're getting too old for this."

He sucked harder in an effort to feed quickly. She flinched and pulled away from him. He lost his balance and tumbled onto the floor.

"Ow! Goddammit you bit me you little shit!" she cried.

A meek voice issued from his lips. "I'm sorry mama." He rubbed the dirt smeared on his face from the floor of their filthy, single-room cottage. She pulled on his arm as he tried to stand, dragging him back onto her lap. She held a long file in her hand.

"Not again mama, *please!*"

"Shut up and open your mouth." She yanked at his jaw, prying his lips open as he squirmed, but it was useless. She worked to flatten the small, sharp canines protruding from his gums with no regard for her son's tears, or the blood oozing from his mouth. She'd filed past the gum line and was shredding his tender flesh. In an effort of self-preservation, he snapped his ruined teeth at her, and shoved her hands back. He'd struck with enough force to push them both backward, toppling over the chair in which his mother sat.

"You were *hurting* me, mama."

She glared at him. "I survived your father. I'll be goddamned if I'm gonna let *you* kill me."

"When is Daddy coming home?"

"He isn't coming home. He *hates* you. So do I."

LUCA WALKED ALONG THE RIVERBANK, HOLDING HIS MOTHER'S HAND. HIS head reached above her hip. She tugged him along, going almost as fast as the water rushing alongside them. It was spring, and the water flowed rapidly, crashing against the rocks and sending up an endless spray of cold white foam.

"Where are we going, Mama?"

She stopped and stared at him with a blank expression. "You're not going anywhere."

She shoved him hard, and he fell into the river. His limbs were frozen. He tried desperately to breathe, scrambling for the surface, but it was as if he were swimming through lead. His lungs filled with water. He stared upward through the clear water, seeing a shimmering vision of his mother's face staring down at him. He stopped struggling, and sank like a stone. The world went black. That was the first time his heart stopped beating.

A deep voice resounded in his head.

Get up!

An invisible force gripped his collar and dragged him out of the shadowy depths. His hands felt the mud of the riverbank. He clawed at it, heaving himself onto dry land. He stood up, confused. He didn't know where else to go, so he went home. He was still dripping when he opened the door. His mother was sitting near their small fireplace. She reeked of liquor.

"You really *are* your father's son, aren't you?"

HE WAS WOKEN OUT OF DEEP SLEEP BY THE MOST HORRIFIC STENCH. HE'D outgrown the blankets that comprised his bed, his bare shins poking out of the thin cotton. His head felt surrounded by a thick haze. He wheezed and coughed, spewing blood all over his shirt. He felt a ring of fire weighing down his neck. Reaching for it, Luca seared his hands, grunting as he lifted the garlic braid off his neck and tossed it across the room.

"Why do you do this?" he cried.

She turned her cold gaze on him, but said nothing.

"What did I ever do to you?"

"You were born," she snarled. "What are you, anyway? You're not a vampire, and you're *not* a human. You're nothing."

"I'm your son," he said softly. "I love you."

He waited for a response. She snorted.

"How could anyone love a monster?" She stood and walked out. He never saw her again.

LUCA WANDERED THROUGH THE FOREST, COMING ACROSS A FAIR-HAIRED teenager about his age, sitting alone.

"Hi," the boy said.

Luca remained silent.

"*Hi*," the boy repeated. "Are you lost?"

"No. Just hungry."

"My dad's in the woods, hunting. I'm sure he'd be willing to share."

"Thank you."

"Say, waiting for my dad is boring as hell. Wanna play?"

"Sure!"

The boy sprinted in the opposite direction. "Catch me if you can!"

Luca gave chase, tapping the boy's shoulder in a minute's time.

"My turn!" He wended his way through the forest with ferocious speed.

"Hey, you're too fast! I can't keep up!"

Luca stood in one place, hiding in the shade of a tall tree. The boy moved warily through the woods, sensing Luca's presence, but not seeing him. Luca jumped out at him, causing the lad to leap back in surprise.

"Shit! I didn't see you there, you're like a damn shadow. And that speed. You're not...a vampire, are you?"

Luca put his hands up defensively. "No, no I'm not!"

"But you're a dhampir, right?"

"A what?"

"A dhampir. A half-breed."

"Oh. Um, I guess so."

"Well, dhampir, wanna go for a dip? Chasing you builds up a hell of a sweat."

"I can't swim," Luca protested.

"Ah, you can watch then. Chase you up those rocks!"

Luca followed as the boy climbed the craggly boulders with his bare hands. Dew clung to the surface of the rocks, making them slick. Halfway up, the boy lost his grip. He plummeted downward, cracking his skull over the treacherous ground below. Luca jumped down, landing on his feet and racing over to his friend. He was breathing and his eyes were open, but Luca could see the brains spilling out the back of his head. The sight nauseated him. But the smell—the smell reminded him of his sharpened hunger. The boy clasped Luca's hand.

"Hey kid," he sputtered, "what's your name?"

"Umm..." He didn't know what name to give. His mother had never addressed him.

"Come on, give a dying guy your name."

He gave the only name he knew. "Dracula."

The boy laughed. "I wouldn't tell people that. That name'll get you killed."

"I don't have another one."

"Use mine, I don't need it anymore. It's Luca."

The boy expired, sending a shudder down Luca's spine. He'd never seen anyone die before. No one was around. And the boy who used to be Luca was already dead. He bent over his friend and opened his mouth.

A bullet whizzed by his nose, embedding itself into the rock behind him.

"Get off my boy!" The bereaved father leveled his shotgun at the dhampir. Luca disappeared into the forest.

~

A YOUNG MAN, LUCA RIFLED THROUGH THE COINS IN HIS PALM AS HE stared at a brunette, leaning against the walls of the city he was leaving.

"There's not enough money in the whole world," she said in a cloying voice, averting her face.

He kept walking.

~

FULLY GROWN, POWERFUL, AND IN TUNE WITH HIS ABILITIES, LUCA SAT atop a chestnut horse. He lived and worked without thinking, retreated deep under his own skin. He looked sternly at the teenager blocking his path.

"Please sir, I don't have any money, but no one in town will help me. Kill the vampire that did this," the dark-haired girl said, pulling at the scarf covering two deep punctures, "and you can do what you want with me."

"You do realize…" Luca said in a low voice.

"Realize what?"

"I'm a dhampir."

The color drained from the girl's face. She cringed.

~

KATE FELT SHE WAS COMING TO THE SURFACE OF AN UNFATHOMABLE depth, her reality just barely out of reach. She saw her own face, looking down at Luca, buried up to his shoulders. The sunlight danced in her hair.

"I'm a dhampir," he said with a heavy heart.

"What's a dhampir?"

KATE OPENED HER EYES. LUCA GAZED DOWN AT HER TEAR-STREAKED FACE.

"My mother said I looked just like him, so I thought I would be able to track him down."

Luca's eyes were glazed with tears. "I blamed him for everything. If only I'd had a different father, I thought, everything would have been different. And maybe, my mother would have loved me."

Kate sobbed. "Oh god, Luca, I'm so sorry."

"You're the only person who's ever truly loved me, and I will love you until the end of time. Even," he hesitated, "even after you've gone, I will cherish you forever." He brought her close, and she buried her face in his chest once more.

"Luca, do you have the power to…make me like you?" she asked.

He looked in her eyes, and considered his answer. "Yes. But no."

"Even if that's what I want?"

"I love you as you are, Kate. I don't *want* to change you."

"But if it were that or nothing?"

Luca didn't answer. It was a hard question, after an already hard morning.

"We'll cross that bridge when we come to it, okay?" Kate said. "But I want you to know that I always want to be with you, no matter what it takes."

No matter what, she thought.

He gazed into her eyes as she dried his tears and pressed a kiss to her lips.

I love you too, he thought back.

Her head jerked back in surprise. She could hear him. Despite his protests, Luca had already taken the first step in bringing Kate closer to his own nature. They both knew it, but let the subject drop for the time being.

"Thank you for sharing this with me, —" Kate hesitated. "What do you *want* me to call you?"

"Luca. That's who I am."

29

IT WAS LATE IN THE MORNING WHEN THE COUPLE ACCEPTED THE invitation to a poolside breakfast. Kate limped as she walked toward a chair near the pool's edge. Luca kept his hand on her lower back to support her. He had kept his promise not to heal her from his bite, but he still did his utmost to keep her comfortable.

"So glad you've finally decided to grace us with your presence." Allistair was alone there, watching his son swim in the small pond at the eastern side of the castle. It was surrounded by tall trees, and had a slim bank that was just big enough to squeeze a couple of chairs, some ottomans, and a chaise. On tiny tables were platters that held the remainders of a sumptuous breakfast of fresh bread and homemade jams, yogurt, and cherries picked from one of the other castle gardens.

"Sorry. Late morning," replied Kate. She wasn't going to spend the little energy she had coming up with a lousy excuse.

"You slept well, I assume?" Allistair gave his sister a sideways glance. When she looked up at him, indignant for even asking, he changed the subject. "I can call for more food if you want," he offered as Kate and Luca picked at nearly empty dishes.

"This is fine, thank you," said Kate.

"Fine. The town is agog with the preparations for tonight. All of Castelmor will be there."

"What about outside of Castelmor?" Kate asked.

"Who did you have in mind?"

"How about the people whose hard work you're honoring?"

"Well obviously, Kate. I'm not completely incompetent. By the way, Julian and Lilla are a no-go."

"What do you mean?" Kate asked.

"Julian was extended an invitation. He declined."

Kate opened her mouth, but Allistair cut her off.

"He didn't say why. Just that he wouldn't be able to make it."

"Hmmm."

"Philip too. Cara's having a really hard time. I think her labor is going to come earlier than anticipated."

"Poor thing. *His* nerves must be shot," Kate commented.

"I can only imagine. Anyone else?" her brother asked.

"Not that I can think of."

"What's left for us to help with?" Luca asked.

"Everything is well in hand. Ted left it to you to decide the menu."

"And what exactly are *you* doing?" asked Kate. Her brother was slumped low in his chair.

"What's it look like? I'm watching my son swim." Kaspar was too busy diving to the bottom of the pond and counting how long he could hold his breath to notice the couple.

"Why not join him?" Luca asked.

"I would like to, but it's so damn hot out here I think my ass has melted into the seat. I can barely move."

"You're hot?" asked Luca.

"Yes, of course, it's hot as hell out here," Kate said.

"Oh. I thought it was just me."

"No, silly. It's just a hot day." Kate walked over to Allistair's chair and tilted it upward. "Let me help you."

"No, no, Kate don't!" Allistair cried.

Too late. She'd tossed her brother into the pool. When he surfaced, Kate crouched by its edge.

"That was for yesterday," she said.

The rest of the day was spent in preparation for the ball celebrating Kate's service and safe return to Icarya. The final menu included many choices made by Luca. Kate catered to his palate, allowing him to choose the things he liked best, which turned out to be fresh fruit and savory spices. When everything was set, they retired to her room.

Kate went about answering a pile of correspondence and mending a pair of boots while Luca relaxed in one of the heavy chairs, reading *Dracula*. As he neared the end of the text, Kate sensed his growing confusion.

"Something wrong?" she asked.

"Dracula is defeated in the end?"

"Yes."

"That doesn't seem very likely to me. You've got an almost unstoppable character with magical abilities, against one of his victims, two scientists, and an 'American,' whatever that is. How could they possibly compete? Let alone triumph? They couldn't even protect their women. *Both* were bitten."

Kate laughed. "It's fiction, Luca. Or at least, some part of it must be. The good guys win in the end because that's what good guys do. This book is sold as entertainment. And most of the heroes are English, so of course they're going to win."

"What's that?"

"What's what?" Kate asked.

"English."

"Oh. It's like the word 'American.' It's a national distinction."

"I see. Kate?"

"Yes?" she ground out. But she knew that Luca couldn't help but ask what to her were the silliest questions.

"What's 'national?'"

"Oh, for heaven's sake, here! I'm trying to *do* something, you know," Kate threw her still broken boot on the ground, stomped over to the fireplace mantle and picked up an old map that rested there in a pile. She laid it out across Luca's lap as he hung one leg over the arm of the chair.

"This is Earth. *Here* is where Dracula's castle is supposed to be." She pointed to the mountains of Transylvania. "And this," she said as her finger traveled westward to the British Isles, "is where the rest of the story takes place. It's called England, and the people who live there are referred to as the English."

Luca studied the map. "Where was I when you found me?"

"I don't know. I couldn't tell without some kind of distinctive marker or natural feature, but I didn't notice any."

"Why did you say the English would win?"

"It was a joke. Just an age-old pride talking."

"You're English?"

"I'm Icaryan. But yes, I was born in England's capital city. For hundreds of years, it was the most powerful empire in the world. It still is, I suppose, considering."

"Considering what?"

"Its permanence. You were able to read my book, were you not?"

"Yes."

"And you understand me just fine?"

"Of course I do, you're speaking the common tongue."

"No," Kate corrected, "I'm speaking in my mother tongue. You're speaking and reading in English. Somehow, through all that time, it survived."

"Oh. That *is* impressive." Luca paused.

But this book still doesn't make much sense.

Kate fell into Luca's lap with a playful grunt, exhausted by this conversation that went nowhere.

"Luca, honey, you're killing me."

His face fell. "Sorry. I'm trying to learn."

"I know. And I don't mind helping you, really. Next time, you can read whatever book you want. I just want to fix my shoes."

Later, Kate and Luca got dressed for the party. Luca fiddled with his robes. Kate smoothed out his shoulders, and his nerves.

"I didn't think it was possible, but you look more handsome than ever," Kate said.

"Thanks," he said, flashing a broad smile.

"I've got to figure out what I'm wearing. Any preferences?" she called out as she opened a wardrobe to the left of her bed's headboard.

"Nothing would be nice," Luca answered.

"Yes, well, I can't go downstairs in nothing."

"We'll stay here then."

She came over to him, pouncing on him and causing him to fall backward onto her plush mattress. "You're not going to help me, are you?" He avoided the question as he sank into a cozy depression. His eyes sparkled.

Kate laughed. "Haven't you had enough?"

"I could never get enough of you." He chomped his teeth at her before Kate bounded off the bed and headed back to her wardrobe.

"You've got some view," he called out, standing up to fix his clothes. He looked again out the window to the right of the hearth, framing lush greenery. Luca could make out a forest path far in the distance, now all covered in soft moonlight.

Kate came out from behind her wardrobe doors, wearing a simple but elegant black dress. Gold embroidery danced around a flattering neckline, which conveniently covered the mark Luca had made in the bath.

There was no mistaking it. It was the dress she had been wearing in Luca's dream. Standing before him now, Luca thought she looked even lovelier than he remembered.

"You look wonderful." His eyes twinkled at her. She felt his affection strongly at that moment, how struck he was by her beauty, and his good fortune to have found his way into her heart.

"Thank you," she said.

"It suits you well."

She turned her head to the right and stared out the window. Her eyes glimmered as she looked out over Icarya. She released a tightness in her chest as her soul waxed sentimental.

"I used to stare out this window, imagining what was going on all over Icarya, wondering who needed my help and what new places there were for me to explore. On some nights, I tied my bed sheets together and snuck out, wandering the forest at night, learning all its ins and outs. I always wanted to be out there, doing something useful and earning the title that had been suddenly bestowed upon me. I trained and trained. I built up my body, and learned how to use a variety of tools and weapons. I studied strategy, geology, magic... when I was ready, I packed up with what little skills and experience I had, and headed out on my own."

Luca put his arms around her, standing up straight and staring out over her head through the window with her.

"I struggled at first and made a lot of mistakes. Once I became comfortable here, I took on new challenges, visiting new places. I've made friends and enemies all over the universe. And now I've finally met someone I feel I can share my life with. All because of the excitement I feel when I look out this window."

Luca bent down, spooning her as she continued to gaze out at the twilit landscape. She held his arms as they held her, wrapping herself in his embrace. He bent his head down, and she turned her face to kiss him.

"I'm glad you're here with me, Luca. This is one of the few ways I know to show you who I really am. This is who I am."

Once again, she had managed to touch his heart.

30

KATE'S HOMECOMING CELEBRATION WAS A GRAND AFFAIR. HUNDREDS OF people in beautiful clothes and perfectly groomed creatures danced in the ballroom, which boasted twenty-foot corniced ceilings inset with gold. In the corner, an Icaryan orchestra played elegant and lively music, inserting a slow, romantic song every so often to keep people from tiring out too soon. Other guests socialized outside, strolling through the softly lit gardens. In the banquet hall, tables set with delicate white linens were filled with people chatting and laughing. The clink of wine-filled glasses and silver flatware created a din that bounced off the walls. The whole castle gave off a yellow glow in the twilight. The day's heat dyed the sky with streaks of pink and deep purple, before the sun sank to make room for millions of stars twinkling in the firmament. It was a glorious night.

Kate and Luca met up with Allistair, who was trying to explain the concept of moderation to Kaspar. He was so excited by all the food that he was liable to give himself an upset stomach. Out of the corner of her eye, Kate spied Ted, who was surrounded by a flock of women who pretended that every word he spoke was more interesting than the last.

"Any bets on which one of them stays the night?" Allistair asked in Kate's ear.

"Don't be ridiculous," she responded. "It'll be more than one."

"God, you're right. What was I thinking?" Allistair said with a laugh.

"Kate, will you dance with me?" Luca asked.

She looked at Luca in surprise. He didn't seem the dancing type.

"Of course, I would love to."

"Save one for me?" Allistair asked before taking his leave of the couple. Kate was still struggling to accept her brother's drastic mood swing. He smiled at her.

"It will be my pleasure."

Luca led her to the center of the ballroom. He brought her to face him, and with his hands at his sides, asked:

"How do we do this?"

"You ask me to dance, but you don't know how?"

"You've been teaching me to do new things ever since I met you. I thought you wouldn't mind teaching me one thing more."

Kate beamed at his compliment. After a brief interlude of simply smiling at each other, Kate took Luca's hands, placing one behind her back and holding on to the other. She kept her eyes locked on him, and they began to sway. Kate took a step back, and Luca stepped forward with her, maintaining the frame she had started them with. She turned, and he turned with her. He wasn't very sure at first, but after a few minutes of matching Kate's lithe movements, it took less concentration on his part. He was surprisingly graceful.

"You're not too bad at this, for a beginner," Kate commented.

"It's not as hard as I thought," said Luca. "It feels sort of intuitive." He finally got his bearings, and the pair floated through the room with ease.

"So," Kate asked, "how do you like Icarya so far?"

"It's beautiful."

"Wait until you see the rest of it. It really is a magnificent place, filled with magnificent creatures."

Luca nodded in agreement on this last point. "Everyone I've seen has been kind and welcoming."

"You've given them no reason not to be."

"The waking hours suit me particularly well too."

"What do you mean?" Kate asked.

"I'm used to villages that shut down after five or six in the afternoon. Here, you stay awake late into the night, when I'm most alert, and only wake up in the morning if you want to. I don't need a lot of hours of sleep, but I don't feel as fatigued as I used to. The sun doesn't weigh me down at all."

"I loved it the minute I set foot here. Once I knew this place existed, it's the only place I ever wanted to be."

"You haven't told me that, you know."

"What?"

"How *did* you come to find this place?" Luca asked as he dipped her.

"By accident, actually. My brothers and I escaped the rain by exploring a nearby cave. We came across a wall that felt funny when you touched it. We realized that the wall seemed to reappear and disappear. When it disappeared again, we walked through it, and instead of being in the countryside, we came out onto a beach. The same beach that you and I landed on."

They continued on like that, dancing and socializing deep into the night. Their fluid movements carried them throughout the ballroom. Eyes locked, every time Luca's fingertips brushed against her skin, every time her hips grazed his, the lust mounting between them grew. When they retired to Kate's bed chamber, Luca noticed that the window had caught Kate's attention again as she undressed. Kate heard Luca rustling the bedclothes behind her. After a few minutes, he came to stand behind her.

Is this tight enough?

She turned around, confused by Luca's question. She looked down, and saw that Luca held three sheets in his hands, tied together at the ends. She looked up at him, and he grinned.

31

IT WAS A SHORT RIDE DOWN THE SIDE OF THE CASTLE WALLS FROM KATE'S window. Luca lowered himself down while Kate hugged his chest and wrapped her legs around his hips. The rest of Castelmor was dead asleep after the night's excitement.

Their feet touched down on lush grass, and they slipped silently through the outer gardens. Kate led the way down the wooded bluff and toward the rocky beach at the bottom of the cliff as they flitted through the forest. Luca stopped her at one point, grabbing onto Kate's arm and pinning her up against a tree. He hurriedly pushed her clothes out of the way and wrapped her leg around his hip, taking a short break from running to make love.

When you found me, he confessed in a feverish haze, *this is what I was dreaming of. You.*

Her consciousness melted into his. His teeth sank into her neck, imbuing her with a burst of energy. They were off again without much ado, traveling until they reached the fog-laden shore. Kate commandeered a small wooden rowboat, untying it from the makeshift marina and shoving off into thick mist.

3 2

DAYS AFTER KATE AND HER CREW HAD DISEMBARKED AT ICARYA'S
southern beach, Rene steered the *Demeter* northwest toward Cathair.
The fog that had obscured Icarya's greenery was thin and wispy as he
approached the harbor. Beyond the stern's edge, the port bustled. Men
slick with seawater tossed each other the morning's catch, while women
young and old swept the dirt entryways to the taverns, inns and shops
that lined the muddy coastal streets.

Rene inhaled the lingering sweetness of the sea as his crew pulled
Demeter to port. He oversaw the transfer of the goods he had ferried
from Gilbraith, Icarya's nearest and friendliest neighbor, known for
their exquisite glassworks. As the final crates of brightly stained
windows were being lifted out of the hold, Rene retreated to the
captain's quarters to fetch a few personal belongings. He pocketed a
watch, his private collection of maps, and the small souvenirs he had
picked up for his family, a set of handheld creatures for his two sons and
a pendant for his wife. He held the singular gem to the light. A deep rosy
hue reflected brilliantly from its countless facets, giving it an interesting
and luxurious shape. His heart leapt as he imagined her surprise.
Though he had committed the contours of her face to memory many
years ago, he never failed to be astonished by her graceful beauty. His

frequent daydreams of her during long journeys paled when faced with the warm and exuberant reality.

When Rene crossed the threshold of his cabin to disembark, he became uneasy. His gaze darted in every direction, desperate to discern what had changed from the pleasant scene of only moments before. The crew had departed. The ship was still. Too still. A horrible foreboding swept over him like a cloud charged with thunder. The instincts of a retired soldier screamed at him from the tips of his hair to the soles of his feet. Had he thought it possible, he would have believed an ambush was imminent. He retreated, reaching just inside the door for his saber. As his fingers groped blindly along the inner framework for the feel of cold, reassuring metal, the shadowy pall hanging over the ship swallowed him whole, closing his slender fingers over the captain's throat.

THE *DEMETER* ROCKED QUIETLY IN THE DOCKS UNTIL NIGHTFALL. THE moons shone sickly yellow as the sea lapped against the hull. The streets were emptied, quiet. A singular light animated the local tavern, but the mirth of its patrons was contained within its four walls. The locals were entrenched in their seaside yarns, singing in unison as Demeter's captain passed through the streets unnoticed.

His steps were slow and deliberate. He drifted through the town like a phantom, staring straight ahead at some unknown, fixed point. A lunar glow reflected in his face, shrouding him in luminescence. The creamy smoothness of his complexion was set in sharp contrast to the blackness that towered over his shoulder. Anyone who might have cast a glance in the unfortunate captain's direction would have perhaps seen the figure biting at his heels, or else would have sworn that Rene was stalked by an impenetrable night mist.

Rene floated through this midnight cloud, past the village and up the abutting hills. His home lay at the wide landing at the peak, edged by a thick wood. The straw-thatched roof emitted no smoky furloughs, the glass-paned windows projected nothing but the night's depth. His soul quickened at the sight, struck by a sudden relief, one rapidly suppressed by his unbridled fear of the rage mounting tangibly behind him.

When Rene opened the door to his home and found it deserted, his unseen follower's wrath grew white-hot. Rene stumbled in the dark, calling out:

"Chrysta, darling? Boys?"

The phantasm looming behind him spoke into the silence. "They're not here, idiot."

"May I turn on the light?"

The man of shadows, assuming his full figure now, replied with a vexation that crawled down Rene's spine.

"It isn't necessary."

Rene pleaded. "I should like not to stumble in your service. The darkness yet hinders me. Please?"

"Please *what?*"

"Please, Master?"

The man who shared Luca's face breathed the dense night air with satisfaction. "As you will."

"*Thank you*, Master." Rene quickly lit an oil lamp affixed to the inner frame of the entryway. The intrusion of light soaked the well-kept cottage in a weak yellow hue. The heat of the modest flame provided no warmth, darting into the darkest corners of the room for sanctuary, finding solace in the coupled punctures that burrowed into the depths of Rene's neck. He carried the flame to the center of the room, where he lit a gathering of thick candles on a long wooden table. The gaping maw of darkness receded as Rene's home took shape. The edges of the table, the sparse bookshelves, and the woven rug were soft, blurred by weak candlelight. Thin ribbons of smoke from the wax pillars furled around Rene's reddened eyelids, setting the outline of his orbitals in deep crimson. He looked akin to a rabid animal, the ferocity in his eyes matched only by the utter confusion of his affliction. He obeyed the command that rang between his temples, and sat at the table, facing the man who resembled Luca in all things, and yet appeared as his exact opposite. The man sat erect, assuming a regal but relaxed posture, strumming his fingers on the bare table. He was the first to speak.

"Where are we?"

Rene stared at his soul's captor, fixing his gaze on nothing in particular. The curve of his strong shoulder. The sleek, loose line of an errant curl. The pointed edges of his coat collar, a rich fabric that he had felt for a fleeting moment against his check, with his head tilted up and back by those smooth hands. He mused at how they had craned his neck with so much force, and yet so gently. But *not* his eyes, not those twin orbs ringed with fire. Anywhere but there. If his pupils ventured too close, he became hysterical. Rene answered the question completely and without reserve, his voice echoing into the void with neither intonation nor emotion.

"We are in my home, at the foot of the Indigo Forest behind Cathair, Icarya's central port."

The ancient demon shifted in his chair.

"I've been everywhere there is, but on no part of Earth have I seen men who look like fish walking along the shore."

"We're not *on* Earth, Sire," Rene answered.

The vampire narrowed his eyes in disbelief. "After millennia of failed conquests, do you mean to say that there were countless *other* possibilities?"

"I found it hard to believe at first as well, Master, but—"

"But you have a small mind."

Rene bowed his head. "Yes, Master, but even *this* small mind came to see the truth. I have been a denizen of Icarya for the past five hundred years."

The prince raised an eyebrow. "Five hundred? You don't look bad at all. For a mortal."

Rene shined with pride at his guest's facetious compliment. The vampire lord mused, stretching his legs under the table.

"It's funny, don't you agree? To only learn something of this magnitude now?"

Rene remained blank. The irony of Dracula the elder's position was lost on him. The night stalker clucked his tongue. "You're not very good company."

"Forgive me, Master," Rene said, his tone grave. His face was awash with terror, as if he'd committed an unforgiveable offense. He offered out his neck to be swiftly separated from his skull. Dracula ignored the gesture, contemplating his situation.

"*How* did we get here?"

"By chance...and magic."

The vampire's eyes narrowed. "Might that have anything to do with this?" He took the crystalline sphere from his coat and placed it on the table. It resounded with remarkable weight for its small size.

"I am a simple man, Master, a humble sailor. Such things are beyond me."

Rene's guest seemed unmoved by his plain response. Dracula sensed his host's deep concern about not being useful.

"I shouldn't have asked," he stated, tucking the orb back into the hidden folds of his coat. Countless blood-stained lifetimes had not robbed him of the decorum of a prince.

He considered whether he should abandon the carefully wrought scheme that had pulled him into this new world by chance. A moment's reflection reminded him that the curse of his failures had followed him to the ends of the earth. There seemed no reason it would stop at its borders. Reassured, he nodded to himself, and continued his interrogation.

"Where is my son?" The vampire saw confusion dominate the face of his freshest victim. He rolled his eyes. "The one who looks like me."

"I'm sorry Sire, I did not notice the resemblance. Now that you mention it—"

"Where is he?" Dracula interrupted, growing impatient. Rene sensed his lord's moodiness, and hastened to satisfy his whim.

"I dropped him off at Icarya's southern shore. His party was headed toward Castelmor, the seat of power."

"Who's the woman?"

"Sire?"

"The one he left with, the curvy redhead." He licked his lips, searching for the word. "Dishy."

"My Lord, that is Katelyn, High Queen of Icarya."

A wry smile spread across Dracula's lips. His chest inflated in vicarious pride. "A queen? What an excellent choice."

"She seemed quite taken with him, Master."

"Of course," he said with a straight face, eternally arrogant. "Your family," he continued, finally perusing the letter that had lain ignored to his right, "they've gone to her mother's." He returned the letter to the table and folded his hands innocently in his lap. "Call them back."

Rene's face twitched, a lost soul straining to break free from his immortal bonds.

"Master," he whispered. *"Please."*

Dracula's face hardened. He extracted from his coat a blank sheet of paper and a pen, and laid them neatly on the table, just beyond Rene's lifeless fingertips. His irises flared. Rene picked up the pen. His distant eyes were tearful, staining the parchment as he scrawled the pen's ink across it.

"Now," the prince said in a low voice, leaning his elbows on the table, "tell me everything."

33

Luca rowed through the night to the westernmost of the Far Islands. It was dense with lush vegetation. Secreted away at the very edge of the jungle was a two-story hut with a straw-thatched roof. The lovers reached the shore by dusk the following day, the sinking sun warming the waves as they pulled in their boat and scooped up scallops resting in the ripples of mud.

Kate and Luca lived in bliss on the island the natives called O'loa through the extended summer months, basking in each other's affections. Kate taught Luca how to swim, which came to him much easier than it had upon his arrival in Icarya. Their glistening muscles hardened from the daily hunt for food, and repairs made to their weather-beaten love nest. They consummated their love at least twice a day, losing themselves in the surf. There was not an inch of Kate's body that Luca had not kissed. Clothes were often unnecessary. Luca let his hair grow wild, and Kate braided small sections, much like her own. The pallor of Luca's skin lost its supernatural edge, replaced by subtle peachy undertones from long hours spent unabashedly in the sun. The steamiest days were spent in retreat from its glare in the countless grottos, floating in the cool waters and expending their energy on the shimmering, moss-softened rocks. Luca's former self fell away.

Kate became a bronzed goddess, her sun-kissed hair soaking in more of its gold. Her wrists and fingers were stained a dark umber in an elaborate design, inked by islanders in exchange for some of her daily catch. She and Luca subsisted on the freshest seafood and the sweetest fruits. She kept a stock of plants with medicinal properties for a time when she might exploit them. Luca drank her blood for pleasure, receiving his sustenance now from food alone. Her blood gave him a power and vigor he'd never known before. For her part, Kate was filled with vitality. Never was she more alive. Their desert hideaway was heaven.

They pulled themselves away from their hidden paradise as the sun's heat abated, with a solemn promise to return. Rowing through the Western Sea and back to the Icaryan coast, Luca set the oars on the inside of the boat, feeling melancholy. He reached for Kate and pulled her body to his as the boat swayed in the open waters.

"I don't want it to be over," he lamented, covering Kate's neck in hot kisses.

"*We're* not over," she assured him. "We never will be."

He made love to her under the overcast sky. They returned to rowing after lunch and a brief swim. Afterward, Kate had to cover herself with the thickest of their blankets to be comfortable.

The sun shone brilliantly over Icarya as the pair traveled at a leisurely pace through the open fields, toward Kate's riverside cottage. As they reached the summit of a small grassy hill, the daylight gave way to Icayra's twin moons. Luca recognized where they were. They were climbing a hill, which had at the top of it a tree with a thick branch, big enough for them to sit on. It was the same tree where they had sat in the back of her Earthbound tent, where he had felt the Icaryan sunrise for the first time, and where Luca had decided to join his life to Kate's. They rested there for a minute.

"How much farther do we have to go?" Luca asked.

Kate's expression turned mischievous as she faced the opposite side of the hill. The rise descended in an almost vertical fashion right beneath their feet.

"Not far at all." She hopped off the trunk, down the edge of the cliff.

Luca leapt over to catch her, then realized that a flat landing was only eight or nine feet below them.

"Come on!" she bellowed. He followed after her, crouching on his knees as he landed gracefully like a large jungle cat.

Kate extended her right hand. The flattened drop of the cliff had a wooden door on it. The hill was the roof of her cottage. To their left was a small, quiet stream that let out into a river. On the opposite side was a small bank that led to a mountain pass.

Kate opened the door to reveal a small yet spacious area. Bunches of drying flowers and herbs hung from the knotted ceiling, tied to tree roots that weaved in and out of the space. Several wooden shelves were home to small glass jars holding oils, roots, berries, grasses, soils, powders, and elixirs. The hill and a portion of the tree's trunk had been hollowed out. Luca stepped through the doorway, and stood at the foot of Kate's small bed, set against the left wall, with a tiny window carved out above it that let daylight into the room. Further in to his right was a long squat cupboard that held linens, cooking utensils, and space for fresh food. Tucked behind it against the wall was a folded up wooden table. The wall behind her bed had a deep recess where Kate kept a few articles of clothing, weapons, and some books. To the right of that was an even deeper and taller recess, covered in stone. That served as her washroom.

"It's not as majestic as O'loa or Castelmor, but it's functional," Kate said.

"It's charming. It would have been nice to have something like this to return to when I was working as a hunter."

"Why *didn't* you have anything like this?" Kate asked.

"One, I never stayed in one place long enough to make it worth the effort. Two," he said as he reclined on the bed, resting his feet, "I don't think my neighbors would have liked it."

"I don't get to stay here as often as I'd like, but when I'm *not* travelling, this is usually where you'll find me."

"How often will we be working?" Luca asked.

"It's hard to say, since there's no regular schedule by which things happen that require my attention. Several months out of the year, at least, but maybe not all at once or even in the same place. Usually I receive correspondence requesting my assistance, or else I travel around Icarya to inspect villages, bridges, stuff like that. It's a lot of work, but not more than I can handle. I just hope some of that quartz has been processed. I need it. Autumn is a good time for conjuring. Even if I don't require anything now, it's good to be prepared."

"That still makes me uncomfortable. Your magic's side effects were not minor, and if you add them up…"

Kate sighed in acknowledgement as she joined him on the bed. It was a little cramped for the two of them, but there was no such thing as personal space any longer, so they managed fine. She laid her head on Luca's chest the way she had the first night they spent together, listening to his heartbeat. Luca stroked her hair.

"Remember Rick, at the inn?"

"How could I forget? You nearly castrated him."

"Yeah," Kate said, sounding somewhat distant. "I don't really remember that all that well."

"What are you talking about?"

"I remember being insulted, I remember smashing his face and jumping over the counter, and I remember you bringing me back to my senses, but, some of the stuff in between—"

"When you drew blood?"

"Yeah," she stammered, "that is fuzzy to me. I sort of blacked out."

Luca sat up. "You didn't pass out. I saw you standing there. You were talking to him, taunting him. You had this weird, cold look in your eyes. I remember thinking how out of place it was. You were cruel."

Kate looked Luca straight in the face and shook her head. "I don't remember any of that. I don't think it was…was me, for lack of a better way of saying it."

Luca thought for a moment about what she was telling him. "What's any of this have to do with your magic?"

"When I get upset about something, sometimes I give off a magical charge. You've seen it."

"The lake of ice."

She nodded. "Sometimes, I feel like..." A surge of sorrow and hesitation emanated from Kate. Luca waited for her to find the words.

"I feel like something *else* takes over. It *is* me, but it *isn't* me. Sometimes I don't even realize it's happening until it's over, and I have the sense that I've lost time."

Luca brushed her cheek.

"I just...fade," she murmured.

"I don't like the sound of that."

Kate pursed her lips and looked at her hands. "When it's really bad, I..."

Kate paused, not sure she was ready to say what was on her mind. She took a deep breath, and bared her soul. He closed his eyes as he sensed her flashbacks—in a matter of seconds he saw, through her eyes, the things she had been forced to relive. Her own tortured childhood. Wars fought abroad that she had won, and lost. Acts of cruelty she had suffered and incurred. The death of Cyrene. The night she spent with Alaric.

Luca's seething jealousy and anger at seeing her so misused nearly choked her.

Tears spilled from his eyes as he opened them. Luca perched his finger under her chin and lifted her face up.

"I don't want you to cast anymore."

Kate's eyes were glassy. "I can't promise that. It allows me to do things that I couldn't do otherwise. It's a sacrifice that sometimes I have to make." She reached for the cupboard on the left, and pulled an unseen handle to open a small drawer. She retrieved an orb, crafted out of a mixture of quartz and other materials. Imbued with a directive, the sphere assumed an opaque gray hue. Luca picked it up from its resting place in Kate's open palm. He rotated it, scrutinizing it while Kate spoke.

"This is *supposed* to act as a barrier, between...between my natural power, and the magic I choose to wield."

"I don't understand," he said.

Kate took a deep breath. "All the spells you have seen me cast— anyone with enough training could do them. They draw on the elements, and written magic. Not inherent talent." She tongued the inside of her mouth, and after a moment's thought laid the orb on the bed and took his hand in hers. Her skin was warm to the touch, and turned to scorching in scant seconds. Flames snaked between their flesh, licking the skin between their fingers.

Luca closed his eyes. There was no pain in his hand, only warmth. Kate pulled her incensed hand from his, closing her fingers into a fist and snuffing out the diminutive blaze. Luca reached for her. Her palm was smooth, and cool. She bit her lip, and water rimmed her eyes.

"I have not done that in a long, long time. I don't know how I can do it, or why, but I can. I've never summoned earth or water successfully, but the rest—fire foremost, air—"

"And ice."

She nodded. "That's the one that creeps up on me. Instead of protecting me, it's almost as if the orbs are making things worse."

"Could the one who trained you help?"

Kate let out a puff of air. "Drigory's answer was not to use my natural talent. What I can do I figured out on my own, which was no easy task." Her expression hardened. "I became aware of it at the wrong time. It's like you said. I was cruel. I misused my gifts. Horribly. Now I don't use them at all. Some of the worst things I've done I never meant to do. I can't risk any more lives."

"Including your own."

She nodded again, resting her head on his shoulder. "I had no one to help me, no one to explain, just a teacher who steered me away from the truth."

He pressed his lips to her copper tresses. "I have had that feeling for longer than you can imagine. It's easy to hate what you never knew. What kind of father encourages brutality, and abandons a boy completely lost in his own muddled nature? But, had my father taken me under his wing, what kind of man would I have become?"

"Maybe that's *why* he didn't."

"I wouldn't give him that much credit," he sighed. "If you ever bestow that gift on me, I will never let a child of mine flounder in the dark, unloved and alone."

She kissed the firm curve of his chin. "Drigory knows much more than he's willing to tell. I think he knows where my real father is. Or at least, *who* he is. I was looking for him when I found my way here. This is all I have," she said, holding out the blue scarf he'd passed on to her. "I was having an awful day, as usual, but he made me laugh. Let me know there was more to my life than it seemed." She swallowed hard, her eyes shimmery again. "He didn't want to leave. I know he didn't. I could *feel* it."

"Come here," Luca whispered, lifting her chin and bringing her lips to his.

Luca picked up the magical sphere, perplexed by its failure to function as Kate intended.

"How do you open it?" Luca asked, his fingers searching for entry. He found only a small imperfection in the curvature, a microscopic hole. He put it to his eye. The opening went straight to the center, leading to thin wisps of dark gray swirling around dried herbs and leaves, a miniature fire with barely heat enough to smoke without flaming.

"You don't," Kate said, taking it back from him. "It's sealed."

"No it's not. Feel it," he replied, guiding her fingers over the minute aperture. She passed her thumb over it and back again.

"I don't feel anything."

"It's there," Luca said firmly.

Kate's gaze shifted to the side, considering the significance of Luca's discovery. She inhaled a sharp breath.

"It's the blood spells—as the orb pours out—"

"The blood gets in," Luca answered.

Kate shook her head and raised her eyes to the ceiling. "When I illuminated the cave, and opened the gate back to Icarya, I was fine. *No* blood."

Luca pursed his lips. Kate didn't allow the question forming there to issue forth before she answered it.

"No more blood spells, then. I *can* swear to that."

Luca breathed a sigh of relief. "Thank you. Can you promise me you'll only cast *anything* when it's absolutely necessary?"

"I promise."

"And only when I'm around if you need me?"

Kate nodded. "I *do* feel better, knowing you'll be there."

Luca cradled her face in his hands, tugging on her lips and touching his tongue to hers, melting her anxiety away. He didn't need to say anything. She *felt* his eternal love.

Kate put her hands on Luca's chest, pushing him onto his back. She was crouched in between his legs, keeping them parted. Luca took off his shirt in one quick motion as Kate unbuckled his belt and removed his pants. She stroked him as they continued to kiss, and squeezed him as he swelled, taking up more space in her hand. He tried to sit up, but she pushed him back onto the bed.

She smiled furtively as she slunk down on his body, and kissed his lower abdomen. The tip of her tongue slowly scaled the length of him, licking him. Luca squirmed in pleasure underneath her. He moaned at the sensation of her soft, warm mouth, and put his hand to the back of her head.

"Ahhh, don't tease me," he managed to whisper between heated breaths.

"I'll do what I like," she countered. Luca smiled as he was forced to acquiesce to her lips. She licked and sucked, and Luca sighed in deep satisfaction as she finally pushed him further into her mouth.

"Ohh yeah, just like that," he moaned, before inhaling a stuttering breath as she bit him. He groaned as he surrendered to her will. Her fervor grew as Luca's excitement filled her mouth, and his breathing became more audible. She feasted on him, and his hot sex felt the back of her throat. Her tongue flicked at him, which drove him wild. He closed his eyes and bit his lower lip, sighing and grabbing the sheets tight between his fingers as she worshipped him.

After getting dressed once again, with the exception of her boots, Kate pulled out a small circular grate and brought it outside, with

Luca close behind her. She uncovered a large hole about a foot and a half wide and two feet deep.

Luca filled the hole with twigs and grass and sparked a fire. He positioned the metal grate on top. Kate tied her hair back and walked into the stream. As she had done countless times before, Kate put her ear close to the water, and stood very still. After a few minutes Luca saw her poise her hands above the surface of the water. A few more minutes went by, and she plunged her hands quickly into the stream. When she pulled them out again, she was wrestling with the body of a small trout, wiggling to break free. Kate threw the fish in Luca's direction. He completed his part of the dance, catching it in one hand and smashing its head on a rock near his feet before slapping it on the makeshift grill.

Kate came back out of the water, drawing a small blade as she did so.

"In the cupboard inside, there should be some potatoes and a sack with some spices in it. Can you get them while I gut this thing?"

Luca returned in an instant as Kate chopped off the fish's head and threw it back into the water. She scaled and split the fish and removed the spine and innards, leaving two nice-sized filets. She surrounded the fish with potatoes, then grabbed a lemon from the spice bag. She bisected the lemon and squeezed it out over their meal. Then coarse grains of salt and peppercorns. She pulled out a head of garlic and licked her lips.

"Mm mmmm! Nothing like potatoes and gar—" She looked quickly to Luca, who was holding his breath and glaring at her through tearing eyes, waiting for her to remember just who she was dining with.

"Whoops! My mistake—no garlic!" She tossed it over her head, and it landed somewhere on the opposite side of her house. A badger picked it up and took it home for stew. Luca exhaled.

"Thank you."

"Sorry," she said, batting her eyes at him.

"Yeah, yeah."

The fish sizzled away, getting a rich caramel color on the skin before Kate flipped the pieces over.

"Kate?"

"More questions?"

"Just a few more for today. Is Drigory nearby?"

"On the opposite side of those mountains. He keeps all kinds of books and records about the history of Icarya. He has a small collection of treatises on magic passed down from the prior ruling family."

"Maybe we should pay him a visit."

"Maybe. My natural magic is very much like the magic that created this place, according to native-born Icaryans. It's as old as Icarya itself."

"Then he should know how to help you, even if he doesn't want to."

"That was always my impression."

Kate was taking the fish and potatoes off the grill and filling clay plates when she heard her name being called from downstream.

"Kate!"

"He doesn't sound very happy," Kate said.

"Hey Kate, answer me dammit!"

"Who *is* that?" asked Luca.

"That," Kate answered, "would be Julian."

34

Julian appeared on their right. He was somewhat taller than Kate, but did not match Luca in height. He was muscular, and his tousled dark brown hair framed his green eyes and chiseled chin, just passing his shoulders. He held three rabbits, tied together in his hand.

"What happened, did you go deaf on your last trip?"

This is your best friend? Luca wondered.

Upon saying Julian's name, Kate expected to be bombarded by Luca's jealousy after claiming to have romantic feelings for Julian while onboard the *Demeter*. She was confronted instead by his annoyance.

"That's no way to greet a friend," Luca said.

"Who are *you*?" Julian asked.

"*He* is Luca," Kate answered before the conversation got heated. "He's my—"

"Lover," Luca filled in.

"Yes, my lover, thank you," Kate looked at Luca, begging him to cool down.

"Your *lover*?" Julian asked. "How long were you gone?"

"Long enough."

Julian looked at Kate and saw Luca's bite marks, still fresh, on her neck. She had not been expecting company, and hadn't had the time to cover them up.

"Gods, what happened to *you*?" Julian cried as his fingers reached for Kate's wound. She swatted his hand away with her wrist.

Julian turned his eyes to Luca, who remained equally tight-lipped.

Kate changed the subject. "What did you come storming down here for? Not to give me rabbits."

Julian let the subject drop. "No, not to give you rabbits. I saw the smoke and figured you were back. These are supposed to be dinner. Lilla is a few minutes behind me."

"You left her to walk by herself? Some gentleman you are," Kate said.

"I rushed ahead so I could yell at you."

"You've succeeded in that," Kate said, aggravated by her friend's less than warm reception. "What are you yelling at me *about*?"

Luca's eyes narrowed on Julian.

"Never mind, it can wait," Julian backed off.

Kate looked at Luca, then looked at Julian.

"No it can't, because Lilla is only a few minutes away. Luca and I have no secrets from each other, so spit it out."

Luca smirked. She sensed his pride, tinged with a hint of possessiveness. Just enough to let Kate know how much she meant to him. She waxed affectionate as Luca's finger stroked her hand.

"How nice for you both," Julian said under his breath. "First of all, you missed my birthday."

"I was a little busy. You didn't come down here to raise a stink over that. What is it?" Kate asked.

"You ruined my engagement."

"*I* ruined it?" Kate asked. "How could I ruin anything? I wasn't even here." She paused, catching herself. "What engagement? Did you ask Lilla to marry you?"

Julian clamped his hand over Kate's mouth but withdrew it just as quickly as her eyes blazed.

"Stop shouting, she'll hear you! Come inside," he whispered.

Kate grabbed their fish. Luca pulled the table and stools out from behind the cupboard and threw a piece of linen over the table. The pair started eating their hard-earned meal before the fish got cold.

"I didn't ask her yet," Julian said, "but I was going to. Remember that garnet ring I'd seen in the market? The one you were supposed to lend me the money for?"

"That was meant as an engagement ring?" Kate asked.

"Yes."

Kate shifted in her chair. "I didn't know that."

"I *know* you didn't know. You wouldn't have lent me the money otherwise."

"Oh, that's nice…" Kate and Luca exchanged glances. Julian ignored his friend's obvious discomfort at his connivance. "That doesn't matter. It's gone now. While you were away, some rich lady came by and bought it for herself. The seller said he tried to tell her it was not for sale, but she offered him four times the price."

Kate tongued the inside of her cheek. "How is that my fault?" she asked.

"It isn't," Julian sighed, his angry façade broken. "I just really wanted to give Lilla that ring. She liked it so much."

"If she loves you, Julian, she doesn't need the ring."

"I know," said Julian. "That's not the point. I just wanted to let her know that I can take care of her, whatever she needs." He fiddled with his hands, looking dour. "I guess I'm being silly. I was just really upset by it. I'd been saving up, and I was going to pay you back, I really was."

Kate remained silent.

"Ah, but I guess it wouldn't have mattered, if this lady bought it for so much more. I couldn't have paid you back that much. Who could it have been, anyway? Who else other than you has that kind of money?"

After a long silence, Kate sighed. "No one."

She stood up, rummaged through her bedside shelves, and threw Julian a small box. "Happy birthday, jerk."

Julian opened the box, and his eyes teared up. "Oh, Kate, it's just what I always wanted for my birthday. A garnet ring!" he laughed. "But how did you—"

"I went to the market right before I left, and saw a merchant about to buy it. I had to pay four times the price to get him to walk away."

Luca looked at Kate. The generous gesture she'd made to her friend, even given their history, didn't surprise him one bit.

"Kate, I'm sorry, I acted like a fool," Julian said.

"You did, yes."

"And made a bad impression with Luca here."

Luca said nothing in response.

"I...I'll pay you back, but it's gonna take some time."

"It's not important."

Julian nodded. "Okay. Kate?"

"What now?" she asked.

Julian hesitated. "Tell me it's alright."

"What?" He had caught Kate off-guard, and it took her a moment to understand what he meant. She shifted her feet, and struggled to find the right words.

"Oh, Julian, I...you don't need... congratulations."

Julian smiled, his eyes shining. "Thank you. You too," he said, looking at Luca.

"Yeah," Kate whispered.

"So, we're good?" Julian asked.

"Mmhmm," Kate nodded. "Always."

"Best man?"

"*Woman*, moron."

The friends hugged as Lilla walked in carrying a basket of fresh berries and vegetables. She wore a plain lilac dress and had flowing dark hair and blue eyes. When she saw the empty plates on the table with little tidbits of fish and half-chewed potatoes, she dropped everything.

"You've already eaten dinner?" she said. "And here we were gonna make you rabbit stew."

"Sure I ate, but what's that got to do with stew?" Kate asked.

"Oh good. Welcome back, I'm glad you're safe." She walked over to kiss Kate on the cheek. Kate made the introductions.

"Lilla, this is Luca."

"Her lover," Julian added.

"Her *lover?*" asked Lilla.

"Yes, my lover!" Kate shouted. "Say it a few more times, maybe it will cease to shock you. See what you started?" She turned to Luca, who was smirking.

"Just stating a fact," he said in a satisfied tone, crossing his legs and leaning back in his chair. He wore a dreamy look on his face, still reeling from her unabashed amorousness.

Kate clucked her tongue at him. She turned her head, eyeing all the food her friends had brought. "I take it those berries aren't for the stew."

"No," Lilla admitted, blushing. "We were hoping you could make us that pie thing you make."

Kate sighed at the prospect. "Ugh, really? *That's* my welcome home present?"

"Oh, please?" begged Julian.

"Yeah, please Kate, it's been so long," Lilla chimed in.

Kate relented. "Oh alright, but you've got to make that stew."

"On it!" said Julian, who took the rabbits outside to gut them.

Kate took the berries and walked over to her cupboard, pulling a slab of butter out of cold storage, along with pouches of flour and sugar. Luca rose from his seat and stood behind her.

"Can I help?" he murmured in her ear, nibbling on it while no one was looking.

"Yes," said Kate, her skin coming alive with Luca's caresses. "You can stop distracting me and mix these together."

She handed him a bowl of butter and flour, which he squished between his fingers to form the base of a dough. Kate took it from him, continuing to work on the pie crust while handing him the berries to season with sugar, cinnamon, and a hint of lemon. Luca tasted the cinnamon on his finger. The aroma reminded him of Kate's hair. He was very generous in adding the cinnamon. Kate coincidentally glanced over, saw what he was doing and tried to stop him, but her fingers were sticky with dough.

"What are you doing, that's really strong stuff! You only need a little."

"I like it, it reminds me of you." He tickled her.

She tried to stop him but didn't want to get pastry everywhere. He trapped her, and she let out a quiet girlish scream that drove Luca mad with delight. They were living in a lover's paradise that put the soon-to-be engaged couple to shame.

"Enough already, you're gonna make me sick," Julian said as he reentered the cottage, carrying a generous pile of butchered rabbit meat. Lilla hushed Julian out of politeness.

"Leave them alone, they're happy," she scolded as she combined the rabbit with the vegetables she'd been preparing into a pot. "We used to be like that," she reminisced. "Now we're not. Why is that?"

"Don't kid yourself," Julian said. "We were never like that."

Kate and Luca turned to face the couple, stunned into silence by Julian's cold response. Lilla looked enviously at Kate, whose waist was still being squeezed by Luca. She tried, and failed, to hide her embarrassment.

"You're lucky, Kate, to have found someone who *actually* cares about you. I'm really happy for you," she said, her voice cracking as she took the pot outside.

Kate wiped her hands on a nearby towel and walked up behind Julian, who was still seated, strumming his fingers on the tablecloth. She smacked the back of his head with the broad side of her hand.

"Ow!" Julian yelled.

"What the fuck is wrong with you?" Kate hissed. She would have liked to scream at her friend, but didn't want Lilla to hear. "Didn't you *just* finish telling us that you want to marry her?"

"Yes, but—"

"But what? You either love her, or you don't. Make up your mind, before she gets hurt. And if you ever talk to her like that again, I'll have your hide." Kate swiveled around to use the bathroom, eyeing Luca as she left the two men alone.

Behave.

Julian kept his eyes on Kate until she closed the door. Luca watched Julian watching Kate, sure that his eyes had lowered to observe Kate's ass as she turned her back to them.

~

WHEN JULIAN TURNED TO LUCA, HE QUICKLY TOOK IN THE SIGHT OF Kate's self-professed sexual partner. He guessed that Kate's adventurousness was not reserved for her waking hours alone. At the thought of Kate loving Luca in ways he only ever dreamed of, his stare took on a particular shade of green.

"You had your chance," Luca said in a low voice.

Julian scoffed at him. "You really *don't* have any secrets from each other, do you?" he asked, feeling a sense of betrayal at Kate's divulging of things he had never even told Lilla. He turned his gaze to the door as Lilla reentered the cabin, searching through Kate's spice bag for the proper seasoning.

"No garlic, please," Luca requested.

"Of course," Lilla replied, replacing the head she held in her hand. "Julian, do you want me to leave out the pepper? I know you don't like it spicy."

Julian looked her straight in the eyes. Even after his off-hand comment, her question was in earnest. She always did everything to please him, and just now he felt sorry for having humiliated her. His countenance softened.

"A little pepper wouldn't hurt," he said. "Here, let me help you with that."

"There's not much to do, I'm just watching the stew simmer," Lilla replied noncommittally.

"Sounds exciting," Julian said, putting his arm around Lilla's waist before joining her outside. He felt the weight of the garnet ring in his pocket. He'd wanted to propose for ages, but had been putting it off to save for the ring. He noticed Lilla was extra sour as of late and he knew the reason why, but he had wanted to do things on his own terms. Now, he knew that the wait for both of them would be over, and they could start trying to turn their family of two into a family of three.

The four relaxed in the grass as twilight fell. Dinner passed quietly, with Kate and Luca telling of their cave adventures and the ball, which Lilla was upset at having missed on account of Julian's poor temper. They in turn related to Kate all the goings-on she had missed while away. All in all, the world was as it should be, so far as any of them knew.

"So, Kate," Lilla asked, "can I count on you for the autumn festival?"

"Not this year."

Lilla was shocked. "No no no you can't do this to me! You always help, I *depend* on you!"

"Yes, and I never get to enjoy it," Kate answered. "Not this time."

"I never knew you to be so selfish," Julian commented.

Kate opened her mouth to defend herself, but Julian lifted his hand to stop her. "It's about time," he smiled.

"What's a festival?" Luca asked.

"What's a *festival*?" Julian repeated. "Where exactly are you from?"

Kate intervened. "A festival is a kind of celebration. The changing of the seasons is considered sacred. In the fall, we honor the gods of the forest, and give thanks for a good harvest." She turned to Julian. "We did have a good harvest, right?"

He nodded. "That we did." He reached into the pocket of his open vest. "Such good rain, in fact, that we even got some of these." He pulled out a rough, dark fungus. Kate's eyes went wide.

"You told me there weren't any left!" Lilla screamed.

Kate lunged for the truffle. Lilla jumped after her, scuffling in the grass. Julian grinned. "Oh, if only they would do that on command."

Luca shot him an angry glance. Kate shoved the whole truffle in her mouth to protect it.

"Oh for heaven's sake!" Lilla cried, giving up, "you just couldn't share, could you?"

Kate choked on her laughter, shaking her head.

"Was that worth it?" Luca asked, nonplussed, as Kate returned to his side.

"Ohh yes. It's a very rare delicacy."

He raised his eyebrow, not convinced.

"Did I mention it's an aphrodisiac?" she added.

He furrowed his brow, lifted only by the impression Kate left on his mind. "Good work."

She smiled.

"And you let *her* have it?!" Lilla hissed.

"She earned it," Julian winked at Kate.

She nodded. "Quite so."

On their walk home, Lilla was extraordinarily talkative. She breathed easy. Over the years, she had not failed to notice the erosion of Julian's normally carefree mood any time a male had expressed a romantic interest in Kate. She had always felt unsure of her place in Julian's heart, but seeing Kate with Luca put her mind at ease. Their rapport had taken on a different aspect in Lilla's mind than any of the brief courtships she had been a witness to, and she was sure that Luca's presence by Kate's side would not be fleeting.

Julian, for his part, was unusually quiet. He was lost in a memory of a night long past, when he had stormed away from Kate's cottage in search of Lilla. He replayed the scene in his head as he drowned out Lilla's chatter.

HE SAT ON KATE'S BED, WAITING FOR HER TO COME HOME. SHE HAD TOLD him before she had left that she wanted to talk. She was supposed to be gone for three weeks. It had been three months. He had spent most of that time with Lilla, giving in to her desire for him in his impatience. He slept with Lilla to keep his libido in check, but the minute he heard Kate had returned, he left Lilla with a lousy excuse and rushed to Kate's cottage.

Kate opened the door to her cabin, not expecting to see Julian waiting for her in the twilight.

The first words out of Julian's mouth were: "That was more than three weeks."

"I'm sorry," Kate said, throwing all her gear to the floor in one heaving motion. "We had a run of bad weather, and it slowed us down. But I'm here now."

"For how long?" Julian asked, rising to his feet. "How long before you go running off again at the first sign of action, leaving me here to fend for myself?"

"That's what I wanted to talk to you about," Kate said. She took a deep breath. "I miss you when I'm gone. And," Kate said, "I don't want to miss you anymore. I'm here to stay." She smiled, expecting Julian to be happy at the news. Though neither had ever spoken of it, both had silently acknowledged that, over the years, they had come to see each other as more than friends. What Julian said next shocked her.

"Bullshit."

"Excuse me?" Kate said, her eyes going wide.

"You heard me. You'll stay until the next time someone needs you. And someone will *always* need you," he said, his voice getting heated as he approached her.

"Well I *am* the queen, Julian," Kate countered, raising her own voice in response. "But that doesn't mean I'm not entitled to a life."

"What's more important, me or *everyone* else?"

"Don't make me choose, Julian," she said. "That isn't fair."

"Fair? And me, waiting for months for one night with you, *that's* fair?!"

"What do you want from me?!" Kate shouted, gesticulating her arms as she stepped closer to Julian.

He grabbed her by the shoulders and rammed her into the wall by the door, kissing her.

"This," he whispered as he brought his mouth to hers again. They kissed each other hungrily, their arms wrapped in a tight embrace. Between caresses, Julian panted. "Lilla...doesn't need...to know..."

Julian's comment made Kate jerk her head back.

"What *about* Lilla?" she asked.

Julian remembered in that moment that Kate knew nothing of his trysts with Lilla, and immediately realized his mistake.

"Nothing," he said, going for Kate's lips again.

She pulled away. "Answer me. What does any of this have to do with Lilla?"

Julian tried to defend himself by becoming indignant. "I have needs, Kate. You were gone for months, what did you expect?"

She pushed him, shocked by his response.

"Nothing, I guess," she said. Her body went rigid.

"C'mon, it's not a big deal."

"Sleeping with Lilla is not a big deal?" Kate cried. "Is that how *she* feels?"

"I want to be with *you*," Julian replied. "And you're here now. None of that matters anymore." He leaned in again. Kate turned her head to the side, her hands tucked behind her back as she leaned against the wall.

She muttered the only word she could muster: "Leave."

Julian was beyond frustrated. "At least with Lilla, *I* come first!" he shouted.

Nothing from Kate.

"Yes, *Your Majesty*," he snarled, bowing low before slamming the door. Once he was out in the open air, he heard a crashing noise from inside the cottage. Behind the door, Kate had kicked the foot of her bed with so much force that she caused the entire frame to collapse.

The next day, he and Lilla had attempted to pay Kate a visit, with Lilla not knowing anything about what had transpired between her closest friends the night before. When they reached her cottage, they discovered that Kate had left again in the middle of the night. They did not see her for several years. It had taken a long time for her and Julian to put what had happened behind them for the sake of their friendship. During that time, he had grown to love Lilla in her own right. But his feelings for Kate had never disappeared. Days like this one reminded him of that.

"Don't you think so, Julian?" Lilla interrupted his reverie.

"I'm sorry, what?" he asked, coming back to his senses.

"I said, don't you think it's great that Kate found someone who's willing to travel with her? It will be better for the both of them. And he seems to make her happy. I've never seen her like that," Lilla said.

"Oh, yes, it's wonderful," Julian grumbled. When they were steps away from their home, Julian grabbed Lilla by the hand, putting a little bit more energy in his gait. "Come on," he said, pulling her through the door and hoisting her onto the bed.

He pounced on Lilla in the dark, tearing at her clothes and grabbing her hair, imagining, as he had so many times before, that the hair tangled around his fingers was red.

"Did you love Julian?" Luca asked.

"How could I?" Kate replied, nestling herself into the crook of Luca's neck and tucking her leg in between his. "Neither of us ever really gave our relationship a chance. To be honest, we've drifted pretty far apart. I'm closer now to Hercules than I am to anyone else, excepting you."

Luca considered Lilla. She hadn't struck him as a particularly interesting female, and she was nowhere near as beautiful as he found Kate. He wondered why Julian had made the choice he did so long ago.

"I've got nothing against your friend," Luca said as his fingers trailed up and down Kate's arm, "But I don't know what Julian sees in her. She just doesn't compare to you."

Kate kissed Luca on the neck in gratitude. "She's level-headed, predictable, and isn't going anywhere. That makes Julian feel safe."

"It sounds pretty boring to me."

"After all your years, you still want adventure?" she asked, her eyes shining at him.

"Don't you?"

"I'm not thousands of years old. I might want to settle down by then."

"It doesn't feel that long. It used to feel like ten times as much, but with you," he said as he kissed her nose, "with you I feel alive. I want a life of adventure with you. See the places you've seen, and maybe discover some new ones. You lead a charmed life. I'm happy to be a part of it." He rested his head on hers. "Don't ever lose your sense of adventure, Kate. It's one of the many things that I love about you."

35

THE VAMPIRE PRINCE SAT AT THE TABLE OF RENE'S DINING ROOM, spinning the remnants of Kate's spell in his hand. Curtains drawn, he bided his time. He intended to venture out at twilight. As painful as he expected the setting sun to be, he hoped to discover whether the sphere could be of any use to him. He sensed an innate, dormant power whenever he held it in his palm. It's what prompted him to keep it in the first place, but he could not decipher how to access or exploit its potential. Its nature was foreign to him, inscrutable. He required assistance, and he knew it. So he would bear the sunlight.

He rose from his seat, crossing over the body of his servant as he lay prone on the chilled wooden floor. He left Rene to fend for himself as night drew near. Fully expecting the sun to sear his skin on contact, he approached the door with caution. The iron hinges creaked, and the vampire was blasted in the face by nothing more than the fresh, sweet sea air.

The undead lord stepped tentatively over the threshold, tilting his head upward, daring to look at the sun. He stared without consequence at the burning star, its outline made hazy by a wispy mist. Dracula absorbed the sight, lowering his lids and filling his lungs with the clean air. He had not been witness to such a scene since his heart had beat its last, so very long ago. His hand instinctively reached into the pocket of his pants, burying itself in his earthen pouch as he dreamed of home. Mischief played at the corner of his lips as he descended the hill and headed for the village. His footfalls were spry, almost jubilant.

His wonder grew as he roamed the streets nearest the docks, mingling unnoticed among throngs of men, minotaurs, fauns, and creatures he couldn't begin to understand, shambling past on a mass of tentacles. The midnight hue of the shingled roofs was nearly covered by congregations of what he could only approximate to birds of prey. Owls and cormorants were agog in lively conversation. Their beaks chattered away, the precise gesticulation of their talons unlike anything he had seen. To his left, rodents of all classes scurried between the ships. Lines of rigging were tossed by small furry hands. Nimble fingers mended fishing nets, fastened mast ties, and sounded wooden planks and metal girders. Anyone who passed the pale, handsome man in black was too busy to notice that he cast no shadow.

Ambling through the seaside hamlet, Dracula reflected on his choices among the local businesses, contemplating which establishments might prove the most fruitful. His first stop was a bookstore. He found plenty of texts in languages he could read, but none that catered to his present interests. He kept his hands in his pockets as he approached the clerk.

"Excuse me, do you have anything on alchemy, magic, or things of that nature?" His cool tone, coupled with his fiery stare, paralyzed the clerk's soul. The vampire raised an eyebrow, impatient as the young man struggled to find his senses.

"N-no, sir, I'm afraid not. We used to, but there's not enough interest in that kind of thing around here."

Dracula's pupils widened, drinking in the light. He seemed to absorb the shrinking rays of the sun, creating a dark, fathomless void where he stood. The clerk disappeared into a back room and returned with a pile of books that had been removed from the shop's inventory. Dracula took the collection, gave a subtle bow of his head, and left. The clerk turned his head, watching him leave. He stared absent-mindedly at the doorway, gazing at the spot where he had last seen the beautifully dark man. He remained there steadfast, peering into the darkness until the sun rose again.

Dracula drifted past a tavern, a shipping firm, and a dressmaker before examining the window of what appeared to be a general store. A small sign of pressed bronze in the corner of the window advertised the wares within: *Herbalist—specializing in healing and protection, and mid-level scrying.*

The vampire grunted as he walked through the door. The invisible seal to ward off enemies that had been woven over the entryway was no more than an annoyance. But he did draw unwanted attention. The proprietor descended a set of stairs set opposite the door, whose side profile constituted the wall behind the counter. The broad, bearded man looked warily at his patron, who had turned his back to him.

"Can I help you?" the owner asked in a husky voice.

"Just looking for now, thank you," Dracula responded. He kept his eyes on the items lining the shelves, scanning jars of dried leaves and powders. Nothing resembled what he possessed. He averted his eyes until the last moment, turning to look at the herbalist once he stood directly in front of him. The man's wary glance immediately transformed to stoicism. Dracula retrieved the orb from his pocket and laid it on the counter.

"Can you tell me what this is?"

The owner's limp fingers closed around it, raising it to his deadened eyes. "A container."

"For what?"

"Uncast spells. Waiting to be activated."

"How do I do that?"

"It will only obey its conjurer." The herbalist examined it closer, in awe. "The craftsmanship is remarkable. I've not seen its like before. Even the casing is hand forged. This one seems empty."

Dracula took the orb and returned it to his coat. "Not quite." As he turned to leave, a buxom girl with dark flowing hair pushed open the door, carrying a large basket of laundry.

"Hello father," she cried, shutting out the sun's dying glare behind her.

The owner remained speechless, staring into the shadow before him. The shadow turned his head, meeting the girl's friendly smile. Her breath caught in her throat. Robbed of their strength, her fingers released their hold on the basket. It landed on its side, spilling the neatly folded linens to the ground in a rumpled heap. Dracula stepped over the clothes and took the girl's outstretched hand. She closed his fingers in hers, keeping their clasped hands pressed to the small of her back as she led him behind the counter and up the stairs to the private rooms above.

The herbalist stood deaf to the intermittent thumping of the ceiling above him, heedless of the rapidity with which his daughter's cries changed from ecstasy to terror. The bereft father stood senseless to the blood soaking through the floorboards, flooding his eyes and staining his beard.

36

Luca adjusted well to the shorter, chillier days of autumn. They made several short journeys to nearby villages, partly to check up on various inhabitants, but mostly to show Luca the sights. He saw first-hand how much Kate was responsible for. By her side, he learned how to reap crops, prepare soil for winter, mediate arguments, manage a ship, repair a burnt out house, and maintain friendly relations along Icarya's borders. His ability to heal was met with gratitude, earning him a warm welcome wherever they went.

In the quiet stretches, Luca spent his days reclined on Kate's heather bed, listening to her melodic voice as she sang her spells and restocked her arsenal. He frequented the nearby university, drinking in their library after reading all the books Kate kept in the cottage. He pored over tomes of history, agriculture, studies of other worlds, and anything else he thought would make him a worthy partner for Kate.

In the small days before the fall festival, Luca came home to a cottage covered in flour, with small, sweet pies stacked in every open crevice, waiting for their turn on the fire. Kate turned as he knocked on the doorframe, the surprise on her face like a child caught doing something naughty.

"It's for the children," she said in a small voice, taking in the havoc she'd wrought for the first time.

"You just *couldn't* help yourself, could you?" he asked in a dry voice, then snatched her up and covered her sweetened skin with caresses.

The fall festival came quickly. Luca browsed the dozens of stalls set up by forest dwellers selling homemade wares and sweets with interest. The miniature pies he had helped Kate finish were gone on the first day. He thanked his luck for getting a taste early. Tests of speed, strength, and agility kicked off. the celebration.

Luca refrained from participating, feeling his supernatural advantage would be unfair. He ate his fill of the harvest at the grand feast that preceded the central ceremony, where costumed creatures re-enacted age-old tales of forest sprites, animated rivers and talking trees at the dawn of the world's creation. They told the story of the forest god who fell in love with a man, and how their daughter, inheriting the power of her mother to become the forest, ruled as the first Icaryan queen. Luca watched with intrigue from the open-air amphitheater. Crouched in the grass with Kate sitting inside his legs, he wrapped his arms around her, resting his chin on her head.

In the climactic scene where the man, played by Julian, professed his love for Lilla, dressed as the goddess in a golden glittering gown, he pulled the garnet ring out of his costume and presented it to her. The crowd erupted in cheers. Kate covered her smile with her hand. All anyone in the audience heard was Lilla's resounding "Yes!" followed by a row of cheers that echoed for miles. Kate cupped her hands to her mouth to compete with the roaring crowd.

"Took you long enough!" she shouted.

Julian faced the audience and bowed.

After the forest settled down for the final act, Luca brushed his smooth cheek against Kate's and whispered in her ear. "You'd look good in white."

She turned to face him with a wry smile, ruffling his hair as he kissed her bare collarbone.

"You make me very happy," he said.

She leaned her head against his chest and swooned, content.

The following week passed uneventfully. After visiting with friends at the university, Luca headed home.

"I'm serious Luca. You should be teaching," the faun to his left said. "Lots of people could benefit from tracking and combat skills like yours. Think about it."

"I will," he said, parting ways with fellow readers, a pile of texts on politics under his arm. He approached the cottage from the rear, smelling the searing bass before Kate came into view. He bent over her, running his fingers through her hair and craning her neck upward. Her open mouth was a warm, sweet welcome. She moaned despairingly as she pulled away from him.

"Don't start something you can't finish," she said, her voice dreamy.

"Who says I can't?" he countered, moving south to her throat. Even as she protested, her body leaned into him, acquiescent.

"Dinner," she answered.

Luca held fast.

"I will not be ruled by a fish."

Her pretense melted away. She pulled on his coat collar, but before she could relieve him of it, he withdrew from her grasp and stood. It was his turn to groan.

"Oh that's just cruel," Kate wailed.

"We have company," he said, following the sound of frolicking children with his eyes. They appeared on the grassy ridge to the right of their cottage, a young boy chasing the smaller one down the hill before they both tumbled, giggling as they rolled near the stream's thin bank. Their mother, a fair-haired beauty with chocolate eyes, followed after them.

"What a surprise!" Kate exclaimed, getting up and tousling the boys' hair. "You've grown since I saw you last!"

"I sure have!" the older boy shouted. "*He's* the same though," he cajoled his brother.

"Am not!" the younger child grunted, pushing his brother back into the stream.

"Alright, settle down," Luca said in a mock stern voice. "Kate, who are these little miscreants?"

"These are Rene's sons, and his wife Chrysta," she said as the woman approached. She fell into Kate's open arms, her energy spent.

"Nice to meet you." Luca extended his hand to the boys.

"He doesn't *look* that strong," the younger one quipped. He turned to face Luca. "We heard Queen Kate was living with a giant, as strong as Hercules!"

"Did you?" Luca answered with a grin. Both boys had their palms in his. He lifted them off the ground without flinching, their wiry legs dangling in the air.

"It's so nice of you to visit us," Kate said to their mother. "I'll have to catch more fish, I wasn't expecting you. Where's Rene?"

His wife stifled a sob, masking the gut-wrenching agony on her face before her children had a chance to observe it.

Luca saw Chrysta's reaction out of the corner of his eye, and brought the boys back to the ground again. He felt Kate's worry, though she put on a better face than her friend.

She backed away from Chrysta, clasping her hands in assurance before passing through the open cottage door. She returned with two jars, knelt by the boys, and poked holes in the lids with a small knife.

"Now listen carefully, both of you," she said, "I have a mission for you. There are tiny little toads around here, with a bright yellow patch right behind their heads. Catch some for me, and I'll show you something special. But make sure they can breathe, okay? They're fast, so you have to be smart." She smiled at them as she handed them the jars.

"Consider it done!" the older boy proclaimed, and they dove into the undergrowth.

"Stay where I can hear you," their mother bellowed, following Kate's gesture and sitting at her table.

"Chrysta, this is Luca, and anything you have to say you can say in front of him," Kate said as the couple seated themselves. Rene's wife pulled a white linen square from her skirt's pocket and dabbed at her eyes. She wrung her hands incessantly.

"Have you seen Rene lately?" Chrysta asked.

"We saw him a few months ago," Kate answered. "He dropped us off at the southern shore, and said he was coming to port in Cathair. Did he have another engagement after that?"

Chrysta shook her head. "Not that I know of. When I heard news of your return, I was at my mother's house. She wasn't feeling well."

"Is she alright?" Kate asked.

"*She's* fine, but I was getting ready to head home, and I received this letter from Rene." She tossed a piece of parchment on the table. Its worn creases suggested many readings. "I've never seen anything like this," she said, sobbing, "and I was afraid to bring the boys home. If I didn't know any better, I'd say Rene didn't write it, it's barely his handwriting—"

Luca felt a knot form in the pit of his stomach. Chrysta's tale was all too familiar. He reached for the letter first. As his eyes scanned its contents, the knot tightened into a noose.

> *My love! I came home to an empty house. I have returned from Cathair <u>not</u> <u>alone</u> and long to see my boys. Protect! <u>Musn't</u> come home quickly darling. Your <u>loving</u> husband misses you.*
>
> *Renn—*

Kate knit her brows and put her hands in Luca's. Hatred, fear, and guilt suffocated him. Suffocated her.

Chrysta interrupted the flow of their thoughts. "I stayed at my mother's as long as I could, but she was starting to ask questions, and the boys want to see their father. Then I remembered that your cottage was on the way. I'm so glad I found you here. I'll feel a lot better going home with you."

Luca hastily folded up the letter, as if looking at it further disturbed him. He chose his words carefully.

"You've already had a long trip. You're exhausted. Why don't you stay here? Kate and I are more than happy to put you up until we get this taken care of."

"Oh, would you?" Chrysta sighed, relieved. "Thank you so much, you have no idea how worried I've been!"

"Uhh, yeah," Kate said, rising to her feet and trying to catch up with

Luca's suggestion. "I have a tent I can set up, the boys will like that. You can have our bed."

"Are you sure? I didn't mean to put you out," Chrysta protested.

"Nonsense. We won't be here, so it won't be an imposition," Kate replied.

Luca touched her forearm. His sweet voice provided him no protection. She could feel his heart sinking, further and further away from her.

"Darling, there's no need for both of us to go. Why not stay here? Keep an eye on things…" his voice trailed off. Even his eyes were unconvincing.

Try again, she hissed at him.

Aloud, she said, "we'll leave in the morning. You'll have the cottage to yourselves."

Luca's stomach churned, but he remained silent.

She could feel his soul being rent in two, but they both kept their cheerful appearances until their refugee family was tucked safely into bed.

Kate spoke into Luca's ear, curling into his arms under the stars. The ominous feeling swirling in his head had not abated.

"Are you going to talk to me?"

Luca stared at the night sky, his eyes filled with a sadness Kate only faintly remembered there.

He placed his hand over Kate's, squeezing her fingers as if convincing himself that she was really there, that the last few months of his life had not been a dream. Lips closed, he conversed with her in the safest, most intimate way he knew.

That letter—the style—I've seen it before.

Kate sat up, looking straight into his eyes. "What?"

Luca sighed. *Your friend is dead. He's fighting for his soul now.*

Kate shook her head. *I don't understand.*

That letter was written under psychic coercion. But Rene managed to break through, a little.

But what does that mean?

It means he's fallen victim to a vampire. And I know which one. His eyes finally dared to look at her. *So do you.*

That's not *possible,* she insisted. *There has to be another explanation.*

No there doesn't. If he's taken Rene, that means that he came through to Icarya the same way we did. We led him here. Or, I did.

First of all, you're wrong. Second, it wouldn't be your fault, even if you were right but you're not.

What do you *think it is?*

The obvious answer is a paranoid delusion. Seems to be going around, she mused.

He raised an eyebrow. *And it just so happens that this person came into contact with us as we moved between worlds?*

It's a lot more plausible than someone following us into that world without either of us knowing it.

Luca blinked, confused. She had a point.

It's too far-fetched, Kate continued. *The very person who you were tracking, unsuccessfully, is actually tracking you? Why?*

I don't know. Still.

We'll go see Rene and find out what this is really about.

No, he pressed firmly. *I absolutely will not subject you to that kind of danger. If something happened to you...*

She felt his inner walls crumbling, and snuggled closer.

You'd distract me. I wouldn't be the best hunter I can be. And I have to be. To keep you safe. To keep everyone safe. He paused. *If he's been here all this time, who knows what kind of damage he's already done.*

I still don't believe you.

He grunted.

But let's say I did. I'm pretty sure I would have heard about a vampire running amok long *before this.*

Luca folded his arm behind his head.

Not necessarily—he's smart, he wouldn't draw that kind of attention.

Do you hear yourself?

Why don't you trust me? he asked, hurt.

It isn't that. I just think that...

He waited for her to finish her thought.

She propped herself up on her elbow to face him.

I think maybe you'd think that no matter what it was. *Do you feel like you left your world behind too hastily?*

No.

That you shouldn't *have left without resolving things—*

No. He caressed her face. *This is where I belong. But if I'm right...I have to take care of it. Any blood he spills here is on my head.*

That would never be true.

I have to do this.

But not alone.

I already said you're not going.

She swallowed hard. *I'll pretend I didn't hear that.*

He shifted in the grass.

I'm willing to give you lots of latitude, she said. *I may not have killed any vampires before, but from what I've heard...*

Her skin warmed under his touch.

...I don't think Daddy would like me. Her comment was Luca's first taste of Kate's aggression. It was a strange sensation—haughty, cold, and yet seething with a fury waiting to be unleashed.

Another reason for you to stay, he insisted as the heat left her. *You've been fine here. I don't want you putting yourself at risk.*

I can't let you go alone. Chrysta came for my help because she knew she could. If you're right, I need to be there, to let others know I'm aware of the threat and I'm dealing with it. Either way, I can't hide behind you.

He absorbed what she said, and she felt his reluctant consent.

I'm sorry. Sometimes, I really do *forget your position.* He sighed.

Not to mention, she continued, *how worried I'd be. You'd let me go crazy like that?* she asked, pressing closer.

This is a nightmare. It had to be him.

How do you know it is?

I can feel it. He squeezed her tighter. *I've built a life with you here. I'll do whatever I have to to protect that.*

She kissed the recess of his neck under his ear. *So will I.*

37

THE DAWN PRESSED AGAINST KATE'S EYELIDS AS SHE LAY SPRAWLED IN THE grass. She exhaled white puffs of crisp autumn air. Turning onto her stomach, she pulled up the blanket to block out the thin mist rolling off the distant mountaintops. Her arms sought Luca, but found only a damp impression in the ground. The snap of crackling fire echoed in her ears as she sat up, rubbing her face. Luca's voice soaked into her head like a warm caress.

I'm on the roof.

She stretched her limbs and made a miserable attempt at fixing her hair. Walking around to the back of the cottage, she spied Rene's boys dueling with a pair of wooden sticks. Luca sat watching them. He held a thick branch in his hand, whittling it to a long, sharp point. She cast a wary glance at him as he looked up, but neither spoke. She cocked her neck, and saw a half dozen prepared stakes lain neatly beside him. She sighed. She turned back to the boys as their voices crescendoed, and realized what they were playing with.

"I'll take those, thank you," Kate said, relieving them of their ill-gotten toys.

"Aw c'mon! How are we supposed to fight the monsters?" the older boy protested. Kate shot a sharp look at Luca.

"Never you mind," she answered, holding the stakes out to Luca.

"It's for their protection," he said.

"Uh-huh. And is that before or after they put their eyes out?" She dropped them at his feet. "Can you clear it with their mother before giving them weapons?"

He pursed his lips, acknowledging his misstep. He restored them to the end of his wooden army and continued working. Chrysta climbed the hill just then, carrying one of Kate's baskets in her arms.

"Luca, I did what you asked. I wrote that Mother's illness has taken a turn, and I'm unable to leave her at present."

He nodded. "Good. This way, he won't be expecting you." Chrysta presented the basket in her arms to Kate. "I saw the blueberries in your cupboard. I hope you don't mind, but I took the liberty of using them—some food for your journey."

Kate salivated, inhaling the delicious aroma of freshly baked muffins.

"Yes. I mind terribly," she said, taking a generous bite and continuing to speak while chewing. "You'll have to come back and do it again sometime, just to make it up to me."

Chrysta smiled.

Kate took a hearty gulp. "Ah, thank you." She pressed her hand to Chrysta's shoulder. "Whatever you need, Chrysta. I'm here."

The unknowing widow kissed her queen's hand. Her bleary eyes reddened again. "Thank you."

"So long boys, we'll be back soon." Kate knelt for her hugs. The younger one came second, a somber look on his face. He whispered in Kate's ear.

"Daddy's not coming home, is he?"

Luca turned his head. Kate struggled to answer.

"My dear boy, why would you—"

"I dreamed it," he said. "When you get to my house, can you sweep it? It'll keep the spiders away."

"Spiders? What?"

"In my dream, Daddy is covered with spiders."

Luca rubbed his hand over his mouth and turned his eyes away.

"I'll take care of everything. I promise," Kate said. She pulled the boy close, kissing his smooth little forehead.

She stood and walked onto the roof, in earshot of a congregation of sparrows nesting in the tree's canopy. She beckoned them to her.

"Watch over them," she requested. "Anything out of the ordinary—"

"We know where to find you," one answered.

She nodded. "One more thing. Do you think one of you could go to Castelmor, see if there's any news?"

"News?" a female sparrow repeated.

"Of disappearances or...deaths..."

"Wouldn't you already know something like that?"

"Yes, but...just make sure."

"Will do," the female replied. She left her perch and headed northeast.

Luca called to her. "Ready?"

"As ever."

Rene crouched in the darkness, staring at the corner of his home where the wall met the fireplace. His gaze bore through a minute crack in the stone face.

His prey emerged, extending its segmented legs in tiny fluid movements. It traveled north toward the ceiling. Rene pounced, clawing his way up the wall. His overt size in comparison to his arachnid quarry was a massive hindrance. He was in the center of the ceiling when he lunged triumphantly at the unfortunate creature, shoving it halfway into his mouth.

The scuffle unnerved a thin layer of dust, falling through the air like ashen snow and collecting itself again on the books strewn across the table, indeed across the rest of the cottage. Dracula sat directly underneath Rene, poring over the volumes of magic at his feet, amassed over the course of weeks. Dust obscured the lines on the page before him. His eyes flared red as he tossed the book against the wall, crushing its spine. He shouted into the darkness.

"You will desist at once!"

Rene scurried off the ceiling and returned to his corner.

"Positively revolting," the dark lord muttered, brushing the dust off his clothes. Rene let the remnants of spider legs dangling from his lips fall to the ground as he clutched his head, wailing. He beat his fists against his skull, ripping out tufts of hair and making deep gouges in his scalp.

The vampire's ire was stoked by his complete failure thus far to learn anything about the orb, pregnant with unspeakable power, if only he could tap into it.

"Shut up and make yourself useful," he snapped. He shoved the orb into Rene's breast pocket. "Guard that with whatever remains of your wretched life, and make yourself presentable. When I return, we'll see about learning how to use those teeth."

Rene perked up. "Yes Master! Thank you!" He scrambled after Dracula, groveling at his heels as the door slammed in his face.

Rene dressed himself in his best attire, using a white silken scarf to cover the wounds on his throat, just as his master had shown him for his jaunts to the bookstore. He wrapped it in several layers to counteract the sheerness of the fabric. Tying delicate knots lent it an appearance of deliberate fashion. He stacked the last pile of books in the newly swept corner. It was late in the afternoon when he heard a reserved knock at the door. He strode to the entryway and smoothed out his clothes before opening the door with a grand gesture.

"OH, RENE," KATE MOANED. THE SIGHT OF HIM IN THE DOORWAY— bloodshot eyes, spindly fingers lined with dried blood no matter how hard he scrubbed, and the uncharacteristic scarf—was enough to convince even the staunchest skeptic.

Luca took a step forward, putting himself between her and Rene. Her grief crawled down his spine as she gripped his shoulder, but she kept her composure.

Rene cleared his throat. "Ah, Kate, Luca, do come in," he said, opening the door wide behind him.

Luca led the way, keeping Kate's hand clasped in his left as they stepped through the doorway. Luca took note of the pristine space. His gaze traveled upward, where the patterns of dust that Rene had overlooked betrayed the events of just a few hours before.

"Is anyone here with you?" Luca asked in a stern voice.

"H-here with me? Why no, just the two of you," Rene said in a saccharine tone. "Who else could there be? Won't you have a seat?"

Luca remained on his feet. So Kate remained on her feet, taking her cues entirely from him. Luca surveyed the room but saw nothing untoward in the shadows. Nothing but books. Books everywhere. All seemingly on the same subject.

"Thinking about becoming a sorcerer?" he asked.

Rene laughed in a hopelessly maniacal fashion. "Heavens, no. What would a humble sailor like me have to gain from learning such things?"

"You tell me."

"As I say sir, nothing. Nothing at all. Please," Rene said, more insistently, "sit down."

"You're not interested in magic?" Luca asked.

"No, for the last time."

"These aren't yours?"

"Of course not."

"Then whose are they?"

The air in the house stood still. Kate felt the heat bristling off Luca, and took a step back. Rene perceived the subtle movement and lunged at her, snapping his mouth. Luca shoved him to the wall. Rene screamed, his wide eyes drinking in the light.

"*Master!* They're here! They're –!"

His cry caught in his throat as Luca pierced his heart with the stake he'd hidden in the sleeve of his coat. The crazed luminescence flickered and faded, leaving Rene with his familiar countenance, much deteriorated.

"K-Kate?"

"I'm here Rene, I'm here!" She rushed to Luca's side.

"M-my fam-family—"

"They're safe," she said.

He clasped her hands, and pressed his blood-stained lips firmly to her clenched knuckles.

"*Merci.*"

Kate shuddered with grief. She struggled to provide stalwart comfort to the dying captain.

"*Bon-chance, mon ami. Va avec Dieu.*"

Rene squeezed her tighter. He turned to Luca and gave a subtle nod.

Luca drove the stake home. Rene's life spilled onto Luca's hands and pooled on the floor.

Kate backed away, too stunned to cry.

Luca's clear voice pealed like a bell, bringing her out of her stupor.

"Wait for me outside."

"No, I—"

"Go."

Complacent, Kate exited the scene, shuffling her feet. Luca worked quickly. He drew his sword and separated Rene's head from his neck in one clean stroke. Both crumpled to the floor. Luca laid Rene's corpse out, shoving his severed head between his legs. He walked to the nearest stack of books and ripped the pages from the spine. He emptied his hands, doing the same to the next book, and the next. As he grabbed the fourth, he stopped. Blood was pounding in his ears. His hands shook. He stared down at Rene's vacant, hopeless eyes, and succumbed to his rage.

He heaved the books in his hands across the room. They smashed into a pair of candlesticks perched on a mantle set into the far wall. The flame leapt from the wax and bit into the dry, aged paper. The walls shook with Luca's wrath as he destroyed the house.

The flames were climbing up the walls as Luca left. Plumes of dark smoke rose in thick columns behind him from the rough-hewn chimney as he walked to the edge of the hill. Kate sat staring into the sea, her knees tucked against her chest. The errant ashes stung her eyes, augmenting the tears that pooled there but refused to fall. He sat beside her as the sun dipped into the sea, staining the sky a vibrant pink.

"Rene was one of my very first friends here," she said. "On Earth, his country and mine were constantly at war with each other, but *we* felt connected, in a way. Connected by that memory. He taught me everything I know about seafaring. He was a good man. And a good father." The word caught in her throat. "Like the one I never had." She closed her eyes, forcing the tears down her face. She let her head fall onto Luca's shoulder as she wept.

Luca kissed her hair. He spoke softly, his tone devoid of the authority by which he'd ordered her out of the house to spare her the sight of it.

"We have to leave," he said.

"Won't he come?"

"I can't face him like this. Not with you here. I need you to be safe."

She looked up, but he pressed his finger to her charged lips.

"Don't argue with me."

In that moment, he knew there was only one way to keep her from harm. Against her will.

Without warning, she felt his heart rend.

"No," she begged, as his psyche crept over her own.

He trembled with guilt, but held firm as he pulled her to her feet, and they hurried to the coast, circumventing the bustling heart of the town. He spoke into her ear as he tugged her along, scouring the harbor for an open boat and staring over his shoulder.

"Tell your brothers, but no one else. Exposing him will cause him to retreat, and will do more harm than good."

She wiped her silent tears as they walked. When she ceased to resist, Luca cursed the day he was born. He squeezed her waist tighter, but she did not, *could* not respond.

He choked on his own heartache, shuffling her into a vacant boat to their right. Their steps were arrested by an incensed howl that pierced the twilight. Several others on the docks cocked their heads in the direction of the forest behind them, but none save Kate and Luca feared its source. The boatman cleared his throat, gaining Luca's attention.

"Where to?"

"Castelmor."

Kate walked docilely to the bow of the small craft. As he began to loosen his iron grip, she sensed Luca's fear, his pain. His voice in her head.

Forgive me.

She turned to him, as if she were looking upon a stranger.

His heart died in his chest.

His movements were arrested for but a moment. He put his determined foot on the stern and shoved hard, sending Kate and the young sailor alone into the Western Sea. Luca stood on the dock, watching Kate's shocked, tearful face fade deeper into the waves. When the boat was reduced to a blur, Luca turned on his heels, and rushed in the direction of the forest.

ON THE EDGE OF TOWN, DRACULA HAD HEARD RENE'S CRY. HE HAD RISEN from his seat and hastened to the cottage, ducking into an alley when Rene's lifeline was severed. The blow had hit him hard, and it had taken several long moments before he could give chase.

The blaze was furious when he barreled through the front
door, blowing it off its warped hinges. He picked his way through the fire and smoke, dodging falling fragments of the wood no longer supporting the ceiling. He tripped over Rene's corpse, his nose crashing into the sunken flesh of his neck. He cursed in a foreign tongue, pushed himself up on his hands, and searched for the orb. Dracula felt the lump in Rene's blood-soaked breast pocket. The orb was slippery with blood as the vampire fished it out of Rene's shirt.

He had the immediate impression that it took up more than the usual space in his hand. Dracula's pupils widened in disbelief. The orb rolled toward the blood puddling in his palm, and absorbed it, expanding ever so slightly.

The undead prince's marvel was interrupted by the ominous cracking overhead. Dracula jammed the orb into his jaw and leapt out the window as the central beam collapsed. His lupine form crashed through the blistering glass.

He was oversized for a wolf, and his dark coat was mangy. He suffered a deep gash to his front left leg, but it closed just as quickly as it had opened. His feral eyes glowered at the destruction. Turning his elongated snout to the smoldering sky, he vented his ire. Foaming, he shook himself off and skulked into the forest at the house's rear, his form swallowed up by the onslaught of darkness.

EPILOGUE

ALARIC STARED AT HIS REFLECTION IN THE OVERSIZED MIRROR PERCHED ON the wall in his room in Likhan. He drank in the sight of the naked woman staring back at him. Her creamy skin was smooth and perfect, culminating in two celestial mounds darkened at the center. Possessing the body of Kate's emissary Christine, he ran his petite hands over his breasts, over *her* breasts, in delight. They were not as plump as the queen's, but when he squeezed, he had his hands full. A daring hand trailed down Christine's sculpted abdomen, groping its way to an ebony patch of hair below her navel. He slipped his fingers inside his own flesh, then withdrew immediately and gripped the high-backed wicker chair behind him, softening his fall into the plush mauve seat cushion. Erotic thrills while trapped in a female form sent his head spinning. It was his sixth night playing the part of Kate's protégé to effect a coup favorable to Icaryan interests. Namely, to ensure Icaryan freedom, and position her brother Ted's unrecognized son as the new seht. Each night, he attempted to pleasure himself before the magical masque that provided Christine's allure dissolved. And each night, he was driven back by a spiraling bout of nausea.

He wrapped his fingers around the woven plant shoots acting as chair arms to brace for the return of his thick limbs and broad chest. He ran his rough hands through his chestnut tresses, falling in waves beyond his shoulders and gracing his triceps.

"I give up," he muttered, finishing off his glass of fermented citrus before turning in for the evening, sleeping above the covers. Sweltering heat billowed through the glassless marble terrace marking the edge of his room, riding a humid wave past the long thick blades of tropical greenery that was his only privacy.

An oppressive wind roused him in the small hours of the morning. He batted his heavy lids in the dense air, and rolled onto his back, covered in a thin sheen of sweat. The red-haired beauty that ruled Icarya, and his heart, stood in the doorway. Without a word, she ascended the bed and straddled him. Her smooth fingers raced across his burgeoning erection, guiding him into her as she ground against him.

"Oh gods *yes*," he groaned, her provocative silk robe falling away with a simple brush of his fingertips. His stretched out his hands and clasped her hips as she drove into him, then reached for glorious breasts as they bounced in her fury. She dismounted, slinking down on the bed and licking his dripping hot sex. Alaric ran his fingers through her hair, tugging as she sucked him hard. She came up for air and their eyes locked. But they weren't Kate's eyes. They were Luca's. The vision of Kate's dark, beautiful lover startled him. Luca grinned. A deep laugh emanated from his throat as he opened his mouth and pushed Alaric's rippling steel past his lips.

Alaric's mouth hung open in protest. He shuddered in silence as Luca lashed his tongue across the length of him and pushed his throbbing edge to the back of his throat. Alaric's heart raced as he submitted, and clasped the silky tresses he held in his hand even tighter.

In an indescribable moment, Luca's tongue scaled his straining length, and the next delved deep into his recesses, exiting his flesh only to tease the burning heat at the doorway to Christine's sex. Luca rose and mounted him, crashing into the female form Alaric possessed as completely as if it were his own. Alaric clawed hungrily at Luca's back, but Luca shook himself free, rolling Alaric over on his stomach and slamming into him from behind.

Alaric's face didn't touch his mattress, but rather collided with Kate, trapped underneath as Luca assailed him mercilessly from behind. His small, feminine hands groped the queen. He suckled her breasts, biting her then licking the pain away. She fought back, sucking on his neck and raking her teeth across his lower lip. His ravenous tongue traveled south, the urge to be inside her again too great. She remained silent as he lapped at her flesh, wrapping her bent legs around his neck as he devoured her. He licked hungrily at her slick arousal. At that, his own lust grew insatiable, shedding his female form and empowering him to pound into her with all the force he could muster before she disappeared again.

At long last, she screamed. She called his name, and ran her fingers greedily through his hair. His heart danced in her validation, and in the grasp imbued with an affection that transcended his lust. He dug deeper, his flat stomach grazing hers. He craned his neck, searching beneath him for her expectant lips, but Kate wasn't there. Near the middle of his chest was Christine's face. She ran her little fingers across his shoulder blades, clawing at him, desperate to pull him close. Her sapphire eyes pleaded with him, her legs refusing to release him. He reveled in her embrace, and glided into her with unspeakable passion until everything else faded away.

He pumped into her with all his might, but could not achieve climax. Awoken with a start, Alaric lurched over the edge of his bed, yanking at his painful erection with incredible speed, the release of his efforts spurting onto the floor. He slumped over, mopping the sweat off his brow with the back of his hand.

His chest heaved in the unabating heat of the night air. Stumbling out of bed, he groped for the nearby chair, making his way clumsily to the carved stone water basin beside the mirror. Alaric submerged his face for relief from the stifling swelter, and to shake off the intense reality of his dream. Returned to his senses but unable to sleep, he sat at the small, deep chestnut writing desk against the far wall, laying out several sheets of thin, clean parchment. Sweeping his dripping locks out of his face, he pulled a metallic green quill from its inkpot and scratched away.

Thank you for reading! Did you enjoy? Please add your review because nothing helps an author more and encourages readers to take a chance on a book than a review.

And don't miss more from Kathryn Troy with <u>THE SHADOW OF THERON</u>. Turn the page for a sneak peek!

Also be sure to sign up for the City Owl Press newsletter to receive notice of all book releases!

SNEAK PEEK OF THE SHADOW OF THERON

It would have been a pleasant day, if not for the hanging.

The sun glistened off the newly constructed gallows—it was not often Lighura had a public execution—and people greeted each other in the square, staking out spots with a good view as they consumed their sweet buns and boiled eggs.

Lysandro was not hungry. He couldn't see how good people could be content to stuff themselves before a man was set to die, before the stench of a man expiring in his own piss filled their nostrils. He could smell it already.

Kato brushed against his elbow.

"You'll be able to see better from here, Don de Castel."

"I can see all I care to from here, thank you."

The innkeeper nodded. "As you say, Signor. But if you change your mind—"

Lysandro nodded and planted his feet on the ground, fists clenched at his side.

The crowd snapped to attention as the door to the magistrate's office opened. Lysandro's stomach soured at the sight of Marek. He exuded a sense of utter disinterest in the events of which he himself was the director. But Lysandro saw the glint of malice in Marek's eyes that he was unable to hide. He relished the power over the life and death of the wretch behind him, his broad chest inflated with self-importance. In short, Lysandro loathed him.

His attention turned to the bound man following the magistrate. Two of Marek's officers stood beside him and another behind, forming a diamond around the condemned. It was clear this man would not go easily to his death.

He writhed and twisted his body to get away from the men holding him, one at each elbow, kicking and flailing his legs out in a childlike tantrum. He was so focused on trying to escape their grip that only inchoate groans passed his lips. When they ascended the steps to the platform, the man's struggling became more desperate, more violent. The crowd gasped when the man wrangled one arm free and it looked like he might escape. But he fell to the ground as two of Marek's men fumbled after him, fighting to keep him in their grip. They forced him to his feet again.

Without saying a word, Marek turned to face his underlings. They redoubled their efforts, squeezing the prisoner tight between them until his feet barely touched the ground. The man's struggling didn't cease, but his range of motion was now severely restricted. The captive's eyes went wide in fear, showing the whites of them like a man held in the throes of a hysterical fit.

Drop back, Lysandro thought. He couldn't stop his mind from racing through all the ways the man might free himself. It he could just loosen their hold on him again, he could run. But he'd never make it. Not without help.

When Marek turned his face to the crowd, his eyes had narrowed to murderous slits, and his jaw was tightly clenched to preserve the façade of a smile that he wore there. He lifted his chin and addressed those who had gathered:

"People of Lighura—Jair Oreyo is guilty of killing Don Aldo Carras, who caught him stealing silver. His crime was discovered by his widow, Doña Sofia Carras, who tripped over her husband's body when responding to his screams."

Lysandro heard the gasps of those around him as Marek recounted the grisly details. Marek was either too stupid or too cruel to show more consideration for Carras's family. They stood huddled together in a tight circle, their faces pointed at the ground, while Marek expounded on the way Don Aldo's brains had been bashed against the stairway of their own home and turned the entryway slippery with blood. The women and children who congregated in the square turned their heads away from the platform as if to shut out Marek's words and shield themselves from the nightmares such lurid descriptions were bound to produce.

Lysandro could feel his face flushing hot. A good man's guts were being strewn about with words. That he couldn't stifle them turned him livid.

Seemingly sated by his talk of violence, Marek shifted to patting himself on the back for a job well done. He turned to his officers and beckoned with a small gesture for the prisoner to be brought forward. His men accomplished it, but with great difficulty.

"Any last words?" he asked in a cool, collected tone.

Jair was foaming at the mouth. Lysandro could see the veins on his neck bulge as his face went purple with rage, and he lunged at Marek.

"Liar!"

Lysandro's ears pricked up. Alarm bells rang in his head like the one in the temple tower—a full-throated clang that deepened his suspicion.

"Murderer!" Jair shouted. "You're just as guilty as me!"

He pled with his captors, who rammed the noose around his neck. "Don't listen to him, he's a liar! *Stop*, or he'll do the same thing to you!"

The knife tucked up Lysandro's sleeve prodded him at the wrist. He calculated the distance and the force it would take to sever the rope swinging from the beam.

He could do it. Avoiding notice, though—that would be another matter entirely. But something else stopped him from sliding the hidden blade into his hand.

You're just as guilty as me.

Jair was a murderer; he just wasn't alone.

The corner of Lysandro's mouth twitched as the officers tightened the noose around Jair's throat, but his fingers remained loose at his side.

The blood in Lothan Marek's veins hissed in fury as his brothers dragged Jairo, kicking and screaming, toward the noose. He was being ridiculous. It was one thing to steal from the poor, and another to murder a pillar of the community and think no one would notice. Lothan had no choice but to act. And Jair had the gall to call him out in front of the whole village.

His behavior worked in Lothan's favor. He was acting like a lunatic with his hair on fire, and Lothan expected people to discount his exclamations as the ravings of an almost dead man. Jair's outrage was Lothan's shield, so long as he kept the anger from his face.

Jair had been effective at his job; his taste for brutality had served him well on occasion. He was perhaps the strongest among them, excepting Lothan himself, and it was a bitter shame to kill him. Almost.

All those who shared his blood were a greedy, groveling, worthless waste of a power that should have been his alone. Today brought him one step closer to the magic scattered across their veins being made whole.

Lothan quashed his annoyance as Jair squealed and squirmed to the last minute, wriggling like a worm until the floor gave way beneath him and silence reigned over the square, heralded by a definitive, satisfying crack. Jair's latent power shivered up Lothan's spine. The surge of energy buzzed through him like a current, crackling at his fingertips and the ends of his hair. It was delicious. But not nearly enough.

Lysandro was grateful for the silence; it was infinitely better than a roar of cheers would have been. The Carras family remained clustered together as the knot of onlookers unfurled itself, and people returned to their routines to try to forget what they'd seen. Lysandro made his way toward them. Marek approached at the same time, holding a large wooden box in his hands.

"Doña Carras," he said, presenting her with the recovered silverware.

He looked so pleased with himself.

Don Aldo's widow stared at him, then took the box into her hands with a dumb expression on her face.

Lothan furrowed his brows. "This *is* your stolen silver, is it not? I imagined its return would bring you some comfort." He had to fight to keep the bite out of his voice.

Lysandro could hold his tongue no longer.

"Perhaps she'd be more grateful if you'd preserved her husband's dignity, rather than turn his final moments into a spectacle."

Marek looked up at him, his eyes bright with challenge.

"Or perhaps they'd have been grateful if you had arrested Jair weeks ago, after he'd already been accused of thievery by the blacksmith. Granted, his family's possessions are humbler than this fine collection," Lysandro continued, gesturing at the box of silver, "but had your justice been swifter—"

The widow sobbed, and Lysandro let his accusation hang in the air.

"The blacksmith's account was not reliable. He was not as—"

"Worthy of your attention?" Lysandro offered. His mouth set into a hard line. "I shouldn't need to remind you that the office of magistrate is bound to protect *all* of Lighura, not just its wealthier citizens."

Lothan scowled.

"What did you lie about?" Lysandro asked.

"Excuse me?"

The abrupt turn took Marek by surprise. Lysandro lifted his gaze over Marek's shoulder to the hanged man. "With his last breath, he called you a liar. What did you lie about?"

Marek huffed through his nose and shifted on his feet like a bull in a pen.

"He called me a murderer too. Do you also accuse me of that?"

Marek fixed him with a venomous stare. Doña Sofia's hand flew to her mouth, and her younger children hid their faces in her voluminous black skirts.

Lysandro didn't flinch.

He waited for an answer with feigned curiosity. Marek had walked into the trap himself. Lysandro wasn't about to help him out of it.

Marek's gaze slid to the widow. "I did my duty here today. No one can say I didn't." He turned his back on them both and left.

Doña Sofia let out a sigh of relief. "Thank you."

"Someone had to say something."

She looked down again and brushed her fingers against the grain of the box Marek had given her as her children came out of hiding. Lysandro smiled at them and ruffled the younger boy's hair before turning his gaze back to their mother.

"Is there anything you need?" he asked.

"We'll be all right. Thank you again."

Lysandro nodded and looked to her eldest son. "Take good care of them."

The young don was a strapping teenager, who tried to act older than he was by appearing to be unmoved by the whole affair. He was managing it badly. The boy's eyes darted from one end of the square to the other, not finding an answer to the question forming on his lips.

"There's so much to go through. So many papers. I don't even—"

"There's nothing that can't wait a few days' time," Lysandro interrupted. "I'll come see you soon, help you get everything sorted. Let's see if we can't make any sense of it."

"Thank you."

"It's my pleasure," he replied. "Take care."

Before departing from the square himself, Lysandro spared one last look at the hanged man, cast in silhouette by the sun's rays as Marek's officers worked to cut him down. Lysandro wondered at all he might have inquired of the dead man—all the questions he could never ask.

The cheerful weather was wasted on the somber mood that hung over the dusty little village until nightfall. Lysandro called on his father for a late supper, having finally found his appetite after a full day's abstinence. He greeted the doorman genially.

"Good evening, Diego."

"Good evening, Don Lysandro. You'll find him in the dining hall this evening."

"The dining hall?" Lysandro asked. "Does he have guests?"

"No, Signor. He simply said he longed for some formality."

Lysandro raised an amused eyebrow. He thanked the man and headed through the familiar hallways of the house in which he had grown up and found his way to his father. Don de Castel the elder was already seated at the head of a long wooden table in an elegantly papered room of cream and burgundy. Cheeses, warm bread, and a stiff fortified wine lay fanned out before him.

"Standing on ceremony today, Father?" Lysandro asked, seating himself at his father's right hand and pouring himself a drink.

"Indeed," Elias answered, not looking up from his plate as he tore off a piece of bread from a larger loaf and soaked it in a spiced olive oil.

"In your dressing gown?" Lysandro asked.

Elias grunted in the affirmative. "It's my best one."

Lysandro smiled and took in the image of his father. His robe was one of fine fabric, luxurious and warm against the chill in the air coming off the sea. The wine-colored gown was elevated by an intricately embroidered scroll pattern, with golden threads woven into the cuffs and collar. His father's face was thin, but sharp, and marked by an imposing chin and a well-kept, respectable beard of silver to match the hair smoothed back on his head. Yes, Lysandro thought, his father looked every ounce a don.

"Marek hung Carass's murderer today," Lysandro said.

"Mm."

"How *he* got to be magistrate I'll never know."

"That's easy. You didn't try for it."

Lysandro sipped at his wine. "Surely there are other able men in this village."

"There's so much influence you could wield, if only you would. There's no one sitting on the Andran Council now for Lighura."

"I doubt the Council would take kindly to my views."

"You still think you should give up all your land, and have it owned by the peasants who live there?" Elias asked.

"I clearly can't manage it on my own. Why *shouldn't* they own the fruit of their labors?"

"Without their rents you would be impoverished."

"I've known many men poorer than I who lead much happier lives."

Elias reclined in his high-backed seat and studied his son's reserved expression. "The social season starts in a few days. Will you attend the opening ball?"

Lysandro's heart constricted at the mention of it. He tried to dodge the question by digging into the slice of pork loin on his plate, but his father's expectant stare was unwavering.

"Why?" Lysandro asked, swallowing. "So I can mix with ladies almost ten years my junior and talk about the latest fashions?" Women saw his wealth and his title, and little else.

"That problem will get worse the older *you* get without choosing a bride. You're almost thirty."

"I seem to have exhausted my prospects."

"You only need to choose one."

If only there was *one*, Lysandro thought. *Just one.*

"You ask too much," Elias said.

"I just want what you had with Mother. Is *that* too much?"

Elias's eyes softened. "No. Maybe some travel would be in order. You've always longed to see Mirêne for yourself."

"Perhaps." Though Mirêne was more attuned to the Goddess's loving and more artful face, and better reflected Lysandro's own inclinations, he couldn't leave Lighura now—not after what had happened. There was a tension in the air, a sense of trouble brewing into something darker. More sinister.

He returned home and descended into the cavernous rooms carved out from underneath his estate. The space was sparsely furnished, with only a small dresser and a low bed covered in soft, dark furs. Wax puddled at the bases of the wrought-iron candelabras that flanked the corners of the room and lent it their dim light.

Lysandro considered what his father had said. He might find more in common with the people of Mirêne, but his heart belonged to Lighura too. Lysandro couldn't leave the fate of its people in the hands of Marek. Lysandro's belief that he was a thief and a murderer was stronger than ever. But he needed proof to remove him. Proof that might finally be within reach.

The trading ship that had quit the port yesterday had left heading north, rather than back the way they'd come. It would be easy for them to round to the other side of the coast unseen, rather than out to sea.

He stripped down to his skin and donned much simpler attire, dyed black to blend with the coming night. The worn fabric often felt more familiar and reassuring to him than the fine clothes he wore in the daytime. Too fancy an outfit would give him away and would more than likely get in his way. He didn't wear any metal or ornamentation that might glint in the moonlight; he had to be able to weave in and out of the darkness unseen. He completed his ensemble with a broad hat, leather gloves, and a sword honed to a fine point. He wrapped a strip of black cloth tightly around his face, revealing only his eyes, and tucked his long hair, kept in an older, more distinctive style, tucked inside his shirt.

Lysandro abhorred violence. In the full light of day, it went against the example of kindness he worked so hard to set. But the edge of a sword carried a certain sense of rightness. So he sought justice from the shadows.

∼

Lighura's coast was too small to be a true harbor. It could only manage two ships at once, three in an emergency. Tonight, as most nights, the port was empty, leaving the water to creep slowly up the narrow beach without disruption. The only sounds for miles were the breaking of the surf and the call of gulls. But Lighura had pride of place in Andras. Aside from its beautiful coast, it was reputed to be the birthplace of the hero Theron, though exactly *where* he had lived had been lost to the passage of time.

As Lothan made his way down the sloping path to the shore, past the grass-covered dunes and toward the thin strip of sand, he spied the merchant vessel he sought approaching from a distance. They were still too far away for Lothan to tell if they carried any genuine relics aboard. If they truly possessed what they claimed, he would know—just as the work of Argoss sang in his veins, the lingering sense of the goddess sent his skin crawling. The only thing he felt in that moment was the blade pulsing against his abdomen. Under his coat blossomed the scent of fresh blood—a river's worth of it.

The drums of the broken metal shard's magic beat furiously between his ears. It was perhaps the only proof in the whole world that the goddess had failed—Argoss may have lost his life, but his sorcery was beyond her ability to destroy. A hot determination overcame Lothan as he brushed his fingers against the makeshift handle at his belt, drenching them in gore. What the goddess's whores insisted did not exist was his birthright, to bend and shape to his will. It had eluded him until now, with no clean or clever way to adhere the bleeding metal to the handle of his cheap knife, no symmetrical point or edge to pull them neatly together. But Jair's energy had come to roost in him, and he willed the broken fragment to cling to the grip. This time, it had obeyed.

The flow of blood racing along its jagged edge made him sticky, lapping at his skin like a wonton lover. It turned his blood feverish, and made his mouth run dry. He licked his lips as a distraction.

The sense of triumph he had first experienced when the shard had come into his possession had waned. What good did it do him if he couldn't find a way to salvage what remained of the once-mighty Blood Sword? It was so small. And he was not a blacksmith or a sorcerer. At least, not in the true sense of the word. He'd managed to find its locations, and had it transported from the farthest edges of Andras without raising suspicion, but that had been accomplished through instinct and sheer luck. The "why" of it eluded him. It was a constant source of frustration. When Lothan jabbed it through the air for the first time to test it, blood didn't fly off the edge in a venomous spray, which was a bit of a disappointment. But this was only one piece—Lothan consoled himself with the prospect of finding more, and one day wielding the full blade without squandering its power as Argoss had.

He had half a mind to slay his brothers right where they stood and take back from them what was his. But he was tied to his post, and much of what he craved lay beyond his grasp. He needed them. Although at this particular moment, the furtive glow of the lanterns on the beach was infuriatingly stationary. Lothan quickened his steps, and almost barreled into Jenner.

"What are you doing just standing there like an idiot? Spread out! Who do you have on the cliff?"

"That was Jair's job, Lord Lothan."

Lothan stared at him, and the man's legs nearly buckled as he spun on his heel and hurried to do the job himself.

They scattered at his command, taking up their positions as the ship made land.

Lothan was incensed by the illicit goods as they received the smugglers. They had only trinkets to offer— illustrated pages and "blessed" bits of junk, useless things that allowed deluded fanatics to feel nearer to the goddess and their hero—but nothing that bore the mark of Argoss. They had promised him more. They had promised him the Cerulean Key. Lothan did not take kindly to being lied to.

He turned to the man standing at his left and whispered in his ear.

"Get Gorin down here."

His brother retreated up the cliff face to recall the lookout. The more of them Lothan had nearby, the quicker he could dispatch the two-faced captain and his crew.

Lothan was still waiting for the pair of them to come back down when Jenner handed the captain his money. The captain in turn handed it to his second, who scurried up onto the boat. Lothan shot a piercing look to the cliffs, but neither man was anywhere in sight. He'd just about lost his patience when a single head popped into view.

"He's gone!"

"What do you mean, gone?"

"Like he's just vanished into thin air."

Lothan's skin prickled. Then he heard a scream, and a splash. That's when he knew they were not alone.

The sailors aboard the ship drew their swords, but it was useless against an invisible enemy. One man came flying in their direction and landed face-first in the mud. Another two, from Lothan's vantage point, seemed to disappear entirely, as if the floor had opened up from under them. Pandemonium erupted on the small vessel, but no one could discern the cause.

"It's him!"

"It's the Shadow of Theron!"

Marek's men watched but made no move to help, their eyes round in the lantern light. They grew skittish, wavering in place like horses ready to bolt.

He screamed at his men —better they fear him than some impostor who styled himself after a ridiculous excuse for a god. But his raging was drowned out by another voice that echoed across the sea.

"Ho, there! Looking for this?"

The Shadow of Theron appeared out of the darkness. He stood balanced on the thin outcropping of the ship's prow, with the sack of coins Jenner had just given over to the captain dangling from his hand.

The realization that he'd snuck past the lot of them without so much as a ripple out of place seized Lothan with a fit of rage. For too long, the Shadow had plagued him. Whenever he had come close to achieving even the smallest of his aims, Theron's Impostor had been there; he always knew the precise moment to strike, and always came away laughing—leaving Lothan chasing after him like an empty-headed fool. He reached for the bleeding dagger at his belt.

Not this night.

"Get him!" the captain shouted.

Jenner lunged for the chest, but the captain kicked the lid shut with his boot and caught him by the hand.

"No money, no trade!" The captain scooped up the ill-gotten treasure and sped back to the ship. The sailors seemed to have the Shadow cornered, stuck as he was on the thin bowsprit poking out over the water, but he batted their swords away with ease, their seething violence no more than a child's game to him. He pretended to lose his balance and flung the coins far out to sea.

A blood vessel in Lothan's neck threatened to burst; the smugglers howled in indignation. But when they charged him, he cut one of the lines connected to the foremast and used it to sail clear across the water to the stern. He bounded off the ship and landed on the beachhead with the grace of a jungle cat. He turned his back on Lothan, not showing a care in the world, and waved the ship off.

"Safe journey! Be careful of those rocks, they're trickier than they look!" Then he returned his gaze to the men on the beach, and grinned.

All Lothan needed was to get close enough to deliver one small slice.

But the Shadow was untouchable. He dodged Marek and his men with nimble steps at every turn, cutting through their number as he stayed always just a hair's breadth out of reach.

In a matter of minutes, Lothan's lieutenants lay sprawled flat in the sand, bloodied and unconscious. Lothan slowly worked to close the circle tighter and tighter as the Shadow danced around him. He was close enough now that the Shadow could see what it was that Lothan held; the broken blade shimmered brilliantly in the moonlight. The Shadow grew more careful, pushing Lothan to the brink of his endurance.

Lothan shot him a grim smile and tried to knock him off his balance.

"Was Theron himself such a coward in the face of great magic, or is that just you?"

But the Shadow was relentless, and deftly avoided his blows.

Lothan was rewarded for his patience. He thrust straight ahead, causing the Shadow to twist away to the side. But instead of righting himself, Lothan stepped into the dodge, leaving himself exposed, and retracted his arm back at rapid speed.

It was a shallow cut on the upper arm, nothing more. But Lothan felt the edge of the blade bite through the Shadow's sleeve, and the soft release as it rent open his flesh. The tang of blood filled the air as the tiny droplets joined the flood along the enchanted metal. The Shadow staggered backward, his chest heaving.

Lothan shivered in triumph. But he didn't stop. He struck again, aiming high for the head. The Shadow of Theron deflected the blow with more force than Lothan thought possible. But the power that pulsed at his fingertips didn't lie. Lothan stood grinning in the moonlight as the Shadow turned and ran for his life, although he was somewhat perturbed by the Shadow's speed. He shouldn't have been able to run at all.

The others were rising from the ground as his enemy shrank back into the shadows.

"Where did he go?"

"Should we go after him?"

"Let him be," Lothan said, a devilish grin on his face. Lothan was giddy, drunk with victory. "I cut him. With this." He held out the vermillion remnant of the Blood Sword of Argoss. His brothers gaped and dropped again to their knees, pressing their heads back into the sand.

"It may not be what it was. But if it has even a fraction of its old force...he won't live through the night."

~

Don't stop now. Keep reading with your copy of <u>THE SHADOW OF THERON</u>

∾

The powers of old are fading. A new Age is dawning.

Holy relics are all that remain of Theron's sacred legend.

Now those relics, the enchanted weapons forged by the Three-Faced Goddess to help Theron defeat the wicked Sorcerer Argoss, are disappearing.

Lysandro knows the village magistrate Marek is responsible, and he searches for proof disguised as the masked protector the Shadow of Theron.

But when Marek wounds him with an accursed sword that shouldn't exist, Lysandro must find a way to stop Marek from gaining any more artifacts created by the Goddess or her nemesis.

The arrival of the beautiful newcomer Seraphine, with secrets of her own, only escalates their rivalry.

As the feud between Lysandro and Marek throws Lighura into chaos, a pair of priestesses seeks to recover the relics and return them to safekeeping. But the stones warn that Argoss is returning, and they must race to retrieve Theron's most powerful weapon.

While they risk their lives for a legend, only one thing is certain. The three temples to the Goddess have been keeping secrets: not just from the faithful, but from each other.

∾

Please sign up for the City Owl Press newsletter for chances to win special subscriber-only contests and giveaways as well as receiving information on upcoming releases and special excerpts.

All reviews are **welcome** and **appreciated**. Please consider leaving one on your favorite social media and book buying sites.

For books in the world of romance and speculative fiction that embody Innovation, Creativity, and Affordability, check out City Owl Press at www.cityowlpress.com.

ACKNOWLEDGMENTS

Thank you to all my friends and family who answer all my crazy questions and get excited for every update. Your love and support keep me sane. A big thank you to all the folks at City Owl, to Keylin Rivers at Fantasy Book Cover Design, and to my street team for helping to launch this book baby into the world. Special thanks to Catrinia for all her wonderful images of my beloved characters, and to Sam and Robin for their enthusiasm and sharing their love of this story. You guys are rock stars.

ABOUT THE AUTHOR

KATHRYN TROY is a history professor by day, a novelist by night. She likes to write what she reads — fantasy, romantic fantasy, gothic fiction, historical fiction, paranormal, horror, and weird fiction. Horror cinema and horticulture are her other passions. When she's not writing or reading or teaching, she's either gaming, traveling, baking, or adding some new weird creepy cool thing to  her art collection. She is a Long Island native with one husband, two children, and three rats.

kathryntroy.blogspot.com

ABOUT THE PUBLISHER

City Owl Press is a cutting edge indie publishing company, bringing the world of romance and speculative fiction to discerning readers.

Escape Your World. Get Lost in Ours!

www.cityowlpress.com

 facebook.com/YourCityOwlPress
 x.com/cityowlpress
 instagram.com/cityowlbooks
 pinterest.com/cityowlpress

www.ingramcontent.com/pod-product-compliance
Lightning Source LLC
Chambersburg PA
CBHW030349020726
47493CB00003B/751